PRAISE FOR CAROLYN BROWN

The Sometimes Sisters

"Carolyn Brown continues her streak of winning, heartfelt novels with *The Sometimes Sisters*, a story of estranged sisters and frustrated romance."

—*All About Romance*

"This is an amazing feel-good story that will make you wish you were a part of this amazing family."

—*Harlequin Junkie* (top pick)

"*The Sometimes Sisters* is [a] delightful and touching story that explores the bonds of family. I loved the characters, the storylines, and the focus on the importance of familial bonds, whether they be blood relations or those you choose with your heart."

—*Rainy Day Ramblings*

The Strawberry Hearts Diner

"Sweet and satisfying romance from the queen of Texas Romance."

—*Fresh Fiction*

"A heartwarming cast of characters brings laughter and tears to the mix, and readers will find themselves rooting for more than one romance on the menu. From the first page to the last, Brown perfectly captures the mood as well as the atmosphere and creates a charming story that appeals to a wide range of readers."

—*RT Book Reviews*

"A sweet romance surrounded by wonderful, caring characters."
—*TBQ's Book Palace*

"Deeply satisfying contemporary small-town western story . . ."
—*Delighted Reader*

The Barefoot Summer

"Prolific romance author Brown shows she can also write women's fiction in this charming story, which uses humor and vivid characters to show the value of building an unconventional chosen family."
—*Publishers Weekly*

"This story takes you and carries you along for a wonderful ride full of laughter, tears, and three amazing HEAs. I feel like these characters are not just people in a book, but they are truly family and I feel so invested in their journey. Another amazing HIT for Carolyn Brown."
—*Harlequin Junkie* (top pick)

The Lullaby Sky

"I really loved and enjoyed this story. Definitely a good comfort read, when you're in a reading funk or just don't know what to read. The secondary characters bring much love and laughter into this book—your cheeks will definitely hurt from smiling so hard while reading. Carolyn is one of my most favorite authors. I know that without a doubt that no matter what book of hers I read, I can just get lost in it and know it will be a good story. Better than the last. Can't wait to read more from her."
—*The Bookworm's Obsession*

The Lilac Bouquet

"Brown pulls readers along for an enjoyable ride. It's impossible not to be touched by Brown's protagonists, particularly Seth, and a cast of strong supporting characters underpins the charming tale."

—*Publishers Weekly*

"If a reader is looking for a book more geared toward family and long-held secrets, this would be a good fit."

—*RT Book Reviews*

"Carolyn Brown absolutely blew me away with this epically beautiful story. I cried, I giggled, I sobbed, and I guffawed; this book had it all. I've come to expect great things from this author, and she more than lived up to anything I could have hoped for. Emmy Jo Massey and her great-granny Tandy are absolute masterpieces not because they are perfect but because they are perfectly painted. They are so alive, so full of flaws and spunk and determination. I cannot recommend this book highly enough."

—*Night Owl Reviews* (five stars and top pick)

The Wedding Pearls

"*The Wedding Pearls* by Carolyn Brown is an amazing story about family, life, love, and finding out who you are and where you came from. This book is a lot like *The Golden Girls* meet *Thelma and Louise*."

—*Harlequin Junkie*

"*The Wedding Pearls* is an absolute must-read. I cannot recommend this one enough. Grab a copy for yourself, and one for a best friend or even your mother or both. This is a book that you need to read. It will make you laugh and cry. It is so sweet and wonderful and packed full of humor. I hope that when I grow up, I can be just like Ivy and Frankie."

—*Rainy Day Ramblings*

The Yellow Rose Beauty Shop

"*The Yellow Rose Beauty Shop* was hilarious, and so much fun to read. But sweet romances, strong female friendships, and family bonds make this more than just a humorous read."

—*The Reader's Den*

"If you like books about small towns and how the people's lives intertwine, you will *love* this book. I think it's probably my favorite book this year. The relationships of the three main characters, girls who have grown up together, will make you feel like you just pulled up a chair in their beauty shop with a bunch of old friends. As you meet the other people in the town, you'll wish you could move there. There are some genuine laugh-out-loud moments and then more that will just make you smile. These are real people, not the oh-so-thin-and-so-very-rich that are often the main characters in novels. This book will warm your heart and you'll remember it after you finish the last page. That's the highest praise I can give a book."

—Reader quote for *The Yellow Rose Beauty Shop*

Long, Hot Texas Summer

"This is one of those lighthearted, feel-good, make-me-happy kind of stories. But, at the same time, the essence of this story is family and love with a big ole dose of laughter and country living thrown in the mix. This is the first installment in what promises to be another fascinating series from Brown. Find a comfortable chair, sit back and relax, because once you start reading *Long, Hot Texas Summer*, you won't be able to put it down. This is a super fun and sassy romance."

—*Thoughts in Progress*

Daisies in the Canyon

"I just loved the symbolism in *Daisies in the Canyon*. As I mentioned before, Carolyn Brown has a way with character development with few if any contemporaries. I am sure there are more stories to tell in this series. Brown just touched the surface first with *Long, Hot Texas Summer* and now continuing on with *Daisies in the Canyon*."

—*Fresh Fiction*

The
Magnolia
Inn

The
Magnolia
Inn

CAROLYN BROWN

 Montlake
Romance

Published by Montlake Romance, Seattle

www.apub.com

Amazon, the Amazon logo, and Montlake Romance are trademarks of Amazon.com, Inc., or its affiliates.

ISBN-13: 9781503904392
ISBN-10: 1503904393

Cover design by Laura Klynstra

Printed in the United States of America

This book is dedicated to my amazing friend Shirley Marks,
for believing that I can always get something done by Friday
and for all the support she continues to give me.

Chapter One

If only . . .

Jolene had played the game in her head too many times, but that evening she did it again. If only her dad hadn't died when she was a teenager. If only her mother hadn't spiraled down afterward into drugs and alcohol. If only Aunt Sugar and Uncle Jasper weren't going off on a long, long vacation in their new motor home. If only they hadn't signed over half the Magnolia Inn to that despicable Reuben, Uncle Jasper's nephew, who had been such a bully when they were kids. If only Jolene had the money to buy his half of the inn.

Sugar held up her shot glass. "To a brand-new adventure for me and for my darlin'."

"Sweet Uncle Jasper." Jolene decided to count her blessings rather than dwell on what-ifs.

"Honey, he's always loved you so much." Sugar patted her shoulder with her free hand.

Three shot glasses clinked against Sugar's—all but Jolene's. She wouldn't touch a drop of alcohol after living through her mother's addiction, and especially after Johnny Ray, her last boyfriend, also turned out to have a drinking problem. She clinked with her glass of sweet tea. The four older women threw back the whiskey like they were bellied up to the bar in an old western saloon. Then they slammed the small glasses down on the wooden table, and Sugar began to refill them.

Sugar raised her gray eyebrow toward her niece. "You sure you don't want one little shot, darlin'?"

"Positive. I'll be the designated driver for these three." She took in Lucy, Flossie, and Dotty with one wide sweep of her hand.

"Don't you worry about that, darlin'," Flossie said. "Jasper will drive us home if we get tipsy." The old girls hadn't aged much since Jolene had seen them last. Lucy still needed rocks in her pockets to hold her down when the wind picked up in East Texas. Her dyed red hair was still cut in a chin-length pageboy, and she still used way too much blush on her thin cheeks. That night she wore gray sweats that hung on her scrawny butt like a gunnysack on a broom handle.

"To a new year full of surprises." Flossie held up her glass, and when they'd tossed them back again, she refilled them.

"After this one, that's enough for me." Bright-blue eyes twinkled in a bed of wrinkles on Lucy's face. She was partial to red pantsuits, and Jolene would bet dollars to alligators that she slept in her high-heeled shoes. The ladies threw back the whiskey again. Jolene was glad Jasper would drive them home if they drank too much. She'd been coming to the Magnolia Inn since she was a little girl, but during all that time, they'd always just visited at the inn, so she had no idea where they lived.

Dotty raised her glass in another toast. "Neither time, nor miles, nor big-ass RVs can sever our heartstrings."

Miz Dotty was five feet tall if she tiptoed a little bit, but with that big blonde Texas hairdo, she reached Jolene's five feet two inches. She'd barely come up to her late husband Bruce's shoulder. And she'd never gotten rid of the deep Cajun accent she'd brought to Texas from south Louisiana sixty years ago.

"Travelin' around the country has been mine and Jasper's dream for forty years." Sugar grabbed a paper napkin and wiped away a tear. "I'll miss y'all, but I'm so excited about our new life on the road. Y'all've got to keep up the Friday-night gossip sessions here at the inn. Promise me."

Jolene glanced at the mirror hanging on the wall—in roughly forty years, she would look exactly like her aunt. Sugar, born Sharlene Mae nearly seventy years ago, was short, slightly curvy, blonde, and brown eyed and held an attitude that mixed sass with independence—Jolene would be damn proud to grow up just like her.

But all the spit and sass that Aunt Sugar had bequeathed her by DNA did not pay the bills. Strange as it was since she was a teetotaler, Jolene was a bartender. She'd probably have to get a job to keep things running at the inn, and that would mean working on Friday nights. But maybe they could move their little support meetings to another night if that happened.

Jolene remembered a few Friday-night support meetings of a very different kind, where kids of addicted parents met to try to understand what was going on in their families. She didn't go to very many of the gatherings. When her boss offered her the opportunity to pull a double shift at the all-night truck stop—well, the money meant more.

Lucy laid a hand on Sugar's shoulder. Dotty and Flossie, sitting across the table, each reached out to hold a hand. Black mascara tears rolled down all their cheeks, settling in wrinkles on their way to their chins.

"Damn it, Sugar. Never mind that." Flossie wiped away her tears. "It's your dream, and we're all tickled that you get to have it. You two just get out there and enjoy seeing the whole United States. Promise to send us pictures and call us."

"Of course I will," Sugar said. "And y'all will keep an eye on Jolene and Reuben here at the inn, right?"

"You got it." Lucy's voice cracked. "I'd rather see you going off in that RV out there with Jasper than having to look at you in a coffin like I did poor old Ezra."

"Ezra?" Jolene asked.

Dotty moved her hand away from Sugar's and patted Jolene's. "Her last boyfriend. The only reason she's drinking tonight is because she's in mourning and because Sugar's leaving us in the morning. She'll wear calluses on her knees tonight prayin' for forgiveness over these shots."

"Go to hell, Dotty," Lucy growled.

"Only if you go with me," Dotty giggled.

"Okay, no fussin' and no more tears," Sugar said. "Jolene, we're ready for it."

"Yes, ma'am." Jolene pushed back her chair, went to the refrigerator, and brought out a container of rocky road ice cream. She set it in the middle of the table and then handed out spoons to everyone.

Sugar removed the top. "This has gotten us through good times and bad."

"Yep, through funerals and farts," Dotty laughed. "Flossie, remember when you ate chili at Bruce's wake and . . ."

Sugar dipped her spoon into the ice cream first. "And I had to sit beside you."

Jolene got so tickled that it was her turn for tears to run down her cheeks. She'd missed the banter during the past few years, but there hadn't been time to make many trips all the way across the state of Texas.

Even though she hadn't visited Aunt Sugar as often as she'd wanted, when she thought about home, her mind always went to the Magnolia Inn. The best memories of her childhood were of the times she'd spent there, and she'd always looked forward to summers in East Texas—except those years when she and Reuben were there at the same time.

Flossie dug into the ice cream. "Well, I was doin' the whole lot of you a favor by letting go of all that gas. Nobody lingered in that church after the last amen was said."

"Good thing no one lit a match. Poor old Bruce was terrified of fire. I used to tell him that he'd better be nice to me or I'd have him cremated and bury his ashes right beside my mother's grave. They never did get along," Dotty said as she got her first bite of ice cream.

"Speaking of fire—to PMS and hot flashes," Sugar said.

"We've put on our wading boots and conquered it all, haven't we?" Flossie nodded.

"And we went through it together. I couldn't have survived any of it without you three to support me." Lucy dropped ice cream on her sweatshirt. "Well, dammit!" She rolled her blue eyes toward the ceiling. "Forgive me, Lord, I'm still transitioning from a sinner to a saint."

"That means her halo isn't fully formed yet," Dotty said.

"If we peeled back all that Dolly Parton hair of yours, we'd find horns hidin' under it," Lucy smarted off.

"With gold glitter on them," Dotty shot right back.

"Y'all excuse me. I can't laugh again or I'll have to go find some dry underwear," Jolene said. "Don't talk about anything fun while I'm gone."

"Oh, honey, at our age, we have to talk about it the minute it hits our minds or we'll forget it," Sugar giggled.

"You sure you and Jasper can find y'all's way to forty-nine states in that RV?" Flossie asked.

Jolene could hear the bantering continue as she went from the kitchen to the bathroom at the end of the foyer. She looked at her reflection in the mirror and tried to smile, but it didn't work. Tears streamed down her face. She'd always said that the walls in the Magnolia were magic, because that's the way she felt when she was there. It didn't matter what was going on in her life—there was always fun at Aunt Sugar's inn.

The inn was now half hers. The title had been transferred, but it wouldn't feel real until tomorrow morning, when her aunt and uncle drove away in the big-ass RV sitting in the backyard. Uncle Jasper had left the other half to his nephew, Reuben, who'd always been referred to as her cousin, although he really wasn't blood kin at all. It wasn't the best of situations, but Jolene was determined to make it work.

She'd miss Aunt Sugar and Uncle Jasper, but Reuben could suck the life right out of the magic the inn had if he was as obnoxious as he'd been as a kid. Hopefully, he'd changed and he had some savings. Surely he did—after all, he'd been a college professor for years. He might have been a bully when they were kids, but he must have put back some money. If he was willing to invest it in the inn, they could do some remodeling and be ready to reopen by Easter weekend. She had the figures all worked out on paper, and he wouldn't even have to live there or run the place. She'd be glad to split the profits with him, even more so if he stayed far, far away.

❋

Tucker Malone pulled the painter's tape from the edge of the crown molding, made sure everything was cleaned up, and locked up when he left. Job finished—year done. Tomorrow was New Year's Day. He stopped by his favorite liquor store on his way home, but the parking lot was full. That meant people were standing in line, and Tucker was too tired for that after working fourteen hours to finish up the job. He drove to a smaller store on the other side of town and found only half a dozen cars in the parking lot.

"Happy New Year's," a bunch of kids yelled at him.

"Not until after midnight, and I bet you got whatever is in that brown bag with a fake ID," Tucker grumbled.

An older man, wearing a well-worn cap with *Army* emblazoned on it, held the door for him as he started into the store. Tucker nodded. "Thank you, sir, and thank you for your service."

"Been a long time since anyone called me sir," the old guy said, hoisting his brown paper bag. "May the new year bring you happiness."

"That would require a miracle, but same to you, sir." The veteran couldn't know that happiness hadn't been in Tucker's world in a very long time.

"Amen to that." The man disappeared into the darkness.

Tucker picked up a six-pack of beer and a small bottle of whiskey. Tomorrow was a holiday. That meant no one would be purchasing liquor that day, and he damn sure didn't want to run out. The lady behind the counter tallied up the price. He wasn't surprised that she didn't ask for his ID. With the crow's-feet around his blue eyes, he looked every bit of his thirty-seven years and felt twenty years older. Tucker stuck his credit card into the chip reader and waited for the beep telling him to remove it. The gold wedding band on his left hand caught his eye as he put the card back in his wallet. If Melanie were still with him, they'd be celebrating the coming of a new year in a totally different way.

"Happy New Year." The lady looked over his shoulder to the next customer.

"You, too." He picked up his purchases and carried them to his truck. He was tempted to get out a beer right then and drink it warm. But drinking while driving was what had gotten him thrown off the Dallas police force. The very next day he'd visited Melanie's graveside and given her his word that he'd never do such a stupid thing again.

He caught the highway headed north and had only a couple of bouts of road rage on the way to the RV park that he'd called home for almost two years. He eased his truck into the narrow space between his trailer and the one next to it. Getting out without hitting the side of his neighbor's trailer took a stone-cold-sober man. Maybe Melanie was watching out from her place in heaven for that, too.

He set his beer and whiskey on the concrete slab that served as a porch and unlocked the door. Sassy, his big, fluffy white cat, darted out from under the trailer and beat him inside.

"Hello, honey, I'm home." He set his packages on the cabinet and picked up a picture from the top of the television. "How was your day?" He kissed Melanie's face and put it back. "I worked late so the job would be finished and I wouldn't feel guilty about taking tomorrow off."

Sassy hopped up on the cabinet and gave him a dirty look while he removed his paint-stained coveralls and tossed them out of the way.

"Okay, you." He shifted his focus to the cat. "I'm sorry I'm late. Your fancy food is comin' right up." He washed and dried a floral china saucer before he dumped a can of food onto it. "I'm sure there's a mouse or two up under this trailer that you could have nibbled on while you waited for me to get home."

She meowed in disagreement.

"Melanie spoiled you. Now you only eat off your own bone china, and you wouldn't get your paws dirty on a mouse." He put the food on the cabinet, and she started eating.

"Now my turn." He got out a package of bologna and made himself a sandwich. He didn't bother with a plate but carried it to the sofa, laid it on the end table, and took off his work boots. He picked up the remote control, found an old western movie, and then wolfed down the sandwich.

Sassy finished her food and hopped up on the sofa arm.

"Don't look at me like that. I only drink on weekends and holidays to fix the loneliness. I'm not an alcoholic."

She stuck her nose in the air, hopped from the sofa to the floor, and with her fluffy tail held high, headed toward the bedroom.

Four beers later and sometime around midnight, he blew Melanie's picture a kiss. "Happy New Year's, darlin'. I miss you so much." Then he fell into an exhausted sleep and didn't even wake up when the park residents set off fireworks.

Chapter Two

*I*f looks could kill, there would have been nothing left of Reuben but a big greasy spot and a pile of bones on the tile floor of the IHOP restaurant. Jolene had hoped that age had changed him into a decent person, but that idea was shattered soon after she'd walked into the restaurant. He still had that eager grin he'd worn as a child just before he bullied her.

A child jackass only grew into a bigger one. But how could he not see the value in her plan, and why had he let her go through the whole spiel before he said no? Did he attach sentimental value to nothing?

Aunt Sugar had told her repeatedly that there was good in every evil person and a little evil in every good person. Jolene glared at Reuben sitting there with a smug look on his face and tried to find a tiny little bit of good. The only thing she could come up with was that he had finished college and held down a job.

"Why won't you invest in this? How can you just throw away what Uncle Jasper entrusted you with?" she asked.

He adjusted his horn-rimmed glasses and squared up his scrawny shoulders. "You'll turn out like your low-class mama. When the going gets tough, you'll turn to drugs and alcohol. And I'm not partnerin' up with you."

"But I'm—"

He held up a hand to stop her. "I never did like you, Jolene."

"What's that got to do with anything? *You* were the bully. That doesn't mean we can't be business partners," she said.

"I never intended to keep my half of the inn. Not from the minute Uncle Jasper called me. He always favored you over me, and I'm his blood kin. I only agreed to listen to your stupid plan as payback for all the trouble you got me into when we were kids. Aunt Sugar spoiled you, and Uncle Jasper took up for you every time we argued."

"You got yourself in trouble by picking on me, and Uncle Jasper is the fairest man ever, so don't blame him," she said.

Reuben's torment of her had gone from simply pulling her hair to breaking Aunt Sugar's dishes and blaming it on her—and even uglier things. She remembered an incident when they were twelve and thirteen. He'd backed her up into the utility room, put a hand on her throat, and run his hand up under her skirt. He'd told her if she ever told on him, he'd catch her down by the bayou and drown her. But she'd told Aunt Sugar, and that was the last time they'd visited the inn at the same time.

"You remember it your way. I remember it mine. At least we won't be partners in this crazy venture, so we'll never have to see each other again." Reuben's smile radiated meanness.

That's when Jolene's touch of evil surfaced—she would have loved to strangle him right there in the IHOP or else throw him in the bayou behind the inn. How did this despicable little rat-faced son of a bitch share DNA with her kind, softhearted uncle Jasper?

Reuben leaned forward and hissed, "Sell your half or live with it. I'm not going into debt for a loan to fix up that old trash heap. I hated the time my folks made me spend there in the summer. I hate fishing, I hate mosquitoes, and most of all, I hated being bored out there in the country. Give me the city and the sounds of civilization rather than owls hooting and tree frogs makin' noise. I contacted a Realtor the minute I signed the papers, and I pity the fool who has to work with you." He tilted his chin up and looked down his nose at her. "But don't worry. You've got a place to live until some fool comes along with enough money to buy me out."

"You'll regret this someday," she said.

He slid out of the booth, getting in one last dig before he strutted out of the restaurant. "No, I won't. Goodbye, Jolene. When my half sells, I'm taking my department on a cruise over spring break. I'm glad that I never have to see Magnolia Inn or talk to you again."

She shot another drop-dead look toward him. If it had penetrated that ugly black overcoat, he would have been sprawled out right there in front of the cash register. She hoped that he'd get such a case of motion sickness that he couldn't eat a single bite of food the whole time he was on the ship or, better yet, that he'd fall overboard and not one of his precious friends would miss him. She was glad that they weren't blood kin, but she wondered how Uncle Jasper would feel when he learned that Reuben had thrown away his half of the Magnolia Inn.

When she left, she wished the restaurant doors would slam like the screen door on the back of the Magnolia, but they didn't even make a squeak. She stomped across the parking lot to her truck, but her athletic shoes didn't make a sound, either. So she slammed the truck door and slapped the steering wheel hard.

Her stomach growled—she always got hungry when she was angry, but she and Reuben had met only for coffee. Thank goodness they hadn't ordered food, because he'd left her with the check as it was. A bowl of leftover beans and a chunk of corn bread back at the inn would have to do for her lunch.

"Happy New Year to me," she grumbled. "I've got a bed-and-breakfast that has barely broke even for the past year because it needs remodeling. I can't get a loan with no credit in my background, and Reuben is a jackass."

She started the truck, and the engine purred like a kitten. She kept it maintained even if it did look like crap. It got her from point A to point B with dependability, and that's all that mattered right then. Maybe the Magnolia would be turning a profit in a couple of years, and that money could replace the old truck.

With the dozen or more bed-and-breakfasts in Jefferson, she'd have to really bill the Magnolia as quaint and quiet since it was five miles out of town. Dozens of catchy phrases came to mind for advertisements, but that took money, and right now, Jolene was so close to broke that she had to pinch every penny twice.

When Aunt Sugar had called to tell her she was going to have half of the inn, Jolene had been so excited that she could hardly sit still. She'd given her notice at the Twisted Rope, the bar she'd worked in since she'd turned twenty-one. Now she had less than a hundred dollars in her checking account, and Aunt Sugar had left enough food in the house to last only two weeks.

She could hope and pray that someone would see the potential in the old place, but until that happened, she had to find a job in order to eat. She knew how to do two things—waitress and tend bar. And she knew of only one bar in Harrison County, Texas, the Tipsy Gator. Dotty's own property.

"I just hope that she'll hire me, even though she'll catch flak from Aunt Sugar if she does. If not, I'll have to start applying for waitress work."

She drove north out of Marshall, right past the lane leading back to the inn, and on toward Jefferson. She'd seen the Tipsy Gator only once, and that had been back when she was sixteen, so she had a tough time finding it now. Her folks had let her stay with Aunt Sugar for a whole month that year. The last Sunday she was there, Uncle Jasper put the boat into the bayou and they went fishing.

"What is that?" Jolene had pointed at a blue building trimmed in yellow. She could see a huge sign above the entrance, and it had an alligator propped up in a lawn chair with a beer in his hands.

"That is the Tipsy Gator. It's a honky-tonk, and I don't ever want to hear that you went in there. It's not fit for proper girls, even if Dotty does own it," Aunt Sugar had answered.

"Dotty owns a bar?" Jolene had almost fallen out of the boat.

"Yes, she does, but we don't hold it against her," Aunt Sugar had said.

Jolene had only planned to find the place from the road instead of the Big Cypress Bayou, and she didn't expect to talk to Dotty that day—after all, it was New Year's Day. She'd come back the next morning. But she sat there in the parking lot admiring the sign for a while. The same alligator was on the front as the back, but THE TIPSY GATOR was written above him in purple lettering. Maybe she should have a big sign designed to go out on the highway to show folks that's where the turnoff to the Magnolia Inn was located.

She'd put the truck in reverse and was about to leave when Dotty pushed the back door open and tossed a bucket of soapy water to the side. Jolene turned off the engine and hurried across the lot, but she was too late. Dotty had already gone back inside, and the door was locked. Jolene rapped on it as hard as she could and shivered as she waited.

Finally Dotty yelled, "Who is it?"

"Just a bartender lookin' for a job," she hollered.

"I thought I recognized your voice." Dotty threw open the door. "Come on in here out of the cold, darlin'."

"I need a job," Jolene blurted out.

"Why? You've got the inn to remodel and run. And besides, Sugar would shoot me on the spot if I put you to work in the Gator." Dotty steered her toward the bar. "Want a beer?"

"I'd love a club soda with a twist of lime," Jolene said. "But it's like this . . ." She went on to tell her about the meeting with Reuben. "Aunt Sugar says that no one is completely evil or completely good. I discovered my bad part when he was so smug. I wanted to strangle him."

"Well," Dotty said, "that little peckerhead could've stood a lot of stranglin' when he was a kid. He like to have driven Sugar crazy when he came for the summer, but he was always sweet to Jasper, so she endured him."

She rounded the end of the bar and made two drinks—the one Jolene had asked for and a strawberry daiquiri for herself. "It's five o'clock somewhere, isn't it, *chère*? Mortgage the Magnolia and buy him out."

"I have no credit. I'm as afraid of a credit card as I am of drinking after what happened when Daddy died. You know that Mama had to sell everything to get out of debt. I have a hundred dollars in my checking account right now. I don't think there's a bank in Texas that would even consider giving me money." She bit back tears. "I just need a job. Please, Dotty."

"You should ask Lucy and Flossie about that. Either one of them would gladly put you to work in their antique stores," Dotty said.

"I don't know a thing about antiques. I've been a bartender since my twenty-first birthday. Come on, Dotty, even if it's just part-time?"

"How about I loan you enough to live on until someone buys the other half?" Dotty asked. "I mean it, *chère*. Sugar will never speak to me if I hire you."

"Why *not* hire me? It's good honest work, and she never fussed at me for what I did all these years. Loans are the same as credit in my books." Jolene had always loved it when Dotty called her *chère* in that deep southern accent. The word meant *dear* or *darling* in French and sounded so sweet.

"But you weren't working in my bar." She took a deep breath and said, "But what the hell? Sugar and I've had our arguments before and we got past them, and she did tell us to take care of you. I was about to put an ad in the paper for a part-time bartender. Friday and Saturday nights. Opening to closing. That'd be eighteen hours a week, ten dollars an hour, and you keep all your tips. And, *chère*, I really like that you don't drink. Last part-time help I had was plastered by the time he went home every evening."

Jolene did the math in her head. Depending on tips, of course, that would pay the utilities and keep her in food. Hopefully someone would see the potential in the inn and buy it before long.

She leaned over and hugged Dotty. "Thank you. I'll be here Friday half an hour before opening to help you get things ready, and I'll do the cleanup after hours, too."

"Now tell me again, *chère*, where did you work and how long? Since Bruce died and I had to take over the whole nine yards of runnin' this place, time gets away from me," Dotty said.

"Ten years at the Twisted Rope out in West Texas. I can handle myself and the customers. You can call my previous employer if you need a reference," she answered. "So you and Bruce ran this together?"

"Yep, he inherited it from his father. Sugar, Lucy, and Flossie almost had a heart attack when we decided to run it ourselves." She leaned closer and lowered her voice. "I think the whole bunch of them kind of lost respect for me, but hey, we made more money in this little shack than we ever did workin' our asses off in office jobs."

"People will always find a place to drink and party," Jolene said.

"Let's celebrate a new partnership with New Year's dinner. I've got a pot of black-eyed peas going in my apartment, and I hate to eat alone. Follow me," Dotty said.

This job is sure starting out different, she thought as she followed Dotty across the barroom floor. Her boss at the Twisted Rope had been a grumpy old man who owned three bars. He'd never invited her to dinner, given her a Christmas bonus, or even told her she was doing a good job. He paid her on Saturday nights, simply handing her the envelope with her paycheck in it. But comparing him to Dotty was like comparing apples to goats. Dotty had been Aunt Sugar's friend since they were little girls. Her other boss had been a stranger, even after ten years.

They went through a storeroom and into another room. As the aroma of food filled the place, Jolene tried to take in the whole residence with one glance, but it was impossible. Sunshine flowed from a skylight into a small living room that could have been featured in *Southern Living*. The smell of beans and bacon wafted in from the galley kitchen off to one side. A doorway opened up into a bedroom that showed off a bright floral comforter on a queen-size bed.

"Oh, my, this is beautiful," Jolene said.

"It used to be a big empty space, but Bruce and I turned it into an apartment. Made sense since we were here so much of the time. It was safer than driving all the way to Tyler at that time of morning, plus it saved gas and time. I've got the traditional meal—black-eyed peas cooked up with lots of bacon, greens with bacon, steamed cabbage, plus some sliced tomatoes and corn bread. Lucy and Flossie were supposed to be here, but they both have a hangover. Poor things never have been able to hold their liquor." She set the table for two as she talked.

"What can I do to help?" Jolene asked.

"Pour us a couple of glasses of sweet tea. It's in the fridge. Ice cubes are in the bowl in the freezer," Dotty said.

"How did you get from Louisiana to here? Sugar said that you were young when you moved here, but you've kept that accent," Jolene asked.

"My mama was Cajun, and that's the language I heard at home. Guess it stuck," Dotty answered. "I worked in an insurance agency for years, and Bruce was a loan officer at a bank. We knew figures and all that when we decided to run this place."

"Regrets?" Jolene asked.

"Not a single one. Let's dig in." She sat down, filled her plate, and picked up the Tabasco sauce. "I like a little kick in my peas."

Jolene reached for it when she finished. "It's the Cajun in us. We might not have put personal roots down in southern Louisiana, but that's where our heritage is."

"You got that right." Dotty smiled. "So how come you haven't married? Your aunt Sugar wants grandbabies. I told her that they'd actually be her great-nieces and nephews, but she wasn't havin' none of that talk."

"Came close," Jolene said. "But then I found his evil streak."

Dotty's eyes turned to slits. "Did some bastard lay a hand on you?"

"No, but he stole my debit card, cleaned out my bank account, and left with the few pieces of good jewelry that had belonged to my mother. His name was Johnny Ray and he was an alcoholic. You'd think I'd learn a lesson from having to deal with Mama, but he was tall, dark, and handsome, and he was a charmer." Jolene flashed back to the first time she'd met Johnny Ray. His sexy blue eyes had looked across the bar at her as if she were the only woman in the whole place. By the time they'd had their last argument over his drinking, those same blue eyes had been shooting daggers at her. She shook the memories from her head and smiled at Dotty. "This is so good. It reminds me of going to visit my dad's folks down around Lafayette. Thanks for inviting me."

Dotty raised her glass. "To love and prosperity in the new year."

Jolene clinked glasses. "I'll settle for prosperity. I make bad choices when it comes to that love stuff."

"Oh, come on now. Don't judge all men by one rotten apple. And besides, you know the Magnolia has magic hidden in the walls. Sugar always told us that, and I believe her," Dotty scolded. "Tell me, though, after all that you went through, didn't you ever think about a therapist? I saw one after Bruce died."

"I did see a real one a couple of times after Mama died. Just didn't feel right. Maybe it was too soon or maybe it wasn't soon enough. Went to a few of those Al-Anon meetings for kids a few times, too. I don't know, Dotty. But I know one thing—it'll take magic and miracles both for me to ever let another man into my heart," Jolene said.

"Well, the future is what it is, and we can't change it any more than we can change the past," Dotty said.

They ate in silence for a few minutes, and then Dotty said, "I wonder how far Sugar and Jasper got today."

Jolene nodded. "They were hoping to get about halfway down Louisiana. I bet Aunt Sugar is making peas and greens, though."

"You can count on it. We old southern women do things right." Dotty handed a plate of corn bread across the table. "You better have another piece to go with a second helping of black-eyed peas for good luck."

"I sure will—this is really good, Dotty. I appreciate the friendship, the food, and the job. After that meeting with Reuben, I needed all of it."

"Oh, honey, that's what friends are for—to share in the joys and half the sorrows." Dotty smiled.

"That mean you aren't going to throw salt in the shape of a cross when I leave?" Jolene asked.

Dotty laughed so hard that tears came to her eyes. "That's a Cajun superstition for sure—I wish it *would* keep certain people away from my house. Are you going to get out the salt for Reuben when you get home?"

"Yep, but according to him, he will never set foot in Jefferson again," Jolene said.

"Well, there, *chère*, is your first miracle, now isn't it?" Dotty said.

It was the middle of the afternoon when Jolene left. After lunch, Dotty had shown her all the basics of the bar. The primary difference between the Tipsy Gator and the Twisted Rope was the location of the liquor bottles. At the Twisted Rope, Jolene could reach for the whiskey, the tequila, or the gin blindfolded. It would take a few weeks at the Tipsy Gator to get that familiar with things.

Five miles south of town, she turned left, inched down the lane to the big Victorian-looking inn set back in the tall pines, and parked the truck among them. She plopped down on the porch swing and set it in motion with her foot. How would it work if someone bought a half interest in the place? Would they want to live there, or would they just be a silent partner?

🪷

Lake Pontchartrain, Louisiana

Sugar clapped her hands when they spotted an RV place right close to the lake that first day of their journey. She loved being near the water, and Jasper couldn't wait to get his fishing equipment out and see if the fish were biting.

"Before you do that, let's call Reuben and Jolene." Sugar touched her phone screen and brought up the contacts, hit Reuben's name, and handed it off to Jasper. "You can go first."

"Hello," Reuben said over the speaker.

"Guess where we are!" Jasper's voice sounded like a little boy's at Christmas.

"Who is this?" Reuben sounded irritated, maybe even angry.

"It's your uncle Jasper," Sugar said. "We've started our trip. We're camped right by Lake Pontchartrain. Have you and Jolene gotten reacquainted? She said y'all were meeting today."

"We met," Reuben said.

"And?" Jasper winked at Sugar.

"I listed my half with a Realtor. I hated that place when I was a kid. Why would I ever want to live there? I'll use that money to take my colleagues on a cruise over spring break, and what's left to buy a new car. So I guess I owe you thanks for that." Reuben's tone had changed from angry to sarcastic.

"I'd hoped that . . ." Jasper looked like he might burst into tears.

"You gave it to me with no strings. I did what I wanted with it," Reuben said. "I really have to go now. I've got plans for this evening. And if some idiot comes along who wants to buy half interest in a money pit, then I'll thank you again for a nice vacation and a new car. Goodbye."

The phone screen went dark.

The RV went silent.

Sugar moved closer to Jasper and wrapped her arms around him. "I'm so sorry, darlin'."

"I should've given my half to Jolene. I just wanted to believe that this would . . ." Tears began to roll down his cheeks.

Sugar's tears mixed with his, because she never could let anyone cry alone. "Let's go fishin' together to take our minds off this. I'll call Jolene another time. She's probably too hoppin' mad to talk right now anyway."

"I love you." Jasper held her tightly. "I thought I was doing the right thing."

"You were." Sugar pushed away from him. "You did nothing wrong. You followed your heart. Who knows how all this will turn out? We're hurting today, but maybe tomorrow we'll look back on this and see that it was all for the good."

"I hope so." Jasper wiped at his cheeks.

Chapter Three

𝒯ucker Malone had just polished off his third beer and was reaching for another when his cell phone rang. He checked the ID, saw that it was Belinda, and ignored it. He wasn't ready to start another job for a few days. He wanted to hole up in his tiny trailer, drink a few beers, eat bologna sandwiches, and watch old reruns on television with Sassy beside him. When he got ready to work, he'd call her.

This was a holiday, by damn, and he deserved a little time off. He looked around at the tiny travel trailer and imagined Melanie in the kitchen, like she had been that last night they were together. They'd spent every weekend they could get out of the big city camping out at the lake—doing some fishing, having a few beers, and planning their future.

He blinked back the tears. He'd lost her, all over a quart of milk. She'd needed it for breakfast the next morning and insisted on driving into town while he fished for their supper. After the auto accident that killed her, he drowned his grief in a bottle.

The weekend drinking had turned daily and cost him his job. That's when he'd gone to the cemetery and promised Melanie he'd only drink on Friday and Saturday nights. The next day he'd brought the trailer from Dallas to Marshall, Texas, the area where she'd grown up, where her parents and two brothers still lived, and where she was buried. He'd thought that living close to where she was raised would help.

It didn't.

But her old school friend, Belinda, a Realtor, had kept him in enough remodeling jobs to buy beer, bologna, and cat food. The trailer had looked like hammered owl shit when he and Melanie had bought it, and it still did. The rust spots had spread in two years, and he'd never bothered to underpin it, but it was big enough for him and Sassy, and it kept the rain off. As long as he could come home to Melanie's picture every evening, he didn't care what the trailer looked like.

He carried his go-bag and a beer over to the RV park bathroom and shivered through a barely warm shower. They'd camped out in the trailer and skinny-dipped in lakes and rivers that were colder than this, but he'd had her warm body next to him in those days. He quickly dried off, got dressed in a pair of old Dallas PD sweats, and jogged from the brick building back to his trailer. Once inside, he pushed Sassy out of the way and dived under a blanket on the sofa.

"Dammit! I left my beer over in the bathroom. Sassy, darlin', be a good girl and go get it for me," he said.

The cat gave him her best disgusted look and settled on the other end of the sofa.

"Worthless animal. I bet a dog would fetch my beer," he fussed at her.

He went straight to the refrigerator, got out another bottle, and headed back to the sofa. He picked up his phone and called the nearest pizza place. It rang five times before he remembered that it was a holiday. He had his finger on the "End" button when someone said, "Pop's Pizzeria."

"Y'all open and delivering?" he asked.

"Yes, sir. This Tucker?"

"Yep. Will you send your delivery guy out here with my regular order?"

"Hand-tossed supreme with extra meat and cheese, and a container of marinara on the side, right?"

"You got it," Tucker said.

He meant to turn off the phone when he finished his order, but he forgot. It rang again, and he checked the ID and laid it back down. Dixie Realty, Belinda's business—it could wait.

He picked up the remote and found a John Wayne western on television. Ten minutes into the movie, as he was reciting the dialogue with the Duke, someone pounded on his door. He stumbled to the door with his wallet in hand, expecting to see the pizza delivery kid bringing his order.

"Dammit! What are you doing here?" he asked when he saw Belinda on the other side of the door.

"Aren't you going to invite me in out of the cold?" she replied.

"What the hell do you want? Don't you know when I don't answer the phone that I don't want to work? This is a holiday," he answered.

She pushed her way past him. "I'm not happy that I had to drive out here—it's a holiday for me, too." She removed her scarf and hat. "Melanie was my best friend, and I know she'd hate to see you living like this. Why don't you get out of this trailer and let me find you a decent apartment?"

"It keeps the wind and rain off, it reminds me of the good times Melanie and I had, and it beats paying rent. But come right in. Make yourself at home. Do the dishes while you're here," he said.

"I'm not your maid, although it looks like you could use one." She tossed a dirty shirt off the sofa and sat down. "I'm here on business. I've got a really good business deal for you."

He leaned against the refrigerator door and waited.

"Well?" she said.

"I'm listenin'."

"Half interest in the Magnolia Inn is up for sale. It's the place where Melanie and I—"

He threw up a hand. "I know that y'all had a senior tea there. She told me all about it. Why's only half interest for sale?"

"Sugar and Jasper, the owners, left the place to her only niece, Jolene, and his only nephew, Reuben. Jolene wants to keep it. Reuben wants to sell. Reuben has authorized me to act on his behalf. You interested?"

"Are you kiddin' me? Half ownership? No, thank you," he said. "I don't share. It hurts too bad when . . ." He let the sentence drop and swallowed the lump in his throat. "You should know that. I don't usually even hire a helper when I do work on your houses. Besides, come on, Belinda—half ownership with a woman? Melanie would haunt me for sure."

"It's business, not love. I've been in the Magnolia Inn lots of times. There are two big bedrooms on the ground floor and six that Sugar and Jasper rented on the second level. You can choose your room, do some repairs, and make a nice profit every year. It's a full-time job for you until spring. After you get the renovations done, you can come back, live back in this ratty trailer, and just rake in the money," Belinda told him. "Or, if you want, you can stay on and help Jolene run the place."

He raked his hand through his dark hair. "I don't cook."

"Surely Jolene does if she's plannin' to run a bed-and-breakfast," Belinda said.

Tucker ran a hand down over his square jaw, which sported two days of dark growth. "I'll think about it."

"I've got another buyer who'd like to invest in the place, so you've got twenty-four hours," Belinda said.

"I'll let you know tomorrow. Call you at the office?"

"I'll be there from nine to five."

The noise of a car stopping too quick on gravel took his attention to the door. "I hear my pizza delivery kid. Want to stay? I've got an extra beer."

Belinda glanced over at Melanie's picture. "I'm serious, Tucker. She would want you to move on, and I can't stay for pizza and beer. Ray and the kids are waiting for me to come home and make our traditional New Year's supper. You better eat black-eyed peas and something green if you want yours to be prosperous." She stood, crammed her hat onto her head, and wrapped her scarf around her neck. "This is a good deal for you, and it'll get you out of this sorry excuse for a home. I hope you don't let it pass you by."

"I said I'd think about it," Tucker answered.

Belinda pushed the door open and disappeared out into the cold night air. She and Melanie had been best friends since they were in the church nursery together, but they looked nothing alike. Melanie had been a tall, slim-built brunette with green eyes. Belinda—a short dark-haired lady—had gained weight with every one of her three kids.

He picked up his deceased wife's picture and ran a finger down the edge of her face. "Don't listen to her, darlin'. We've got an understanding that she don't know jack crap about."

Someone rapped on the door. "Got a delivery for Tucker Malone."

The kid handed him the pizza, and Tucker gave him a ten-dollar bill and a five. "Keep the change."

"Thanks." The kid turned around and jogged back to his car.

Tucker set the pizza on the cabinet, and Sassy immediately opened her eyes. She jumped from the sofa arm to the cabinet and tried to open the box with her claws.

"Go get back on the sofa and we'll share. There's plenty," he said.

The cat glared at him.

"Okay, okay, I'll get your fancy plate down and cut up a piece in bite-size chunks." He picked the black olives, onions, and peppers off her slice. "Peppers are green and olives aren't too far from the color of black-eyed peas, so that takes care of the silly southern superstition, right?"

Sassy purred in agreement until he set the bone-china plate on her favorite place on the cabinet, and then she set about eating. He stacked up four slices of pizza on a paper plate for himself and got out a beer. He carried it to the sofa and watched the rest of the movie as he ate. When it ended, he stared at Melanie's picture sitting on the tiny table at the end of the sofa.

"What should I do, darlin'? I've got all that insurance money, more than enough to buy half the Magnolia Inn and to remodel it. But it's your money and I'm not sure you'd want me to use it to buy half interest in a place where a woman owns the other half. I remember how jealous you were. So tell me what to do. I can't make this decision to spend the money from your death without a sign from you," he said.

He laid his forehead in the palm of his calloused hand and shut his eyes. The distant roll of thunder brought him to full alert, but he couldn't bring himself to believe that was a sign from his beloved Melanie. Sassy hopped up on the sofa beside him, licked her paws, and curled up on her favorite throw pillow. Not a sign by any stretch of the word.

"Guess you'll be sleepin' on Melanie's pillow tonight—that sounds like rain comin' on," he said.

Sassy meowed once and sighed.

"That's not a sign, either." Tucker finished off the pizza and went to bed.

He didn't dream that night and awoke in a bad mood. All he'd asked for was a little indication that he should even consider buying that run-down place. Melanie could have visited him in his sleep like she often did—but nothing, nada, zilch.

He jerked on a pair of possibly clean jeans and pulled on a stained, mustard-colored work coat over a long-sleeved knit shirt frayed at the wrists. Covering his eyes against the bright sunshine, he hurried out to his truck, climbed inside, and flipped the visor down to get his sunglasses. Once he had them on, he shut the door and started the engine. He grabbed a bag of sausage biscuits at a drive-through window and then drove north toward Jefferson. Maybe something would hit him and tell him whether or not to buy the place—or at least half of it.

When he turned down the lane toward the Magnolia Inn, he braked and turned off the engine. He opened the sack and removed a sausage biscuit. He'd never been inside the inn, but Melanie had talked about going there for a tea that the Chamber of Commerce had put on for the girls when she was a high school senior. She'd gotten a dreamy look in her eyes the first time she pointed it out to him from the highway. He smiled as he remembered their conversation that day.

"Someday we're going to have a house like that, and a dozen little Malone boys will slide down the banister from the second floor to the first one," she'd said.

"And what if we have a dozen little Malone girls?" he'd asked.

"Then they will sit on the porch in fancy dresses and you can polish up your shotgun and wait on the swing to scare off the boys," she'd giggled.

A picture of three or four teenage girls on the porch and a couple of boys playing football in the front yard popped into his mind. But that would never happen, because if he bought the house, it would be to run the place as a bed-and-breakfast. Melanie had been his soul mate, and he'd had five wonderful years with her. It was insane to think that a man ever got two chances like that in a lifetime.

"You could help me out here, Melanie," he said.

He'd barely gotten the words out when Sassy crawled out from under the passenger seat and stuck her head into the sack of biscuits. She cocked her head to one side and then the other before she turned to meow at him.

He'd had to tranquilize the stupid cat to move her from Dallas to Marshall, and even then she'd awakened before they arrived. He could still hear her moaning and groaning from the carrier in the back seat of his club-cab truck. So why was she hitching a ride when she was supposed to be staying at the trailer?

"How did you get in here?" he asked.

Then he remembered putting on his sunglasses and his gloves before he shut the door that morning. But still, she should have been throwing a fit by now.

"Is this my sign, Melanie?" he finally whispered.

A bird flew down from the pine trees and landed on the hood of his truck, and Sassy made a noise in her throat as she tried to tease it into coming closer. She'd love it out here in the country, maybe as much as Melanie had thought she would when she'd talked about living in a place like this.

"Okay, I hear you," Tucker said as he pulled his phone from his hip pocket and dialed Belinda's number.

"What's he askin'?" he said when she answered.

"Hello to you, too," Belinda said. "There's a house in Jefferson about that size that's up for two hundred and fifty thousand. But it's in pristine condition, so I've already told him there's no way he'll get but maybe a quarter of that amount for the Magnolia, since it needs a complete overhaul. You seen the inside yet?"

"Nope. Tell him I'll go seventy-five thousand for half of it," Tucker said. "Cash, so we can make it happen sooner than if I had to go through the bank for a loan."

"He's pretty anxious to sell." Belinda drew out the words.

"Then tell him sixty-five," Tucker laughed.

"I'll relay your message. Should have a counteroffer within an hour or two. You should go inside to get a look at what all it needs before you make a second offer," Belinda said.

"I'm looking at it right now from where I turned down the lane. I don't need to see any more than this right now." Tucker hit the "End" button on the phone, laid it aside, and ran a hand over Sassy's fur. "So you didn't want to leave Dallas, yet you want to move here. Whoever said that you own a dog but feed a cat sure knew what they were talking about."

He gazed down the lane at the two-story house with its wide front porch. He envisioned guests sitting on the porch in the summertime. They'd have glasses of lemonade or iced tea, and maybe there would be a little cart on wheels with cookies on it. In the spring, there would be tulips or maybe even rosebushes. Sure, he was eager to see the inside, but he really didn't care how much work it would take to renovate the place. That was irrelevant. The feeling in his heart of doing the right thing was what he'd been looking for, and it was definitely there.

"So what do you think, Sassy? We can pull our trailer back behind the house and live in it while we do the remodeling. Maybe I *should* go in and take a tour of the place." He removed his hat and ran his fingers through his hair. "It's pretty damned impulsive to buy a place without even looking at it, isn't it?"

The cat cold nosed his chin. He hadn't laughed so much in weeks. "Okay, I get the message. Buy it. From the outside, it doesn't look so bad, and they were renting rooms up until a few weeks ago, so it can't be completely falling in. And besides, the Big Cypress Bayou runs behind it, so I can fish every evening."

He grabbed his phone from the passenger seat and called Belinda. She answered on the second ring. "Dixie Realty."

"Call the woman in the house and make her the same offer. Maybe she doesn't realize how much her half is worth. Hell, offer her a hundred thousand and see if she'll go for it," he said.

"I don't think she will, but I'll give it a shot," Belinda said. "Be in touch in a little while."

He drove back to his trailer with Sassy sitting like a queen in the passenger seat. If this Jolene woman was willing to take his offer, he would restore and flip the place and make a nice profit. Once inside, he shed his coat and cowboy boots and began to pace. Sassy turned around three or four times in the middle of his bed before she settled down and went to sleep.

"So you've done your duty and now you aren't going to worry with me?" Tucker asked. "Now that I've seen it again, I want it really bad. You could at least stay awake and keep me company."

Sassy's whiskers didn't even twitch in reply.

He wished he had a job to keep his mind off the two offers he'd made. He'd even be willing to remodel a bathroom to keep his hands busy, and Tucker hated working in the tight spaces. They reminded him of all the times he'd had to crawl under houses in search of things he'd rather not think about anymore. He slouched on the sofa and leaned his head back, shutting his eyes, and second-guessing himself about what he'd just done.

He fell asleep, and in his dream, Melanie was sitting on the swing on the front porch of that big house. She ran out to meet him as he drove up, slung her arms around his neck, and kissed him. He awoke to the sound of the phone ringing, and before he answered it, he just knew that it was good news.

"Hello, Belinda. That was quick," he said.

"Got good news and bad news. Which do you want first?"

"Give me the bad." He raked his fingers through his dark hair and realized he really needed to visit the barber.

"Jolene says no way in hell, and that if she had the money, she'd buy Reuben out. Good news is that Reuben didn't even want to counteroffer. He took the sixty-five thousand and said to tell you to consider it yours. I'll have the papers ready for both of you to sign on Friday morning, but as of now, you can sell that trailer and move into the house if you want."

"I ain't sellin' my trailer. I might drag it out there and park it behind the house by the bayou, but a million bucks couldn't take it from me," he said. "I'll see you Friday. What time?"

"Nine o'clock," she said.

"I'll be there."

"Bring your checkbook."

🌸

Jolene had taken stock of what was left in the pantry, and there was plenty to last a couple of weeks. By then she'd have money from the bar to pay the utility bills. She paced the floor, wondering if the guy who'd offered would really buy Reuben's half of the inn. She went from the foyer up the wide staircase, checked each bedroom, and finally sat down on the top step.

The person who was interested in the place might not finalize a deal on only half. If he backed out, she decided that she was going to open for business, no matter what. She'd take a month to get the place in shape, do the spring cleaning like Aunt Sugar did every year, and take reservations starting the first of February. If she lived on a shoestring, maybe she could save enough to hire someone to remodel one room at a time that way.

Now that she had a plan, even if it wasn't a good one, she was eager to get started, but seven o'clock at night wasn't the time to start washing woodwork. She grabbed a quilt from the back of the sofa and carried it outside. Wrapping it around her body like a long shawl, she sat down on the porch swing and set it to moving with her foot. Within minutes she was second-guessing herself about selling her half. A picture of Aunt Sugar's smile flashed through her mind.

Even if she could have more money than she'd ever had at one time and be on her way to a new life—maybe down near Lafayette, where she still had beaucoup cousins—it wasn't going to happen. She'd made up her mind, and she was going to stay focused on moving forward with the plan.

A big, fluffy white cat hopped up on the swing with her and laid a paw on her leg. It was friendly enough that Jolene wondered if it belonged there and Aunt Sugar had just forgotten to mention it in her excitement to leave the day before.

"Well, what's your name, pretty thing?" Jolene asked.

"Sassy is her name," a deep voice said right behind her.

Startled, Jolene whipped around so fast that she almost fell off the swing. "Who are you, and what are you doin' here?"

Now is that any way to act toward a potential customer? Aunt Sugar's voice popped into her head. *He might stay a week, and you'd make enough money to pay the electric bill.*

"Right friendly, ain't you?" Sarcasm dripped from the man's tone.

"I'm sorry. You scared me. Is this your cat? How did you get here?"

"Drove my truck right up the lane and parked my trailer out in that little clearing by the bayou." His deep drawl left no doubt that he was definitely from Texas. He topped six feet easily in his well-worn cowboy boots. His hair was dark, and the porch light lit up his piercing blue eyes.

"We don't have a trailer park." How had he gotten past the house without her hearing the truck?

"Nope, don't reckon you do." He sat down on the porch step, and the cat hopped off the swing and went to curl up in his lap.

"Then what are you doing here?" she asked again. "Would you like to rent a room?"

"Nope, but I wouldn't mind a tour of the house," he said.

"Why would I do that?" Her fear radar shot up several notches.

"Because, honey, I'm Tucker Malone, and I own half of this place now—or at least I will on Friday when I sign the papers."

Chapter Four

$\mathcal{T}$ ucker had planned on knocking on the door like a gentleman, introducing himself and telling the lady why he was there, but Sassy kind of beat him to the punch. Now Jolene was staring at him like he had horns on his head and maybe a long spiky tail. She was downright cute with those big blue eyes and blonde hair. With that small waist and those curvy hips, most men would be drooling over her.

"I thought maybe Belinda would have told you that Reuben said I could go ahead and move in today. My trailer rent is up tomorrow, so I took your cousin up on staying," he explained.

She stood up and paced to the other end of the porch, the quilt dragging behind her. She whipped it around as she turned. "She called, but there was no talk of you moving in. But I guess since you own half this place, you've got the right to do what you want."

"I thought maybe this first little while I'd just hook up to the electricity and stay in my trailer," he said.

His detective training on the Dallas PD kicked in as he watched her pace nervously across the porch. She was short, maybe an inch or two over five feet tall, and soaking wet she might hit 120 pounds. Her slightly pointed chin didn't detract from her delicate features. Even with no makeup she was a looker—someone he might have hit on in a bar before he settled down with Melanie.

"That's crazy. What would you use for a bathroom?" She continued flipping that quilt around every time she turned to pace to the other end of the porch. "The house is warm, even if it's shabby right now. We need to go inside out of the cold and talk if we're going to be partners."

"What's there to talk about? We both know it needs to be remodeled, so we'll go halves on everything. Close it down until spring and have a grand opening when everything is done," he said.

She eased down on the step beside him and put her head in her hands. "I have about a hundred dollars in my checking account. I hope you have a little more than that, or else your credit is good enough to get a loan."

"Sweet Jesus!" he gasped.

"Here's what I offered Reuben. Hear me out, okay?" She started talking before he could even answer and finished with, "Whether you have the money or you can get a loan, we can put it all in a contract so you won't feel like I'm taking advantage. I'm willing to work right beside you until we get the place back in shape. I can paint, sand, or do anything if you'll only show me how. The Realtor told me that you are a crackerjack carpenter."

"Can you cook?" he asked when she finally wound down.

She nodded.

"And you'll work right along with me without bitchin'?"

Another nod.

He stuck out his hand. "Then you've got a deal. We'll draw up something on paper tomorrow morning and each of us will sign it. And I don't need to get a loan from a bank. Got a safe in the house?"

"Just a little one in the utility room," she answered.

"We'll put our paper in there when we get done with it," he said. "So you can cook for real?"

"Yes, why?"

"I'm hungry," he said.

Even though Jolene looked like she might have traveled a few rough roads, she didn't sound like she was conning him. And he really was starving. That slice of cold pizza he'd had for breakfast had long since digested. He'd been so busy getting the trailer ready to move that he'd forgotten all about lunch.

"What do you want?" she asked.

"I love breakfast for supper. So I'd like biscuits and gravy, pancakes, and maybe an omelet with hash browns on the side." He straightened up and headed across the porch with Sassy right behind him.

"Are you testing me to see if I can make a good breakfast for the inn when it's up and running again?"

"Nope. I just happen to really like homemade breakfast food, and I thought I'd push my luck," he answered.

"I can have it ready in thirty minutes while you do a walk-through of your new property, Mr. Malone," she said.

"Are you serious? An omelet with some toast would be fine. Just call me Tucker. Unless you want to stand on formality, and then I'll call you Miss Broussard." He waited for her to catch up, and then held the door for her and Sassy. "Hope you ain't allergic to cats."

"No, sir. Love them, as a matter of fact. Not much into dogs. You go on and see what you think while I get some food going, and I'll show you that I can put a decent breakfast on the table—Tucker." She hurried off to the kitchen as he started up the wide, curved stairway.

🌼

Jolene's hands shook as she stirred up biscuit dough from Aunt Sugar's recipe file. If he had enough money to redo this place, why in the hell was he living in a travel trailer? Why would he want to buy half ownership? And this all had happened in two days—wasn't that too quick?

Questions upon questions raced through her mind, but there wasn't a single answer to any of them. She shook flour on a piece of waxed paper and kneaded the dough a few times. Once it was cut into a dozen perfect circles, she stomped her foot. She should've only made half a recipe. There was no way two people would eat twelve biscuits.

She slid the pan into the oven and then crumbled half a pound of sausage into a cast-iron skillet. Going back and forth from stove to cabinet, she kept it stirred in between whipping four eggs up in a bowl and dicing up some tomatoes, onions, and peppers for a western omelet.

She glanced out the kitchen window, and a dark shadow proved that he had indeed parked his trailer back there. In the dim light, it looked a lot like the one she'd lived in for a few years when she'd moved out of her mother's place. Since he hadn't signed the papers, he might take one look at what all needed to be done and grab his cat, and she'd never see him again.

Jolene's mind was going in a hundred directions. Jumping from showing him that she'd be a good cook for the bed-and-breakfast to wondering how things had ever happened so fast to just how much money he was willing to invest. She didn't even hear him enter the room.

"We've got a big job on our hands. You got a deadline in mind?" Tucker came into the kitchen and watched her cook from the other side of the kitchen island.

"Not really. Aunt Sugar usually closed up the place a month or so in the winter to do some heavy cleaning. It was kind of slow right after Christmas anyway. We might have a decent year if we could have our grand reopening by mid-April."

"That sounds doable. Smells good in here. Can I wash up in the kitchen sink?"

She shrugged. "The place belongs to you as much as to me."

He'd already removed his coat. Now he was rolling up the sleeves of his body-hugging knit shirt and heading toward the sink. When he finished, he glanced around the kitchen. "Paper towels?"

"Real towels." She tossed him the one from over her shoulder.

"Faucet is dripping. I'll get on that tomorrow after we draw up a plan. Once this place is fixed up, it'll be a gold mine. Reuben is an idiot," Tucker said.

"That's paying Reuben a compliment," she said. "He's worse."

"Maybe so, but I'm glad he didn't want his half." He dried his hands, rolled up his sleeves, and sat down at the table.

"Hey, if this is a partnership, Mr. Malone . . ."

"I told you it's Tucker. Mr. Malone sounds like you're talkin' to my grandpa," he reminded her.

"Okay, then, Tucker. If I'm going to help you remodel, then the least you can do is get your own plate and fork and pour your own coffee," she scolded.

He might have agreed to save the inn, but by golly, he could damn sure help out. She pointed at the cabinet door above the coffeepot.

"Aunt Sugar organized her cabinets. Coffee cups are up there above the pot. Plates are to the left of the sink. Glasses to the right. Mixing bowls under the bar. The big pots and pans, slow cookers, and food are in the pantry," she said.

He chuckled as he pushed the chair back. "Kind of a smart-ass, ain't you?"

"I am what I am. You've got until Friday to live with it or change your mind and pull that trailer off my property." She started melting butter for the omelet.

"And if I don't like working with you and leave, are you going to sell me your half? God knows you ain't goin' to do much around here with a hundred bucks." He poured a mug of coffee, got a plate and a fork, and carried it all to the table.

"You ever go to church?" She stirred flour into the skillet with the sausage and then added milk.

"Few times," he said.

"Ever hear that story about the widow woman who only had enough for one meal until the prophet came along? He wanted the bread she was about to fix, so she gave it to him, and"—she snapped her fingers—"they had enough food to last for months because the oil and flour never played out."

"I'm not a prophet," Tucker chuckled. "You think God is going to keep the pantry full for you?"

"Maybe. I went to church in the summers when I was here with Aunt Sugar. Mama wasn't nearly as God-fearin' as her older sister." She stirred the gravy and set it aside while she made hash browns and started the omelet. When those were done, she made half a dozen pancakes and then carried everything to the table.

"I hope you don't intend for me to eat all this. I'm hungry, but that's a lot of food," he said.

"Hey, you asked for it, so here it is. And besides, I haven't had supper, either." She went back to the cabinet for a plate and fork.

He split two biscuits and covered them with gravy. "I'm not much of a morning person. Give me a bowl of cereal and two or three cups of coffee and I'm ready to work. But I do love this kind of food for supper."

"Comfort food." She nodded. "That's the best kind. So where do we start on this job and when?"

"I'd say on the second floor," he answered quickly. "Finish one room completely and go on to the next. I peeled back a corner of the carpet. Did you know there's oak hardwood under it?"

"Had no idea, but that would sure be easier to clean than carpet." She flipped two pancakes onto her plate and poured hot buttered syrup over them.

"I'll get out my notepad, and we'll set down a plan after we eat. It's been a long time since I've had a home-cooked meal like this, so I intend to enjoy it first."

"So exactly how much money are you willing to sink into this project?" she asked.

"Enough to finish it," he said and changed the subject. "If you do cook like this every morning when we have guests, they'll be booking for another visit before they ever leave."

"Thank you." She nodded. "But this is just a sample of what Aunt Sugar did for breakfast. I've got her menus and recipes for fancy muffins, waffles, and all kinds of things to vary it."

"So she was your mother's sister?" he asked.

"That's right. Her older sister by a different mother. Aunt Sugar's mama died when she was a teenager, and her dad remarried a woman named Victoria that next year. They had my mother about the time that Aunt Sugar and Uncle Jasper got married. There's a picture of my aunt in her wedding dress holding my mother."

What was she doing? He didn't need to know about her personal life. Besides, he could easily change his mind and take his trailer and cat away by Friday. Then she'd be back to square one, needing someone to buy half a bed-and-breakfast.

❀

Usually folks told Tucker what they wanted done, and he gave them two or three options. He'd start at the high end and go down to the bare-bones price that the job would cost. But that evening after they'd had supper, he knew he didn't have to figure in labor, and that was at least two-thirds of the cost of any job.

"Okay, this is what I've got in mind," he said. "The bedrooms are big enough that we can easily take a few feet off each for private bathrooms. People want more privacy now than just two bathrooms at the end of the hall. If we want to keep the plantation feel to the place, then I've got a contact down near Tyler that refurbishes old claw-foot tubs. We could probably get a real good deal on half a dozen."

"That will take a lot of money. It would involve new plumbing and more than one year to pay back," she said. "I was thinkin' new drapes and maybe updating the linens, and hopefully the carpet."

"You got to spend money to make money," he said. "It's a long-term investment. We'll get repeat customers by giving them privacy, comfort, and good food. Maybe when we get rolling we can think about buying half a dozen canoes for the clients to use. The bayou is right behind us. We could also furnish the equipment for fishing."

"You've given this a lot of thought," Jolene said.

"I see a lot of potential in this place. I can even see offering the huge dining room for small weddings. The bride could have one of the upstairs rooms for dressing and the groom could have another. We could call in a photographer and a caterer and give it to them as a package deal." Walking through the rooms had fueled him with ideas that he couldn't wait to share.

"Good grief! That's really ambitious," Jolene gasped.

"The sky is the limit, so why keep our feet on the ground?" He quoted one of Melanie's favorite sayings.

Sassy hopped up on the table and curled up next to the sugar bowl. Jolene reached over and stroked her long white fur until she started to purr. That gesture went a long way in Tucker's books. Any woman who didn't pitch a bitchy fit because the cat got on the table was an okay partner as far as he was concerned.

While she was paying attention to the cat, he stole sideways glances at her. Something stirred in his heart. He hadn't felt anything for a woman since Melanie died. Feelings like he had for his wife came along only once in a lifetime, and they sure didn't happen at first glance. This was probably just excitement.

He must have overwhelmed Jolene enough—showing up unannounced the way he had and then going on and on about the potential he could see in the place. So he picked up his notepad and carried it and a tape measure upstairs.

"What are you doing now?" She'd followed him—an unexpected choice. "Planning on building another wing on the inn so we can turn it into a hotel?" Her tone twined jealousy and sarcasm.

"No, ma'am. This place is just the right size for a bed-and-breakfast. Keeps the cozy feeling. Besides, you probably don't want to make breakfast for more than twelve people, do you?" he asked.

"Aunt Sugar offered a rollaway bed if a couple wanted to stay with a child or if three ladies came down to go to the antique stores for a weekend," she said. "But three to a room was her limit."

"Then eighteen at the most. Any more than that and we might have to call the place the Magnolia Hotel." He opened the door to the first bedroom, dropped down on his knees, and removed the tape measure from his belt. He pulled the tab out and then handed it to her. "Stretch this to the other side of the room."

"My first job as a carpenter's helper," she said.

"It's not any worse than my first one as a B&B owner. I had to set the table for supper," he shot back.

"I guess we've both got a lot to learn." She pulled the metal tape to the other side of the room. "Twenty feet, and it looks to be square to me."

"We'll measure for sure, but I agree with you. We can take six feet off the side of this one and have a nice-sized bathroom and a closet to put the rollaway bed in as well as give the guests a place to hang clothing. Do you realize not a single room has a closet?" He reeled in the tape measure and drew out a rough plan for the two bathrooms.

She peered over his shoulder. "That's what the armoires are for, and there's two rollaways in the closet under the stairs."

"The armoires are pretty beat-up. Let's get rid of them. That'll give us more room for something like a rocking chair by the window. How in the world did two old folks ever get those rollaways up the stairs?"

"Growing up, I always thought Uncle Jasper was the strongest man in the world, but now that I think about it, I bet getting those things up and down has been a chore for him for a while. Maybe they didn't use them very often." She smiled just thinking of her aunt and uncle.

"Or maybe those beds were the reason they decided to retire." His eyes left the notes and focused on her. She was downright beautiful, especially when she smiled.

"I told Aunt Sugar the reason she left after Christmas was so she wouldn't have to do the spring cleaning on this place."

"Guess the remodel will take care of a lot of the cleaning business. Hey, do you ever do much shoppin' in the antique stores in Jefferson?" he asked.

"Two of Aunt Sugar's closest friends run a couple of them. Lucy has Attic Treasures, and Flossie owns Mama's Place. Why?"

"See that oak washstand over there in the corner? Two bedrooms have those, and we could use one as a vanity in each bathroom. I kind of pictured this place with an old plantation home flavor," he said. "What did you have in mind?"

"Tara from *Gone With the Wind*." There was that smile again.

"Isn't there already a place called that in Jefferson?"

"It's still a museum, restaurant, and gift store, but it's no longer a bed-and-breakfast. I meant the aura. It should always have that old-world magnolia charm," she said.

"Want to plant some magnolia trees?" he asked.

"Aunt Sugar tried that, but they didn't survive."

He sat down on the top step and patted the floor beside him. "She ever tell you why it's named the Magnolia Inn?"

"Aunt Sugar's mama came from southern Louisiana, where magnolias are everywhere. So when her parents rented rooms, she named the place that. Please don't tell me you were thinking of changing it. That's one area we'd have to fight about," she said.

"No, I kind of like the image of peace that it brings," he answered.

Tucker hadn't figured on being comfortable in the house, or that he and Jolene would hit it off. He'd thought he'd plug into the electricity and live in his trailer, but now he was entertaining notions of moving all the way indoors. He shut his eyes and brought up a visual of Melanie.

What do you think, darlin'?

It's been time to leave the trailer for a long, long time. Her voice was loud and clear in his head.

When he opened them, Jolene was watching Sassy pick her way up the stairs, one at a time. "She's never been in a two-story house?"

"Nope. Only step she has had to deal with is the one to get inside my trailer," he answered. "So back to those washstands. You didn't state an opinion."

She threw up her palms. "Hey, you're the one with the money."

"But you are my partner, so we're going to share things, right?"

"I never thought something like this would even be possible. I know you paid a lot for your half, but you really need to tell me what our budget is, Tucker. I'm willing to take a small salary out of what we bring in and put the rest of the profits toward paying you back, but I need to know. As it stands, it's pulling in a low six-figure gross a year, before taxes, insurance, and utilities. Like you said, we're partners."

Tucker's eyebrows drew down into a solid dark line. He didn't want to tell her how much money the insurance company had given him when Melanie died, but she was right. They were partners. He did a rough estimate of what it would take to put the bathrooms in and to do some cosmetic work on the downstairs and added several thousand dollars to that. It wouldn't deplete the money in the savings account by any means, but it was a rough budget.

He quoted her the amount, and she gasped. "Good Lord, did you rob a bank? Why are you working odd jobs?"

He shrugged. "Even when I was on the Dallas police force, I flipped houses, so I had a nice nest egg, but there was insurance money after my wife was killed in a car accident." It pained him still to think of profiting from her death. He drew out his tape measure and figured the size of the armoire. That kept his hands busy while he regained his composure and swallowed the lump in his throat. "We've got the finances to do this job right. Now, if we take this thing out, it'll give us quite a bit more room. Washstands could be an old sideboard or buffet—they'd fit in. But they couldn't be much bigger than what's up there in the first room we'll start working on," he said. "Anyway, I thought maybe you could do some lookin' around to see what you could find."

"I'll check in with Lucy and Flossie," she answered and then abruptly changed the subject. "Were you even in this house before tonight?"

"Nope, but . . ." The story about Melanie's senior tea was his private memory, and he cherished it too much to share. "I've remodeled a lot of these old places, and I kind of figured it looked the same." He straightened up and started down the stairs. "Lucy and Flossie sound like what you'd name kittens."

"There's also Dotty, but she doesn't have an antique shop. Those are their nicknames." Jolene followed him.

That evening was the longest one-on-one visit Tucker had spent with anyone in a long time. It usually took about an hour to work up a rough estimate for a job, and most of the time that involved a guy, not a woman. The walls had begun to close in on him. His chest tightened. "I'm going out to my trailer now." He laid his yellow pad on one of the four round tables in the dining room, twisting his torso as if to release a breath.

"Aunt Sugar left two sets of keys. Yours is on the foyer table. See you tomorrow. When it's just us, breakfast is at seven. But for guests, it's on the bar from six thirty to nine."

He grabbed his coat. "I'll be here."

He picked up the keys and hurried outside into the bitter cold wind whistling through the tall pines. With no electricity to keep the tiny space heater going, the trailer wasn't much warmer than outside. He jerked the chenille bedspread from the bed and wrapped it around his body as he fell back on the sofa and stared at the ceiling.

"What have I done, Melanie? I wanted to buy this property for you, to fix it up in your honor, but now I'm having second thoughts." He shook off the bedspread, and in two strides, he opened the refrigerator. He fumbled around in the dark until his hand closed around a bottle of beer, but then he changed his mind and left it there.

"I need something stronger." He opened the cabinet above the stove and carefully felt around until he recognized the shape of the whiskey bottle. Using the light of the moon flowing in from the kitchen window, he poured about two fingers into one water glass. He sat on the sofa and drew the spread over him.

Even though he couldn't see Melanie's face clearly in the dark, he held her picture to his chest. "Talk to me. I've got a couple of days to back out of this deal. I can always drag this trailer back to Marshall and go on with my life."

The whiskey warmed his insides, but it didn't do much for the outside, which continued to get colder by the minute. "Are you tellin' me to go back to the house?" he asked. "I don't know if I can. You're here with me in the trailer."

You got a choice. You can get up off your butt and go get into a warm bed or freeze to death. Her voice sounded so real that he looked over his shoulder.

He tossed back the last sip of whiskey and threw the bedspread on the sofa. It only took a minute to pack a small duffel bag with a change of clothing and his toiletries. He hoped that the two socks he'd found matched, but if they didn't, he could always come back for more when it was light.

The house was dark when he opened the door and slipped inside. Stumbling over furniture, he tried to find the light switch, but no amount of running his hands across the walls turned one up. Finally, he decided to make his way to the kitchen, and that's when a spiderweb hit him smack in the face. Tucker Malone would do battle with a burglar hopped up on drugs quicker than a spider, so he did some fancy footwork trying to brush it away.

It wasn't until a string got tangled in his fingers that he realized it wasn't a spiderweb after all. With a nervous chuckle he gave it a jerk, and presto, the foyer lit up. Glaring at the wooden thread spool hanging from the end of the string, he said, "Enjoy this, because you will be rewired to a switch by the end of next week."

It took a moment for his eyes to focus when he looked away from the light bulb, but when he did, both of his hands went up in surrender. Jolene stood in her bedroom door with a small pistol pointed at him.

"That cord is part of the old-time feeling, and something Aunt Sugar would never change. And neither will I," she said.

"Whoa, girl! It's just me," Tucker said. "I didn't know about the light, and I thought I'd run into a spiderweb."

She lowered the gun. "Scared of spiders, are you?"

"Terrified," he answered and wished he could cram the words back into his mouth. Melanie was the only one who knew about his phobia.

"Well, you'd better be more afraid of me mistaking you for a burglar and shooting your sorry butt. Turn out the light before you go to bed. No need in jacking the electric bill up—unless a big, brave cowboy like you is afraid of the dark, too," she said.

"No, ma'am, just spiders. You afraid of anything?"

"Not one thing long as I have this little friend close by." She kissed the barrel of the pistol and disappeared back into her bedroom.

He'd checked out the whole house earlier and knew that the other bedroom on the ground floor opened right across the foyer from her room. He felt around on the wall just inside the door and breathed a sigh of relief when he found the switch. One flick of the wrist and the room was lit up. Before he did anything else, he went back to the foyer, got his bag, and pulled the string to turn out the light.

"Save on the electric bill." Melanie had said that too many times to count. He eased the door to his room shut and scanned the place, as much for spiders as for furniture placement. Antique lamps were centered on a couple of nightstands flanking the queen-size four-poster bed. A rocking chair snugged against a pole lamp, and a dresser provided four drawers and a mirror. No closet, so his clothing would have to be stored in the dresser drawers. Not that he had that much—one drawer would hold his work clothes, and one would take care of his two pairs of Saturday-night jeans and pearl-snap shirts.

Evidently, he and Jolene would share the tiny downstairs bathroom. He shook his head. "That ain't goin' to work. I'll take one of the bathrooms upstairs. Maybe the one with *HIS* painted on the door. That way I'll stay out of her way, and she can stay out of mine."

He picked up his bag, left the light on in his bedroom, and made his way up the stairs. Even if the bathroom dated back several decades, he was grateful to find a light switch right inside the door. But no shower. He groaned. "I bet the guys who got dragged in here by their wives just loved that."

He turned off the light and went back downstairs to the little bathroom that had a shower, a wall-hung sink, and a toilet crammed into what appeared to be the original linen closet. He bumped his shoulder twice in the process of getting his shoes and clothing off. By then the water had warmed up enough that he could at least get inside the smallest shower on the planet. Thank God there was soap, because he hadn't thought to bring his from the trailer. When he had to bend just to rinse the soap from his hair, he swore that the first thing he would do was get a decent bathroom ready upstairs—one with a nice big walk-in shower. Besides, it would be good for any handicapped folks who stayed at the inn.

"No, that won't work," he grumbled as he got out and reached for a towel from the stack on the back of the toilet. "Without an elevator, we can't say that we are equipped for handicapped folks, unless I take one of the upstairs rooms and open up the one on the ground floor for that." The gears in his mind began to churn again, and by the time he finished drying off, he'd already redesigned the rooms.

He wrapped the towel around his waist and peeked out the door to make sure Jolene wasn't in sight before he sprinted across the foyer. When he was safely in his room, he dropped the towel and crawled in between the soft white sheets. It had been a long time since he'd slept in a queen-size bed, and it felt like it covered an acre. He tossed and turned, wishing he had a switch to turn off his mind.

He laced his hands behind his head and decided that his plans for the private bathrooms had to change. Forget the claw-foot idea. Each bathroom would have a tub with a shower above it, giving the guests a choice. The vanity could still be an antique washstand or some kind of dresser like that—maybe with a bowl-type sink. But there was no way he was going to punish guys by not offering them a shower.

Finally, he drifted off to sleep, only to dream again of that last night he and Melanie had spent in the trailer before the accident that took her life. They'd been camping out by a lake near Dallas, and she'd wanted to make a grocery run into town. In the dream he told her they could live on love, and he'd go to get food later. When he awoke with a start, he wished for the hundredth time that he'd really done that.

He touched his phone and the screen lit up—six o'clock. The smell of coffee already brewing brought him fully awake. That's when he remembered that he'd left his bag in the bathroom and he had nothing but a towel to wear. He pushed back the covers and shivered, picked up the damp towel, draped it around his waist, and hurried to the end of the foyer where the bathroom was located. He quickly dressed in well-worn work jeans and a long-sleeved shirt and almost shouted when his socks matched.

"Good morning." Jolene poked her head out from her bedroom as he was headed toward the kitchen. "You can have that bathroom if you want it. I've got my things strung out in the ladies' room upstairs. It's got a tub and a lot more room. There's a basket for your dirty clothes in the utility room."

"Thanks," he grumbled. "I'm not much of a morning person, but I do like a cup of strong, hot coffee."

"Me, either, so we should get along just fine," she said.

Tucker went through the dining room and kitchen and into the utility room, where two big front-load washers and dryers were located. At least Sugar and Jasper had kept up with the best in that area. He tossed his dirty things into the empty red basket and noticed that the white one beside it was almost full.

Jolene held a cup of coffee out toward him as he entered the kitchen. "So what's on our agenda after breakfast?"

"Let's move the furniture out of the bedroom we measured last night—" he started.

"And tear up that old carpet?"

He took a couple of sips of the coffee. "That's right. What's for breakfast?"

"You said a light breakfast. I'm used to a bowl of cereal, the kid kind that's got lots of sugar," she answered. "When we have guests, I'll serve them the whole big thing, but I'll probably still just have junk. For us, though, dinner is served at noon and supper in the evening here at the inn."

"That's fine."

"And we eat leftovers," she said.

He nodded and topped off his cup with more coffee. "I don't mind leftovers, but quittin' time is five o'clock. I work from eight to noon, take an hour off, and quit at five. Saturdays I stop at noon, and I don't work on Sunday."

"I can live with that, since you're the one with the money," she said as she set two boxes of cereal on the table.

"So what's your story, Jolene? Boyfriend on the side? Ex-husband?"

"You show me yours, and I'll show you mine. You first," she answered.

"I was married. I'm not now because she died in a car accident. And that's all the showing I'm doing right now." He went to the refrigerator and got out the milk.

"No boyfriend at the present or ex-husband in the past, and that's the extent of my show-and-tell, too."

Chapter Five

Mobile, Alabama

arlin', why don't you go up to the RV store and get us a pint of ice cream?" Sugar asked as soon as they were parked in a really nice RV park that evening. Ice cream worked for her and the girls in a crisis, so just maybe it would help Jasper out of his depression.

She paced from the cabinets to the tiny bathroom and back again while the phone rang four times. She was ready to weep by the fifth ring. Just when she was expecting the call to go to voice mail, Jolene answered.

"Aunt Sugar!" she practically yelled. "I'm so glad to hear from you."

"Oh, honey, I've wanted to talk to you so bad, but not with your uncle Jasper beside me. He took it hard when Reuben did what he did, putting his half up for sale. He's still down in the dumps."

"Poor Uncle Jasper. It's a good thing it's against the law to shoot folks. But . . ."

"Hold on. I hear him whistling. We'll have to talk later. When he feels better, I'll call; we'll put it on speaker and have a good visit."

"Okay, but y'all take care of each other and don't worry. A wise lady told me once that things work out for the best even if we can't see it at the time," Jolene said.

"Love you." Sugar had hung up and picked up a travel brochure by the time Jasper returned with ice cream.

"Rocky road." He held it up and smiled for the first time all day. "It always makes things better."

Sugar went to the cabinet and took out two spoons. "Yes, darlin', it does. And the pain gets a little less achy every single day."

He dipped into the carton. "I hope so. Let's talk about our destination tomorrow. We're not far from that place where we sprinkled Elaine and John's ashes in the water. Want to visit there?"

"Yes," Sugar said. "I'd love to. I loved that white sand."

Jasper seemed a little better the next day. He wanted to walk barefoot in the sand and even suggested that they dip their feet in the water. "We'll get our toes in the Gulf and then in the Atlantic and all the way back to the Pacific before this trip is done."

"That sounds wonderful." Sugar removed her shoes and left them sitting on a towel. And then she and Jasper went, hand in hand, to dip their feet in the salty water.

"I feel close to Elaine, standing here where we left her ashes. She was troubled, but then she had good reason. Her mom was so full of herself—that's the role model my sister had."

"She was so different than you, darlin', that I'm surprised y'all shared any genes at all," Jasper said.

"Half genes, I suppose. From our dad—not her mother—but you know all this." She stepped back out of the water.

Jasper draped an arm around her as they made their way back to the towel. "Yep, I do, but sometimes it's good to drag out the memories and talk about things again. I'm just glad that she shared Jolene with us all those years. That child stole my heart from the first time we got to keep her," Jasper said. "Her visits were the highlight of our summers."

Back then, Jasper had boasted a full head of dark hair, but now it was mostly gray. His angular face wasn't as smooth as it used to be, and he'd decided to grow a beard. At first Sugar figured if she ignored it, he'd soon get tired of it and shave it off, but now she'd grown to like it.

"The day that Victoria took Elaine from us, I went down to the bayou and cried until my eyes were swollen. I was afraid she'd never take care of Elaine properly. But she hired a nanny, got remarried, and . . ." Sugar inhaled a lungful of ocean air.

"And that's why you two are so different, even as relations." Jasper squeezed her hand. "Your stepmother and your sister both had the maternal instincts of a Doberman."

Sugar wiped the sand from her feet and put her shoes back on. "You never said that before."

Jasper raised his shoulders in a half shrug. "Just now dawned on me. A Doberman is a fine dog, but the females sometimes make poor mothers. One of my bowlin' buddies had one several years ago. The mama dog got tired of her babies and wouldn't let them eat. They had to bottle-feed those little pups until they were big enough to sell."

"You think Jolene will inherit that?" Sugar shivered.

"No, darlin', I don't. She looks like you and acts like you. Every time Victoria came to get that child, I went to the bayou and cried, too." Jasper dropped her hand and draped an arm around her shoulders. "Main difference in y'all is that you had amazing taste in men and she doesn't."

Without words, she cupped his face in her hands and kissed him.

🌸

Jolene was all for throwing the heavy furniture out the bedroom window and setting fire to it after she'd helped Tucker move it out into the hallway. The four-poster bed weighed as much as a baby elephant. The dresser was most likely created from concrete and only covered with a thin layer of oak. It was no wonder Aunt Sugar didn't move the furniture around in the rooms—she didn't own a forklift. Once Jolene and Tucker had gotten those two pieces out, she slid down the wall and panted like a puppy dog.

Tucker just grinned and went back to bring out a nightstand. He acted like it was nothing, but he didn't fool her one bit. His biceps strained the fabric of his shirt, and the sweat on his brow told a different story.

"Little wimpy, are you?" he asked.

"That would be the pot calling the kettle black," she said between short breaths.

He sat down on the floor beside her. "At least I'm not huffing and puffing."

"Maybe not right now, but when you get that other nightstand and the washstand out, we'll see if you've got enough air left in your lungs to call me wimpy," she said.

He brought out the other stand. "Now *you* can get the last piece."

"Yeah, right! I'll get you a can of spinach and you can play like Popeye and bring the furniture out with one hand," she told him.

"You aren't old enough to know anything about Popeye," he said.

"I'm thirty-one, and Aunt Sugar had lots of old VHS cartoons for me to watch when I came to visit. You ready for that muscle-building spinach?" she asked.

"Hello!" a trio of voices yelled up from the foyer. "Jolene, where are you? We brought cookies."

"Who—" Tucker started.

"Aunt Sugar's friends." She giggled as she rose to her feet. "Lucy, Flossie, and Dotty."

She raced down the stairs. "What a wonderful surprise. How are y'all and how'd you get away at this time of day?"

"We're on our noon break, and we decided to have cookies and milk today," Flossie answered. "And Dotty don't even start to work until evening."

"And we're mad at Sugar for going off on that trip. That's the second stage of grief, you know." Dotty yawned. "Sorry about that. I've only been up long enough to do my hair and makeup. But we've been talkin', and Sugar going away hurts us almost as much as if she died. Thank God she didn't, but it still hurts. And we're going through the stages— so here we are with cookies."

"We're also prayin' that she didn't make a mistake. Who's that up there?" Lucy pointed up.

"Now, *Sister* Lucy."

"Don't you *sister* me, Flossie. Just because I go to church don't make me a nun." Lucy shook her finger at her. "Is Reuben up there starting some remodeling?"

Jolene shook her head. "Reuben sold his half of the inn to Tucker Malone. He's the one making all the noise."

Lucy quickly made the sign of the cross on her chest. "Sweet Jesus in heaven. You aren't lettin' him live here, are you?"

"He owns half the place. What choice do I have?" Jolene asked. "Come on in the kitchen. We'll have milk with our cookies while the coffee is making."

"Of course." Flossie removed a stocking hat and fluffed back her kinky hair. She led the way into the kitchen with Lucy right behind her.

Dotty fell in next and Jolene brought up the rear. "Don't pay no attention to Lucy. She's in another of her church phases," Dotty whispered over her shoulder. "She always does this when she loses a boyfriend, whether by death or to another woman."

"Another church phase?" Jolene asked.

"It runs in cycles. If she's got a boyfriend, she don't have time for church except on Sunday, when the only thing that'd keep us from sittin' beside Sugar would be if we was sick nigh unto death. When they either break up or he dies, then she has to get right with the Lord for all her sinful ways with the boyfriend, and that means she's at some church every time the doors open for services. Right now, she's in the process of gettin' right."

"Catholic?" Jolene asked.

"Nope. She mixes all the religions up together so that she gets the right one." Dotty giggled.

"How does that work?"

"Wait and see," Dotty said out of the side of her mouth.

Flossie had taken the plastic wrap from the paper plate piled with chocolate-chip cookies and set them in the middle of the table.

"We remember Tucker from when he came to church with Melanie on occasion. He's such a tortured soul. And he drinks on weekends." Lucy brought out the milk and four glasses.

Dotty pursed her lips. "Gawd Almighty, Lucy. We're livin' in a brand-new world. If Tucker needs a little something to get him through the tough times, that's his business. And if Jolene wants to sleep with him, then that's her business."

Lucy slapped her hands over her ears. "I can't listen to you take God's name in vain. I swear you didn't used to be like this before you and Bruce left perfectly good jobs and went to keepin' a honky-tonk."

"Whoa, ladies," Jolene said. "I'm not sleeping with my partner, and what's this about a tortured soul?"

"He's like my poor dead Ezra. He felt guilty because his wife died, too." Lucy shook her finger under Dotty's nose. "And don't you giggle again, Dotty. I'm past the denial stage about our precious Sugar leaving, and I'm well into anger, so watch what you say to me."

"Well, honey, you did your best to console Ezra when he was alive, so you shouldn't have any regrets. He probably died with a smile on his face because he was dreaming about all the sex y'all had," Dotty said.

"There's that bar talk comin' out again. You used to be a fine Christian woman before you owned the Tipsy Gator," Lucy said.

"I'm still a Christian. I believe in God and Jesus, even though I run a bar. And I go to church almost every Sunday, so don't fuss at me." Dotty shook her head.

"We didn't come here to argue and fight about religion or the Gator." Flossie picked up a cookie. "And I doubt that Ezra made it past the Pearly Gates anyway, so I don't know why you're all up in religion, Lucy. That old scoundrel never went to church in his life. If he went to heaven, he'd be miserable up there."

Dotty reached for a cookie. "Flossie's right. We didn't come here to fight. We came to check on Jolene and tell her about the Easter Tour of Homes."

Jolene busied herself making coffee, but not a word of what they said escaped her. "Why is Tucker a tortured soul? And I'd love to be included in the tour."

Dotty lowered her voice. "I can still hear him upstairs. Come on over here so we can talk about him. He lost his wife, Melanie, a couple of years ago. She was from down in Marshall, but her daddy was raised here in Jefferson, so they came to church with Sugar and us." She paused. "Anyway, she went away to college and made a teacher out of herself. She met Tucker once she went to work in Dallas. He was a cop there."

"She was his whole life," Lucy whispered. "Then she died in a car wreck, and bless his heart, he's never got over it." She clucked like an old hen gathering in her baby chickens. "I just can't believe he bought half interest in this place. It takes a people person to operate a B&B, and from what I hear, Tucker is almost a hermit."

"I guess we've all got our own emotional baggage," Jolene said.

"Wait until he hauls his damn sorry ass home drunk and you've got guests in the place," Lucy declared.

"She loves Jesus, but she still cusses a little," Dotty said with a wicked grin.

"He's a fantastic carpenter. He's got money to put into the inn. And I'll cross the drinkin' bridge when it happens. And . . ." She glanced over at Dotty, who shrugged and winked.

"And just so y'all know." Jolene took a deep breath. "I'll be working at the Gator starting Friday night."

"Lord have mercy," Lucy groaned. "Have you talked to Sugar about this?"

"Visited with her last night and was going to tell her, but . . ." She went on to tell them how disappointed Jasper was with Reuben's choice.

"I was afraid that would hit him hard," Dotty said.

"Of course it did, but we're not through talkin' about this horrible idea of you working in a bar." Lucy threw a hand over her forehead in a dramatic gesture and then shook a fist at Dotty. "You're leading our sweet girl down the path of unrighteousness. Jolene, I'll give you a job in my place of business. Full-time with benefits if you'll quit the Gator right now."

"I know bartending, and I can only handle part-time work with the inn, but thank you," Jolene said and tried to change the subject. "Do I have the recipe for these cookies in Aunt Sugar's files?"

"I'm sure you do, *chère*," Dotty said. "But now let's talk about this tour of homes. Surely Sugar mentioned it?"

"Oh, that." Jolene was glad Dotty had changed the subject. "She always wanted to be included in it but figured the Magnolia was too far out of town."

"It might be, but we want to add it this year," Lucy said.

Dotty went on. "The three of us are on the Chamber of Commerce committee together for the first time. We carry the majority, and we've decided to vote for the Magnolia Inn to be on the tour. It would be a big thing if you could have it all spruced up by then. The chamber puts lots of advertising and promotion into the tour. Folks come for miles and miles to get a peek inside the bed-and-breakfast places. It could really help you out."

"That's, what, like three months from now?" Jolene asked.

"The tour itself is the Saturday before Easter, so that makes it April 20," Flossie answered. "That'll give you a few months to get things up and running. And if you'll come to work for me instead of"—she shot a dirty look toward Dotty—"working as a bartender, you can choose your hours."

"You'll want to start booking rooms pretty soon for the summer and fall." Dotty ignored Flossie's comment. "The tour would be a wonderful opportunity for folks to see what you've done and get their reservations made. I always wanted to include the Magnolia, but I kept getting voted down since only Lucy and I were on the committee. But this year we've got Flossie, so we'll see to it. Sugar will be so tickled. She always wanted to get to show it off."

"Yes," Tucker said from the doorway. "We'll have it ready by then."

Jolene felt heat rising from her neck to her cheeks. How much had he heard? She motioned to the coffeepot and then to the cookies. "Come on in and meet my friends."

"Always ready for cookies and coffee. I'm Tucker Malone." He stuck his hand out toward Lucy.

Her expression said that she'd rather be sticking her hand in a rattlesnake pit, but she put her frail hand in his. "You probably don't remember us, but we remember you from when you used to come to church with your wife. I'm Lucy Rogers. I own Attic Treasures, an antique store in Jefferson."

"Jolene told me that a couple of you ladies own antique shops. That's wonderful." Tucker brought her hand to his lips and kissed her knuckles. "I'm right glad to make your acquaintance, ma'am. I hope to do some business with y'all as we work on this place. We'd like to keep the antique ambience but use modern things like tubs and showers to make things nice for our guests."

From Lucy's expression, Jolene could've sworn she'd rather have been shaking hands with the devil. "Well, I'll be sure to give you a real good price on anything that you can use."

He turned to settle his crystal-clear blue eyes on Flossie.

"I'm Flossie Simmons, and I own Mama's Place in Jefferson. My antiques are better than Lucy's." She winked. "And since Jolene is like a daughter to all of us, I can beat any deal Lucy would give you."

"And I'm Dotty Beauchamp." Dotty's southern accent thickened. "I'm a Louisiana girl from the other side of the Big Cypress Bayou, and I own the Tipsy Gator. I've seen you a few times in my bar. You always sit on the last stool in the shadows, right, *chère*?"

"Yes, ma'am, I sure do," Tucker said.

Jolene was totally blown away. One minute they were ready to crucify her for letting Tucker live there, and the next they were flirting with him. Good glory! They had to be seventy or older, and he wasn't a day over thirty-seven.

"We should let you two get back to work," Dotty said with a broad wink toward Jolene. "And since you're going to be out of pocket on Friday night, then Sunday afternoon will be our meetin' time."

They pushed their chairs back and paraded toward the foyer. Lucy stopped at the hall tree for her coat, and Tucker hurried over to help her into it. She frowned up at him and shook her finger under his nose.

"Get thee behind me, Satan. You almost got me with your slick ways, but I know the devil when I see him, and you won't entice me with your slyness. Jolene, when you realize that you are doing wrong, you pack your bags and come live with me. I will lead you to Jesus and salvation," Lucy declared.

Tucker chuckled as he stepped back and helped Flossie into her bright-red coat. "Thank you for the cookies."

"You're welcome. Good luck with all this remodeling." Flossie gave Jolene a quick hug and whispered, "I hope you know what you're doin'."

"Y'all come back anytime," Jolene said. "If you'll give me an hour's notice, I'll even have the cookies made."

Tucker picked up the last coat from the hall tree and held it out to Dotty. "It's been a real pleasure to meet you ladies."

Dotty nudged him on the arm. "Honey, don't you pay any attention to Lucy. She'll find a new boyfriend in a couple of weeks and fall off the religion wagon."

Jolene sank down on the bottom step of the stairs and sighed when Tucker shut the door behind the ladies. One bedroom was torn up. The upstairs hallway was a mess. She'd never get even that much put back together if he changed his mind and didn't buy half the inn.

Tucker sat down beside her and propped his forearms on his knees. "So you work in a bar?"

"Ever since I was twenty-one. Until then I did waitress work," she answered. "How much did you hear?"

"I got there when Lucy was offering you a job to quit working in a bar," he answered.

"Sounds like you heard most of it, then. I'll be working at a bar on Friday and Saturday nights. I understand that you drink a little on weekends."

He got to his feet. "I'm going to get a couple more cookies and another cup of coffee to take upstairs with me. And, honey, I drink a lot on Saturday nights."

"Just so long as we understand each other." Jolene stood up and headed toward the kitchen. "Right now we could take fifteen minutes off and call it a midmorning snack."

"Got chocolate syrup?" He followed her into the kitchen.

"For the cookies, the coffee, or the milk?"

"Milk, and then I dip my cookies in it," he answered.

The ladies had called him a tortured soul. Jolene stole glances at him as she got out the chocolate syrup. It was a shame that he'd lost his wife so suddenly. He might never get over it, but she sure wasn't looking forward to dealing with another weekend drunk—like her mother or that last worthless boyfriend.

Tucker never would've figured Jolene for a bartender. Maybe an elementary school teacher or even a bank teller. She wasn't big enough to be a bartender, for one thing, and she was way too cute. The drunks would have her in tears in minutes.

Surely she worked somewhere like the Southern Comfort, a bar at the country club over in Tyler. He could visualize her in a place like that. Melanie's dad had a membership there, and Tucker had gone with him to that place one time after a game of golf. That night a tall redhead had been working the bar, and she'd been flirting with a man in a three-piece suit. He remembered it well because the man had taken off his wedding ring and shoved it into his pocket.

He looked down at his own ring and felt yet another wave of guilt. Every time he and Jolene were in the same room, something warmed his cold heart. He wouldn't betray Melanie by letting another woman take her place. Melanie had always told him to remove his own ring when he was working with tools, but he just couldn't do it. He looked down at his ring now and felt another wave of guilt.

"You sure are quiet," Jolene said.

"Thinkin'." He finished his milk and carried the glass to the dishwasher. "That was a crazy bunch of old ladies. One's religious. One's kind of fussy, and the other one owns the local bar."

"They were Aunt Sugar's best friends from the time she was a little girl, way back before they bought antique stores and inherited a bar." Jolene poured two cups of coffee and handed one to him. "Dotty's husband, Bruce, died years ago. None of the four, including Aunt Sugar, ever had children. I think that's why they were so close, and why Aunt Sugar's going off on this long, extended trip has left a hole in their lives. She kind of held the group together, especially after Dotty kept running the bar even after her husband died. I wouldn't be surprised if Lucy isn't on her religion kick from missing Aunt Sugar as much as the fact her latest boyfriend died not long ago."

Tucker's brow wrinkled in a frown. "She's still dating at her age?"

"Lucy likes men"—Jolene's shoulders raised in a shrug—"but Aunt Sugar going away can't be easy. They are all in their late sixties, so this is a drastic life change."

"Did your aunt live right here her whole married life?" he asked.

"Not just her married life. Her whole life—period. Her grandparents owned this property. When they passed on, they left it to her father. He'd just gotten married, and he and his wife had Aunt Sugar that next year. They opened the inn up for business right after she was born. Grandpa nicknamed her Sugar when she was a baby, and it stuck. When he died he gave this place to Sugar and the equivalent of its worth to my mother."

Jolene's soft, lilting voice soothed Tucker, so he kept asking questions. He wasn't really interested so much in her past. For all he cared, she could read the Bible or even the phone book to him. "How'd your mama feel about that?"

"She never liked this place, so it didn't bother her one bit. She and Aunt Sugar had always kept in touch even if they weren't good friends, mainly because of me—or at least that's what Mama said," Jolene answered. "You ready to go back to work? I've got enough energy to help you get that last piece of furniture out of the room and then we can pull up the carpet."

He put their dirty dishes in the dishwasher. "You got brothers or sisters?"

She shook her head. "Nope, and my folks are both gone. All that's left of my family is me and Aunt Sugar. Daddy went with a heart attack when I was sixteen, and Mama . . ." She hesitated for several seconds. "Mama got addicted to pills and alcohol. She overdosed when I was twenty." She headed out of the kitchen.

The pain in her voice mirrored what he felt when he thought about his precious Melanie. He could hear the hurt and pain in Jolene's tone, and a fresh wave of guilt washed over him, but at least he wasn't hurting anyone by his weekend binges.

"By blood, this place should be all yours." Tucker followed her as they climbed the stairs.

"But by hard work and working as a fishing guide on the bayou in the lean years, Uncle Jasper should have the right to give half of it to his kin—even if I never did like Reuben and I'd still like to shoot him, it's only fair."

"Why didn't you like Reuben?" Tucker picked up one end of the washstand.

"He always was arrogant, and he's a sissy. He wouldn't even bait his own hook when we went fishing. Besides, he pulled my ponytail every chance he got, blamed me if something got broken"—she hesitated— "and when I was twelve, he cornered me in the utility room and shoved his hand up under my skirt."

"You didn't kill him?" Tucker asked.

"Aunt Sugar took care of it, and we came to visit at different times from then on. Look, I think he's insecure and angry because he can't find his place in the world, but I still don't like him."

Should've offered him ten thousand less than I did, Tucker thought.

Chapter Six

ucker arrived ten minutes early for the appointment that Friday, and Belinda motioned him on inside her office. She sat behind her desk with a stack of papers in front of her and nodded toward a guy who was already seated. "Tucker Malone, this is Reuben McKay. Reuben, this is Tucker. Are you both ready to get this deal finalized? Either one of you decide to back out?"

Reuben stood to his feet and stuck out his hand. "I'm ready to close this."

"Same here." Tucker had shaken hands with six-year-old boys who had a firmer grip.

Reuben sat back down, took off his glasses, and cleaned them with a fancy cloth he pulled out of his pocket. His eyes shifted all around the office as if he was afraid to look right at anyone. Tucker's cop training kicked in, and he'd bet dollars to stale doughnuts that Reuben had been bullied when he was a kid. That would explain why he was so mean to Jolene—he'd been looking for someone that he could bully so he'd feel strong.

Tucker wanted to kick Reuben's chair out from under him for being mean to Jolene. No one deserved to be bullied, but especially not Jolene. Tucker was a good judge of character, and that woman was kind, sweet, hardworking, easy to get along with, and a whole list of other accolades, including cute, kissable—

Whoa! Melanie's my wife. Jolene's a partner.

Belinda flipped open a folder and scanned through the pages. Tucker eased into a chair at the end of her desk where he could study Reuben to get his mind off Jolene. The man crossed his legs and kept a constant foot movement going. He was so nervous that he looked like he might bolt at any minute. Tucker had dealt with lots of men like that in interrogation, and the majority of the time, they were guilty of something—usually more than pestering a girl.

"Everything is in order," Belinda said. "Reuben can go first. Sign beside the yellow tabs." She shoved the set of papers over to him and turned to face Tucker. "I understand that you've moved your trailer out to the property, and you and Jolene have started some remodeling."

Reuben chuckled and gave each of them a smug look.

Tucker's hands knotted into fists. "What's so funny?"

"Be careful of starting anything with that woman," Reuben said.

Tucker's hands relaxed. He leaned back in the chair and crossed an ankle over his knee. "Oh, really? Why?"

"She never has amounted to anything. Went to work in a bar soon as she was old enough, and her mama was a junkie with an alcohol problem, don't you know?" Reuben spit out the words like they tasted nasty in his mouth. "The apple never falls far from the tree."

It was Tucker's turn to laugh.

Reuben stopped writing and glared at him. "That funny to you?"

"It don't take much in the way of detective work to see what kind of tree you fell out of," Tucker answered.

"Okay, boys"—Belinda raised her voice a little—"you can have a pissin' contest if you want, but not in my office. You're here to sign papers, transfer deeds and money, and then leave. After that, if you want to bloody the streets with your fightin', then that's your business."

Reuben set his jaw, finished signing the papers, and shoved them across the desk to Belinda.

"Tucker, you sign where the red tabs are located while I tally up my commission so Reuben can write me a check," she said.

Tucker hoped that she tacked on a few extra dollars for stupidity. He signed all the places and then handed her the check he'd brought—already filled out with the amount they had agreed on. He stood up and settled his cowboy hat on his head. "Am I done?"

"Yes, you are. I'll take it all to the courthouse and file it for you. You can pick up copies of everything next week," she answered.

Tucker turned toward Reuben. "I want to thank you for selling me your half of the Magnolia Inn. Jolene and I intend to make a booming business out of it, and I'm glad to be half owner. Maybe someday you'll book a room with us for a weekend so you can see what you missed out on." He flashed his brightest fake smile.

"Don't hold your breath. I hate that place. Always did and always will. The only good thing is now I've got payment for all those miserable weeks my mother made me spend in that mosquito-infested swamp," Reuben said.

"To each his own." Tucker tipped his hat at Belinda. "Be seein' you around." Then he looked down at Reuben, who was still seated. "But the truth is, I imagine Jolene will be glad not to see you around, after the way you treated her when she was a child."

"That was rude," Reuben muttered as Tucker left the room.

Tucker chuckled and kept going.

❀

Jolene poked her head in the door of the Tipsy Gator. "You busy?"

Dotty looked up and waved from behind the cash register. "Not as much as I will be tonight. What brings you out today?"

"Tucker's signing the papers, and I'm not even ready to see Reuben walk down the sidewalk. So, with a free half an hour, I thought I'd check in to see if you've got the tax forms ready for me to sign," she said.

Dotty pulled a couple of sheets from under the bar. "Got them right here. Take about two minutes to fill out, and then we're good to go. We'll be busy tonight. You know, if I'd had a dozen girls with your looks and pretty eyes, I could've gone into the escort business and retired ten years ago."

Jolene cracked up. "Yeah, right. Aunt Sugar would have sent you away to a convent if you'd even let the idea float through your mind."

"Ain't it the truth? I'm glad you're goin' to help me tonight so I don't have to wear my little short legs out runnin' up and down this bar," Dotty laughed with her.

"So we're going to be really busy, huh?" Jolene filled out the papers and gave them back.

"Oh, honey." Dotty smiled. "To start with it's the first weekend of the month. And then folks have had all the family stuff they can stand from the holidays. Everyone is ready to get out and kick up their heels a little. I don't mind busy. I just hope we have happy drunks and not mean ones."

"The happy ones tip better, so I'm with you. I should be going. Just wanted to stop by and check in with you," Jolene said.

"So how's the work coming along out at the inn?" Dotty asked before Jolene could slide off the barstool.

"Great, but it looks like crap. We've got the furniture stacked up in the hallway. The carpet is torn out, and we're going to the lumberyard in a little while to get stuff to start building walls for a bathroom and closet." Jolene started toward the door. "You should come out and see it before and after."

"I'll be there Sunday, remember." Dotty put the paperwork away and hopped up to sit on the counter. "You are welcome here at the Gator anytime. You don't have to wait until the nights that you're scheduled to work to stop by here. It gets kind of lonely sometimes during the days. That's why I spend time at the antique shops with Flossie and Lucy pretty often. If I'm not here, you can find me there."

"Thank you, and the same goes for you coming out to the inn. See you later." Jolene waved over her shoulder as she left.

She got into her truck and listened to the local country music station as she drove to town. She kept the engine running when she parked in front of the lawyer's office. Expecting Tucker to slide into the passenger seat, she was surprised to see Flossie.

Jolene turned the radio off. "Well, good mornin'."

"Tucker is in there right now finalizin' the deal," Flossie said. "I been watchin' from the window of my shop. Reuben got here first. I thought you might wait in the shop. Where'd you go?"

"Down to fill out tax papers and talk to Dotty about bar stuff. Tonight is my first night. I don't expect it'll be much different than the Twisted Rope," Jolene answered.

"I owe you an apology," Flossie said.

"About what?"

"I should've bought half of the Magnolia Inn. I put in a bid, but I was too late. Belinda had already given Tucker twenty-four hours to make up his mind. I should've upped his bid by a few thousand. If I hadn't been so stubborn, we could be partners and my money would be invested in something pretty nice," Flossie sighed.

Jolene was pretty sure that if Flossie had purchased half the property, she'd still be working with Tucker, since he was the best carpenter in the area, so there didn't seem to be much difference in the situation.

Flossie went on, "I never did like Reuben. He was rude to Sugar more times than I can count on my fingers and toes. And then for him to sell out as soon as the papers were signed last week made me furious. Not that I wanted you to have to deal with him every day. Hell, no! But I didn't want him to make a penny more on the sale than Tucker offered."

Jolene reached across the console and patted Flossie on the shoulder. "No hard feelin's here. Who would you have hired to do the remodeling?"

"Tucker, if I could get him. He's the best," Flossie answered.

"So I'd still deal with him every day. It is what it is, Flossie. Don't punish yourself." Jolene smiled.

Flossie laid a hand on Jolene's arm and squeezed it gently. "You're so much like Sugar that you should've been her daughter instead of her niece. Got to go now. There's a customer goin' into the store, and I'm runnin' it alone today."

"Why?" Jolene asked.

"Janie, my part-time help, has that stomach bug that's goin' around. She'll be back tomorrow," Flossie replied as she got out of the truck.

Tucker was behind her before Flossie could slam the door. "It's not often that a pretty lady opens the door for a ragged old cowboy like me, so I thank you for making my day."

Flossie flashed a bright smile toward him. "You are definitely a charmer. Jolene would do well to keep a close eye on you. We'll be out to check on things Sunday afternoon. We'll bring dinner for everyone with us and be there after church."

"Thank you. We'll look forward to it," Jolene said.

Flossie darted across the street.

Tucker crawled into the passenger seat and fastened his seat belt. "I guess that means I have to get over my hangover by noon on Sunday?"

"Yes, it does. And . . . like I said before, I won't abide drunks."

"Reason?" he asked.

"Mother and boyfriend, and we'll leave it at that," she said.

"I've never asked for help with my problem, and it won't affect you."

"See that it doesn't," she said.

She wanted to know what had happened in Dixie Realty, but after that little exchange, she kept her mouth shut.

❀

The detective in Tucker wanted to ask more questions about her life with an addicted mother, but if she wanted to talk about her past, she would. He'd listen when and if she ever did. If not, then that was her business—just like drinking was his. Saturday night had been his and Melanie's date night, and he'd always worked at making it special. He still had all the memories of those wonderful dates. She deserved that much and more for putting up with him and his demanding job. Drinking didn't always erase the memories, but it did soften the edges and the pain of her being gone.

"Did you have a long wait?" he asked when the silence became uncomfortable.

"What?" She frowned.

"At the lawyer's office. You said you had an errand to run. I'm asking if you had a long wait for me to finish up."

She shook her head. "Sorry. My mind was miles away. No, I was only there a couple of minutes, and Flossie kept me company."

"You don't have to go with me. Drop me off at the inn and I'll go on in my truck." After seeing Reuben, he wanted to wrap Jolene up in his arms and tell her that he'd protect her.

Are you stupid? Jolene has been taking care of herself for years. She doesn't need your protection. She needs your support and friendship. Melanie's voice was loud and clear in his head.

"Partnership," he muttered.

"What was that?" Jolene asked.

"Nothing. I was just thinking of my first partner," he answered.

"Are you ashamed to be seen with a woman driving you?" she asked.

"It makes me uncomfortable," he admitted. "My first partner on the force drove me crazy. She wouldn't use the cruise control and she talked nonstop, using her hands to tell a story—both of them, most of the time, and driving with her knee. My next partner and I made a deal—if he'd let me drive, I'd pay for our first cup of coffee every morning. I'd as soon be behind the wheel as sitting in the passenger seat."

She pulled off on the side of the road. "Then you drive."

"Are you serious?"

"We're partners, aren't we? So you're afraid of spiders, and you like to drive. I hate mice with a passion, a rat will send me into cardiac arrest, and I enjoy sitting in the passenger seat. It's no big deal. Partners take care of each other," she said.

"Sounds good to me." Tucker got out and walked around the truck and let Jolene slide over. He adjusted the seat and pulled out onto the highway. "And I got to tell you, I got the same feeling about Reuben that you did. He was so nervous, I thought he might pass out right there. I bet he was bullied, and he did those mean things to you so he'd have some power and feel less insecure. I kind of felt sorry for him until he badmouthed you and your mother."

Jolene nodded. "He sure knows how to ruin any sympathy, doesn't he?"

"Oh, yeah." Tucker pulled into the last remaining parking spot in front of the lumberyard. He would have been a gentleman and opened the door for Jolene, but she was halfway to the building before he could undo his seat belt. When he made it inside, she was nowhere to be seen.

"That cute little blonde that just asked about the bathroom fixtures with you?" Billy Joe asked. The salesman pointed toward the back of the store.

"Yep, that's her." Tucker nodded. "I've got a big list. Think y'all could make a delivery to Jefferson today? Actually, it's pretty close to the county line, not in town."

"Sure thing. We've been slow all week. What are you doin'?"

"Remodeling the old Magnolia Inn. I bought half interest," Tucker answered.

He'd thought that he'd feel something like happiness or maybe even elation when he was the owner, but it was just another day. He wondered, as he handed the long list off to Billy Joe, what kind of emotions Jolene had that moment. Now they were bound up in this partnership until one of them got tired of it. Was she happy to have the money to bring the inn into the modern world and keep its charm at the same time? She could have said something—anything—but she hadn't.

"Hey, what do I need to do now?" she asked as she walked up behind him.

"Go look at all the bathtubs and shower units." His hand brushed against her shoulder when he pointed, and there was definitely a spark. Not a big, overpowering one, but it was there and it worried him. "Basically, that's all we have to pick out today. The rest of the list is already in Billy Joe's hands."

"Who?"

"He works here. I do a lot of business with all of the employees," he answered.

When they reached the display, she stopped and crossed her arms over her chest. "There's not a lot of difference, is there? This one is the cheapest."

"And there's a reason it's the least expensive. We'd be replacing it in a year if we have a lot of guests. They're lined up by price. Keep going all the way to the end and feel the difference with your hands. Check the thickness of the wallboard and, more importantly, check the warranty. Think about how often you want to tear out walls and replace the unit," he said.

Buying fixtures is like getting into a relationship. Melanie's voice popped into his head. *You need to be sure that the one you get has a fifty-year warranty and won't fall apart with use.*

We had that kind of relationship, darlin'. He stood perfectly still, hoping that she'd say something else, but she didn't.

73

"This is going to involve a lot of plumbing," Jolene said.

"Before we get done, we'll probably have the whole house refitted. And maybe most of the electrical wiring redone." He was a little aggravated that Jolene had broken the magic by speaking. It might be weeks before Melanie said anything else. And what did she mean by that comment about relationships? What they'd had couldn't be compared to bathtubs and showers—not by any stretch of the word.

What we had, with "had" being the key here. There was her voice again. *I keep telling you to let me go and move on, Tucker.*

"I can't," he said out loud.

"Can't what?" Jolene frowned. "Who are you arguing with?"

"Myself, I guess," he muttered and quickly changed the subject. "Move on to the last one in the line. That's the one I'd pick. It's got a lifetime warranty and . . ."

She laid a hand on his arm. "Okay, partner, if you're sure."

"I'm not real fond of redoing bathrooms. Putting in a new one isn't so tough, but trying to redo one in such a tiny space is a bitch."

"Well . . ." She dragged out the word. "Then you can pick out this stuff and I'll work on the antiques and pretty things."

"I can agree with that, but I would like to see what you pick out before you buy it," he said. "It's not that I don't trust you to choose gorgeous things, but I want to be sure the pieces will fit where we want to use them."

"Deal." She stuck out her hand.

There was another bit of chemistry when he took her small hand into his, and he didn't like it one bit. He couldn't be unfaithful to Melanie again—he'd felt guilty as hell the few times he'd had one-night stands in the past couple of years. They hadn't done a damn thing to ease the pain, anyway. He certainly hadn't felt anything for those women. So why was he feeling sparks now?

$\mathcal{G}$ ive a bunch of stir-crazy folks some loud country music, a few beers, a pool table, and maybe let them do some two-stepping or line dancing, and they're happy. By the looks of the parking lot that Friday night, there was going to be a full house at the Gator.

When Jolene rapped on the door, Dotty opened it immediately. "I thought you might be here soon. We've got a few minutes until opening. Want a root beer while we wait?"

"Yes, ma'am, with a shot of vanilla. But why wait?" Jolene tied an apron around her slim waist and tucked a towel in her hip pocket. "I'll get it. Since there'll be two of us tonight, which end do you want me to work?"

"I can see you've worked with more than one bartender." Dotty twisted the cap from a bottle of icy-cold root beer and gave it a shot of vanilla.

"You haven't?" Jolene took a long gulp.

"Couple of times, but it never worked out. We got in each other's way too much. I've held down the place with only my ever-changing bouncers since my Bruce died."

Jolene hopped up on a barstool beside Dotty. "We split the bar down the middle. I'll take one end, and we stay out of the other's way, unless one of us gets a rush and the other one hasn't got a customer.

That way we don't get confused about who we've served. Do you run tickets or is it cash when ordered?"

"Cash," Dotty said.

"How do we do the register?" Jolene asked. "I used a code at the Twisted Rope. The journey tape let the owner know at the end of the night how many drinks were served and how much tip money belonged to each of us."

"Well, in this establishment I'm going to trust you, *chère*. We sell. We get paid. We put it in the register and make change if we need to. Tips go in our pocket and we don't take time to count them until the night is done," Dotty told her.

"That's a lot of trust. I could rob you blind," Jolene said.

"But you won't or I'll tattle to your aunt Sugar." Dotty smiled.

"You are a tough one, Miz Dotty."

"Had to be with this job. I'm going to open the door now. You get the far end, and I'll work this one. Get ready for the first rush."

"Thank you." Jolene hugged Dotty. "For not letting Flossie and Lucy talk you into firin' me."

"Us Cajuns got to stick together." Dotty hopped down off the counter and crossed the wood floor.

She was right about the first rush. Thank goodness most everyone started off the night with bottles of beer or pitchers. A half an hour had gone by before someone even asked for a Jack and Coke. It was after that when Flossie perched on a barstool on Jolene's end of the bar and asked for a strawberry daiquiri.

"What in the devil are you doin' here? After the fit you and Lucy threw about me working here, I'm surprised that you even set foot in the Gator." Jolene made the drink and put it on the bar.

Flossie handed her a bill. "Havin' a daiquiri. Listenin' to a little music and . . ." She leaned across the bar and crooked her finger for Jolene to come closer. "Makin' sure that Lucy ain't here. Some old gray-haired guy came today and flirted with her. Said he was comin' to the bar to do a little dancin' tonight."

"And if she is? Isn't that her business?" Dotty joined them from the other end.

"Hell, no! It's my business." Flossie sipped her daiquiri and gave her a thumbs-up sign. "If she's on her hallelujah wagon, then we have to go to different churches with her every week—Wednesday night, Friday night, and every other event. I'm the one that catches the flak, since you have to run this bar. If Lucy's not on the wagon, then we only have to go once a week."

Dotty patted Jolene on the shoulder. "And when she's on her wagon, I have to get up early on Sunday, because some of them churches have two services and she wants to go to the early one," Dotty said. "You know she won't come to the Gator, Flossie, because she knows what I'd say. She's probably down at the Southern Comfort."

Flossie's drink sloshed as she slapped the bar with her bare hand. "Well, crap, I didn't think of that. If I find out that she's out drinkin' and screwin' around, I may not speak to her for a month."

"Aww, if she's doin' that, then she'll go to more than one service on Sunday and pray for a crop failure," Dotty laughed.

"Crop failure?" Jolene asked.

"Honey, you go sow wild oats on Friday and Saturday nights, then you go to church to ask God for a crop failure so them wild oats don't sprout up and grow." Dotty giggled.

"Hey, sweet thang, could I get a pitcher of Bud Light?" A man waved a ten-dollar bill over the top of Flossie's head.

Jolene grabbed it, drew up a pitcher full of beer, and passed it between Flossie and the guy next to her. "Change?"

"Naw, dawlin', you keep that." He winked.

"Thank you." Jolene put the price of the pitcher in the register, shoved what was left of the bill into her apron pocket, and used a bar rag to clean up the spilled drink. "So do you see this guy that's about to push Lucy off the amen bus?"

Flossie spun around on the stool and scanned the bar. "Nope, but I sure wish I did. I'm going to finish this drink and go home. Next weekend I'll check out the Southern Comfort if she mentions going out with him again."

Flossie found a table with some folks she knew near the back of the bar. Jolene didn't even notice that she was still there until a few minutes after midnight, when Dotty handed her another vanilla root beer. "Thank God you're here. I swear this is the busiest we've been in five years. You must be a magnet."

"Don't know about that, but I'm sure glad I wasn't workin' the bar alone tonight," Jolene said.

"That's just another reason why you should quit this place and come to work for me." Flossie parked herself on an empty barstool. "I won't work you nearly as hard, and I'll pay you a better salary."

Dotty snapped a towel at her. "That's enough out of you, or I'll tell Lucy you was checkin' up on her."

Flossie ignored Dotty and focused her attention on Jolene. "Make me one of these things to go." Flossie held up her empty glass. "If I've got to sit through Mass on Sunday, I should at least have something to ask forgiveness for."

"You okay to drive?" Jolene asked.

"Honey, I come from a long line of moonshine runners. My grandma and grandpa moved over here from Kentucky after Grandpa made a fortune in 'shine. I can hold my liquor and sell a dead man a new coffin, and Lucy ain't the only one who can please a man in more than fifty ways. I'll see you Sunday after church."

"That ought to be fun." Dotty grinned. "Lucy will have you and Tucker both saved, sanctified, and dehorned before we finish eating. Dammit! I wish she'd showed up here tonight so I didn't have to go to early-morning Mass on Sunday."

"Why don't you just tell her you aren't goin'?" Jolene asked.

"Only way she'll come to the inn is if we go to church first, so she can ward off that devil Tucker Malone. She thinks he might seduce *her*." Flossie laughed so hard that black mascara streaks rolled down her cheeks.

Jolene laughed with her as she handed her a fistful of napkins to wipe her tears away. "I can't believe you said that."

"Well, it's the truth." Flossie dabbed at her cheeks. "I'm leaving on that note. They say to always leave the crowd laughin'."

"Well, you drive careful, and I'll have the table set when you arrive," Jolene said.

Flossie put on her coat and waved. "It's been fun. See y'all Sunday."

A lady staggered up to the bar. Her jet-black hair was styled even higher than Dotty's, and what was left of her lipstick had settled into the wrinkles around her mouth. "Give me two Jack and Cokes, and would you please bring them to the table? See that stud over there? He's goin' to dance with me and take me home." She slurred every word. "And then the real party starts."

Jolene poured a couple of drinks and whispered to Dotty, "Should we take her keys and call someone to take her home?"

"No, she didn't drive here. She came with a friend and she'll leave with that man." Dotty nodded toward the gray-haired cowboy at the table with the woman. "This happens about once a month. Same friend, but a different guy takes her home every time."

"I wonder if she's got a daughter at home waiting for her," Jolene whispered.

"Reminding you of your mother?" Dotty asked.

Jolene nodded and headed down the bar to wait on another customer. She'd never followed her mother to a bar, because she had to work every night. And her mother had never dyed her hair black or worn it styled like that, but the story was the same. There had been a few times that she'd brought the same man home, but not often. When she did get involved for more than one night, it was because the man promised her the moon.

Staring between two men at the bar, she kept an eye on the woman. Jolene had been working a bar not so very different from the Gator for ten years, and she'd seen lots of women make complete fools out of themselves. So why did the memories of her mother surface that night? Maybe it was being back in the area where her mama was born. Or perhaps it was because Jolene needed to get closure.

Dotty touched her on the shoulder. "You okay, kiddo?"

"Fine, just old memories came haunting me," Jolene admitted.

"It happens." Dotty gave her another pat and went back to her end of the bar.

❁

Tucker brought the picture of Melanie in from the trailer and set it on his bedside table. The antique lamp didn't throw enough light to use for reading, but it lit the framed photograph up very well. He stared at it, remembering the day that it had been taken. They'd met at a Fourth of July party given by mutual friends, and the picture had been taken the next year when he proposed to her in that same spot. His eyes grew heavy, and finally he fell asleep, but she didn't sneak into his dreams.

At three o'clock he sat straight up in bed, every nerve on high alert. Someone was in the trailer—no, the house. He was in his bedroom at the Magnolia Inn, not in the trailer. He eased off the bed, slipped into his jeans, and removed his pistol from the drawer of the nightstand. Holding it to his side, he opened his bedroom door just enough to peek out. A shadow moved toward the center of the foyer. He brought the gun up, and a flash of light almost blinded him.

"What the hell?" he said.

Jolene whipped around. "Sorry I woke you. I tried to be quiet."

He slung the door all the way open. "I can't make the same promise when I come home late, but I'll do my best. How'd the first night at work go?"

"Busy. Made two hundred in tips. That'll pay the electric bill and put some food in the pantry." She sat down on a chair at the end of the foyer table and pulled off her boots. "I'm hungry. You want some cereal? There's the chocolate kind and the fruity one."

"Sure," he said. "Give me a minute."

"To put the gun away or get a shirt on?" she asked.

"I can go as I am," he offered.

"I might spill the milk." She headed toward the kitchen in mismatched socks.

"Why?" he asked.

She turned around and shrugged. "I don't pour too hot with a gun pointed at me or if I get distracted by a man's sexy chest, so you'd do well to put on a shirt and get rid of the gun."

"Yes, ma'am," he said.

The gun went back in the drawer, and he jerked his shirt over his head. She was setting out boxes of cereal on the table when he made it to the kitchen. A memory of Melanie in the kitchen flashed through his mind. He'd loved that woman with all his heart, but the kitchen had looked like a war zone after she cooked. And the high-pitched squeal of the smoke alarm always meant that dinner must be close to ready.

He got the milk from the refrigerator. "Don't suppose you want coffee just before bed, do you?"

She shook her head. "No, but as tired as I am, it probably wouldn't keep me from sleeping."

They ate in silence for the most part. She frowned a lot and cocked her head from one side to the other several times before she shook it in disagreement with whatever voices were in her head. It kind of reminded him of when Sassy needed to be treated for ear mites.

"Are you about to have a seizure or something?" he asked.

"No, there was a woman at the bar who . . ." She paused.

"Who what?" he asked.

"Mama," she said. "She reminded me of my mother. Not in looks, but in actions. I tried to close that chapter in my life a long time ago, but it keeps risin' to the surface."

"Want to talk about it?" Tucker understood exactly what she was talking about.

Jolene was quiet for so long that he figured she didn't want to say anything, but then she began to talk. "She was on a guilt trip from the time my daddy died. He probably had the heart attack because he was stressed out, working two jobs to keep her in her fancy jeans and a new car every year. And even that wasn't enough. His insurance policy paid off the credit cards, but she lost the car and the house. We moved into a trailer and she went to work at a grocery store there in town. Her guilt sent her into a vicious merry-go-round of drugs, alcohol, and men."

She refilled her glass and went on, "I love milk. We didn't always have it in the house those last couple of years, but Mama had her pills. When the doctor quit giving them to her, then she got them from the street. Every Saturday night she'd go out. Before she left, she'd get all dressed up and take two or three pills. That woman tonight reminded me of all that. I hated to see her like that. She'd always been . . ."

Just thinking that he'd been looking forward to hitting the bar the next night filled Tucker with his own share of guilt. He shouldn't put her through all that again—not even if they were just partners. She was a good woman, and she damn sure deserved better.

"How long was it until you lost her?"

"Four years after Daddy died. But truth is I lost her when the doctor gave her that first bottle of pills to help her get through the funeral. She'd always liked her liquor and usually started on cocktails long before five o'clock. Mix those with enough pain pills and—" Jolene's shoulder rose. "I thought when I got a job as a waitress after school every day that things would be better."

Something pinched his heart and tightened his chest. On Saturday nights when he often drank too much, he was looking for a way to make things better, to forget. And yet he hung on to every memory that he and Melanie had shared.

She went on, "The only thing that changed when I went to work was that Mama said she'd pay the bills with her paycheck, and I was responsible for bringing home the food."

Jolene should have been enjoying her senior year of school, Tucker thought. Pep rallies. Time with her friends and a boyfriend who'd be her first love. Not working for grocery money. Jolene deserved a good life just to pay for what all she'd been through.

"Did you hold up your end of the deal?" He wanted to move closer to her, wrap her up in his arms and hug her, but he couldn't make himself do that. It led to other things, and he'd vowed to love Melanie to death—that meant his as well as hers.

She picked up the dirty bowls and carried them to the dishwasher. "Didn't have much choice. Pretty soon I was doing double shifts on Friday and Saturday nights and paying the utility bills, too. Her paycheck was going for pills, booze, and lottery tickets."

"Why'd you stay?" Tucker asked.

"She was my mama, and I had a roof over my head even if I didn't have friends or any time to call my own. I got homework done in the kitchen at the café between customers. I don't know why it's all coming back so strong now. But I hated for her to go out, because it meant there'd probably be a strange man in the house the next morning. And he'd be eating up the groceries I'd brought in for us." Jolene rubbed her temples with her fingertips. "I'm sorry, Tucker. You didn't need to hear all that in the middle of the night."

"What's said in the Magnolia Inn stays in the Magnolia Inn, just like what they say about Vegas." He laid a hand on her arm and wished he could do more to take away some of the pain.

"Thank you. You'd never guess who showed up at the bar and stayed until midnight." She dropped her hands to her lap.

He removed his hand and took a guess. "Lucy with her new boyfriend, and they ordered some weird drink that you had to look up in the book to even know how to make?"

She refilled her milk glass. "Nope, Flossie, but she was there hoping that Lucy would show up. And you'll never guess why." She didn't give him time to answer. "Because if Lucy arrived at the bar, that would mean she was through with her religious phase."

"And then they wouldn't have to go to church with her, right?" Tucker asked.

"Exactly." Jolene yawned. "And now I'm going to bed. I can't get to sleep if I stay up until dawn. See you about noon, and we'll get in a few hours of work before I go back to the bar."

"Oh, no." Tucker shook his head. "I quit at noon on Saturday. Five and a half days a week is my limit. So sleep as long as you want. I plan on drawing up plans for the other bedrooms, and then Monday morning we'll get back after it."

"Whatever you say, partner." She started for the door but turned before she got there. "Thanks for listening. The song is out of my head now."

"You're welcome," he said. "I charge more for therapy. You'll get the bill next week."

"I'll pay it by cookin'."

"Sassy, ain't you?"

She laughed out loud. "No, sir! That's the cat."

Chapter Eight

Jolene parked near the door of the bar on Saturday night and dug around in her purse until she found her phone. She'd programmed in Dotty's number the night before so all she had to do was hit a button, and it started ringing.

"Please don't tell me you've changed your mind or you're not coming in tonight," Dotty answered.

"Not at all," Jolene said. "I'm parked right outside. Would you open the door for me?"

"I'm on my way," she said.

Jolene slid out of the truck, tucked the phone into the hip pocket of her jeans, and slung her purse over her shoulder. Dotty was waving from the door before Jolene rounded the end of her vehicle.

"Get on in here before that wind blows you right over the bayou into Louisiana, and we know what that means." Dotty laughed.

"It'd be tough to leave, right?"

"You got it, darlin'. My daddy loved his home state almost as much as my mama did." Dotty followed her across the floor.

"Like my dad. He talked about Louisiana a lot," Jolene said.

"Where're they buried?" Dotty asked.

"Aunt Sugar, Uncle Jasper, and I scattered their ashes in the Gulf of Mexico near Panama City Beach. They'd honeymooned there, and

I wanted to take them where they'd both been happy," she answered. "Know what you do when life gives you lemons?"

"You add tequila." Dotty snapped her fingers and did a three-second rendition of a salsa dance.

"Or throw them in the trash and make a chocolate cake," Jolene giggled.

"Now you're talkin' my language. I love chocolate." Dotty started across the floor. "From that full parking lot, it looks like we're in for another busy night. Guess word got out that I've got a hot new bartender."

"Oh, come on now." Jolene smiled.

"It's the truth, *chère*. They're coming to try to see if you'll go home with them." Dotty opened the door, and the first rush began. Within five minutes all the barstools were full and the jukebox was going full blast. Jolene drew up pitchers of beer to Blake Shelton singing "Kiss My Country Ass." Every time he sang the song title, everyone in the bar raised their glass and sang along.

"Got us a rowdy bunch tonight," Dotty said.

"Looks like it. Where's Bubba?" Jolene looked around the place for the bouncer from the night before.

"He called in this afternoon and quit. See that big old boy over there in the shadows by the door? That's Mickey, and he's promised me that he'll stick around awhile," Dotty answered.

Jolene glanced that way. Even though Mickey wasn't a tall man, he threw off an aura that said he could take down one of those muscled-up television wrestlers.

"Not what you expected?" Dotty asked.

"He looks like he can do the job," Jolene answered.

"Yep, he can." She smiled.

"And you know this because?" Jolene wiped the bar.

"He's got a reputation with several bars in this area for bein' a good bouncer. Trouble is he don't like to stay in one place very long. But I think he's shacked up with a woman," Dotty told her.

Jolene made a Jack and Coke for a customer. "That's his business. Long as he keeps a little peace in here, that's all you're interested in, right?"

"Amen to that!" Dotty gave her a thumbs-up. "I was thinkin' maybe Mickey might ask you out when I hired him."

"Ha! He does kind of remind me of my first boyfriend, though. I was thirteen and he was fourteen. He gave me my first kiss. His grandma brought him with her to the inn that summer for a whole week."

"Did Sugar know?" Dotty asked.

"Nope, I didn't tell her," Jolene answered.

"How old were you when you had a serious boyfriend?"

"Sixteen. Right after Daddy died, but we broke up after two months. He wanted me to drink, and even then I wouldn't touch the stuff," Jolene answered. "What about your first boyfriend?"

"That's a story for later," Dotty answered.

Another bunch of customers pushed into the bar, pausing in their conversation with the new noise. Jolene turned around to see Lucy and Flossie claiming two empty stools as soon as their occupants left and headed out the door. Lucy's hair had been freshly done, and they both wore jeans, boots, and western shirts with pearl snaps.

"What can I get you ladies?" Jolene asked.

"Two of them things you made Flossie last night. She's been talkin' about them all day," Lucy answered.

"I can't believe you are here, Lucy," Jolene said. "And drinking, too?"

"One drink won't hurt me. Jesus drank wine Himself. And I need to know that Dotty is takin' care of you proper," Lucy said.

"Lucy admitted that she's got a crush on the preacher who did the funeral for her last boyfriend," Flossie tattled. "We ain't never goin' to shake the religion out of her this time if she sweet-talks him into her satin sheets."

"Oh, hush," Lucy said. "Y'all excuse me. I've got to make a run to the ladies' room."

"What happened to the man who was going to meet her at a bar?" Dotty asked when Lucy was out of hearing distance.

"She says that he was sent to tempt her like the devil tried to tempt Jesus," Flossie said. "I'm afraid this ain't a phase. We might have to talk some sense into her—we'll have it right here in the bar some afternoon."

"Why here?" Jolene asked.

"Because," Flossie sighed. "We couldn't have it at the Magnolia since . . . well," she stammered.

"Is it Tucker?" Jolene asked.

"We'll be draggin' out a lot of wine and maybe some whiskey, and we don't want . . ." Dotty hesitated. "We understand why Tucker drinks on weekends, what with Melanie's death, but . . ."

"I thought tomorrow after Sunday dinner," Flossie said. "The sooner the better. You got any ideas about how to get her out of the house and down here, Jolene?"

Jolene fought against rolling her eyes. Sure, it was sad that Melanie had died and that Tucker couldn't seem to get over it, but he didn't need to be mollycoddled. He was a grown man. And he'd probably hate that these old gals were feeling so sorry for him.

"You've had these talks before?" Jolene set a couple of daiquiris on the bar.

"Yep." Dotty nodded. "They had one for me after my husband died. I was drownin' my sorrows in the wine bottle. So I was speaking from experience when I said that I understood Tucker's problem. He's been in here real often, *chère*, like almost every Saturday night, and he drinks a lot. Don't bother nobody, and he's never drunk enough that I have to take his keys, but still he don't need to be in on what we're about to do with Lucy." She leaned over and whispered, "I've been told that he drinks a lot at home after he leaves here."

"Why don't you drop that *chère* shit?" Flossie said. "You're in Texas and have been for more than sixty years, so say *darlin'* or *honey* like the rest of us, Dotty."

"Don't bitch at me over my endearments," Dotty said.

"There's a lot of difference in pouring out a bottle of wine and talkin' a woman out of what she sees as the love of her life," Jolene said. "And Tucker is a big boy. I don't know why you couldn't talk to her while we have dinner at the Magnolia."

"Bottle, nothing." Flossie almost snorted daiquiri out of her nose. "We poured out six of them cheap boxes of wine. There was enough for us to baptize Dotty in, as little as she is." Flossie gasped and pointed. "Do you see who's sittin' at the end of the bar now?"

Jolene tiptoed to see over their collective heads. When she did, she locked eyes with Tucker.

"Sweet Jesus," she muttered. "He's here."

"She's prayin' in a bar," Flossie laughed. "We might need to have a long talk with her and Lucy both."

"And he's on my end of the bar, so don't you worry about it." Dotty hurried off to take care of her customer.

🪷

Tucker took a sip of his drink and blinked. He was seeing things. That couldn't be Jolene. She was working at the Southern Comfort. She was way too classy to be tending bar in a honky-tonk like the Gator. He blinked again.

Well, Dotty owns this place, and she's Sugar's friend, so why wouldn't she give Jolene a job? Melanie was back in his head.

Dammit! He should have asked Jolene for more details. He racked his brain trying to bring back the conversation he'd overheard. She'd said that she worked in a bar Friday and Saturday nights. She didn't say which bar. He had made a rookie detective mistake and assumed it would have to be a club and not the Gator. He started to slide off the stool and simply leave, but it would seem awkward, and besides, he liked this place.

But what about next week? Melanie's voice whispered. *I've told you that you shouldn't be using liquor for an escape.*

"Now you talk to me," he mumbled.

That's all he got from Melanie, and after another whiskey and Coke from Dotty, he gave his barstool to a guy who'd just arrived. He nodded at Mickey on his way out and bypassed the house when he got home. He sat in the truck for several minutes before he got out, went inside the cold trailer, and slumped onto the sofa.

He finally dumped a dozen pens from a mug that Melanie had given him and poured it full of whiskey. "Who needs a bar?" he muttered.

Sometime after midnight he staggered from the trailer to the house. The key went into the lock, but it wouldn't turn no matter how many swear words floated away on the cold wind. Finally, he figured out that he was trying to open the door with the key that went to the trailer.

"Well, dammit!" He found the right one and the door swung open.

Sassy met him in the foyer and followed him into his bedroom.

"It's been a helluva night, Sassy girl," he slurred as he kicked off his boots. "Did you know that the trailer can be a bar? Well, it can. I got whiskey. I played music on my phone until the battery ran out, and I didn't even have to plug money into the jukebox. I hate that Jolene is working at the Gator. She's way too classy for that."

With one jump the cat was on the bed and curled up on the pillow where Melanie should have put her head. Tucker threw himself backward on the bed and shut his eyes.

When he opened them again, bright sunshine was pouring into the room. Both of his hands went to his face to block out the pain. He flipped over on his stomach and covered his throbbing head with a pillow. It was going to be a long, long day for sure, and he needed coffee—lots of it.

He tossed the pillow away and slung his legs over the side of the bed. With something between a groan and a grunt, he stood up and reached for his jeans, only to realize that he'd slept in his clothes. He padded toward the kitchen for his first cup of coffee with Sassy right behind him.

"Good mornin'," Jolene said cheerfully.

"What's so good about it?" he grumbled.

She pulled out a chair. "Sit down."

"Not before I get a cup of coffee."

She pointed at the chair. "Coffee is not first. Sit!"

"I'm not a dog," he argued, but he eased down into the chair.

"One time only," she said, "you get my famous hangover cure. But only once—so write it down or suffer from now on. The ladies are coming for lunch, and we're going to have a talk with Lucy about the way she's acting. You don't need a headache."

She picked up a bottle of honey and squeezed it out into a tablespoon until it was almost overflowing. "Open your mouth and take this like medicine."

"I'll gag," he protested.

She moved the spoon toward his lips. He could either open his mouth or honey would drip all the way down his shirt. Not sure if he had another clean one until he did laundry, he opened his mouth. The honey was so sweet that it did almost gag him, but he got it down.

"That's supposed to work better than coffee?" He didn't need her bossing him around, and he had his own hangover cure—black coffee and lots of it, and then a couple of aspirin.

"That's just step one." She handed him two aspirin and a cup of coffee. "Drink that while I get step three ready."

"This I can believe in." He picked up the coffee and downed the aspirin with the first sip.

She folded her arms across her chest and eyed him from toes to nose. "Three will do," she said.

"Three what?"

"Scrambled eggs. You got to figure them by size. Mama took one, but you'll need three," she answered as she cracked eggs into a bowl.

"You've got to be sober because the ladies are having an intervention thing with Lucy today. They were worried about bringing out booze since you drink on weekends, but I told them it would be fine. So it's going to be." She raised both eyebrows.

"Yes, ma'am." Sarcasm coated each word.

There was no way he could eat eggs. They wouldn't stay down, and he didn't need to be there while those women had—what was that word she'd used? He tried to think of it, but his head pounded. He almost snapped his fingers in victory when he thought of the word *intervention*.

"You think you're magic, do you?" he asked.

"Nope, I'm not magic, but I lived with a drunk long enough to know how to take care of a demon hangover. I did this lots of times for my mother, but you're not kin to me, Tucker, so I'm only doin' it once. I don't have a lot of sympathy for drunks with hangovers, but I want you to be your charming self for my friends this afternoon."

By the time he'd finished his first cup of coffee, she'd put a plate of eggs and two pieces of toast in front of him. One bite and it was all going to come right back up—he had no doubt. But to prove himself wrong, he shoveled one bite after another into his mouth.

"More coffee?" he asked when he finished.

"Not yet," she said.

"I need at least one potful, maybe two," he groaned.

She laid a banana on the table. "Last step. You eat every bite of that and then go take a warm shower. When you come back, you can have another cup of coffee."

He could feel his nose curling in disgust at the thought of taking even one bite, much less eating the whole thing. "You've got to be kidding me—a banana?"

"When the dance ends, it's time to pay the fiddler. You had your night, and now you need potassium. Eat the banana and then go to the shower. I usually just lined all this stuff up for my mother on the cabinet

Friday night. If she wasn't up by the time I had to go pull a double shift on Saturday, she knew how to do it."

"So if it works for me, will I find everything on the counter next time?" Dammit! She was beyond cute that morning with her take-charge attitude. Melanie might be right about her being a strong woman who didn't need his protection.

"No, like I said, this is a onetime deal," she told him and changed the subject. "Did you sleep in those clothes?"

"Yep." He peeled the banana and took a small bite. It wasn't nearly as bad as he'd thought it would be. "And once I get out of them, I've got laundry to do. Want to do it together or separate?"

"Might as well save on the water bill and do it together. Mine's already in the utility room. Bring yours, and we'll get it sorted after your shower," she said.

He finished the banana and pushed the chair back. "That is the last step, right? You're not going to make me eat a toad when I get out of the shower, are you?"

"Never thought of that. It might put more drunks on the wagon than my remedy," she said. "But to answer your question, yes, that's the last thing on the list. You can have coffee when you get out. Our ladies will be here with our Sunday dinner in an hour, and believe me, you'll be hungry by then."

"We'll see." He headed toward the bathroom.

He turned on the water in the shower and laid his clothing on the edge of the sink as he removed each item. By the time he was ready to pull back the curtain and get into the cramped space, the water was hot. He adjusted it, wondering the whole time just how warm he should leave it. So far that crazy remedy of hers was working pretty good. His headache was gone, and he didn't have a bit of nausea.

Once he finished, he wrapped a towel around his waist and stepped up to the mirror that covered a medicine cabinet above the sink. After he'd shaved, he poured a little Stetson aftershave in his hand and slapped it on his face. Then he combed his dark hair back.

"Time to get it cut or else start wearing a ponytail," he said. "I'll be damned! That crazy routine works. I feel good."

He peeked out the door and made a quick little jog to his bedroom, where he threw off the towel. He put on a pair of jeans that could've used a good pressing and found a clean shirt in his duffel bag.

"You think it's time to bring all my stuff from the trailer, Sassy?" he asked the cat, who'd come back to the extra pillow on his bed.

She opened one eye and then closed it slowly.

"Not even a little meow? I got a partner who can cook and who knows how to cure a hangover. That's pretty damn good." Tucker vaguely remembered telling Sassy about his feelings the night before. No wonder she was pissed. She'd been Melanie's pet, and she sure wouldn't want to hear about another woman in his life—even if Jolene did let her lie on the kitchen table.

He left his boots behind and carried a basket of dirty clothing through the foyer and the dining room and was headed across the living room floor when he noticed tears running down Jolene's face. The basket made a thud when he dropped it.

"Is it your aunt Sugar?"

She shook her head and turned her back as she wiped at the tears. "No, just a song on the radio that . . ." Her voice cracked.

He took her by the shoulders and turned her around. "What song? What memory?"

She pulled her phone from the hip pocket of her jeans and hit a few buttons. "It reminds me of my mama. She was in a hotel room when she overdosed, and this was playing on her phone when they found her—over and over again. I should've cut her some slack, but I was just a kid and I didn't understand the darkness or the sadness."

He drew her close and held her as they listened to Sarah McLachlan sing "Angel." His sadness was very different from Jolene's or the singer's, but he could relate to the pain that it caused, because the end result was the same.

"Songs speak to me," she whispered. "They always have. They get down into my heart and strike emotions so deep that I wonder where they come from."

"Me, too." He had to swallow several times for the lump in his throat to disappear.

She took a step back and his arms felt empty.

"What song reminds you of the Magnolia Inn?" he asked.

She drew the tail of her T-shirt up to wipe her eyes. "You'll think I'm crazy."

"Hey, we listened to music all the time when I was on the police force. You'd be surprised what songs bring back memories to me." He wasn't about to tell her that he couldn't even listen to Jamey Johnson sing "Lead Me Home," because that's what they had played at Melanie's funeral.

"Aunt Sugar would dance around the dining room with Uncle Jasper to Mary Chapin Carpenter singing, 'I Feel Lucky.' When I hear that song, I think of how much they were in love and they didn't have to go outside this inn to . . ." She paused for a breath. "And I'm not sure how to explain."

"Maybe the inn really *is* magical." Tucker reached for her phone and brought up "I Feel Lucky," laid it on the counter, and held out a hand. "Can I have this dance, Miz Jolene?"

She put one hand in his and the other on his shoulder. She was a very good swing dancer. When he spun her out and brought her back to his chest, she didn't miss a single beat. By the time the song ended, they were both breathless, and there wasn't a tear in her eyes.

In that moment, he realized that Jolene was more than a partner. She was his friend, the first one he'd made since Melanie died. With sideways glances, he studied her. She was definitely what they talked about when they said dynamite came in small packages. She'd endured so much at such a young age, and yet she was kind, sweet, and the hardest-working woman he'd ever known. She and Melanie would have been good friends for sure.

"I bet Uncle Jasper and Aunt Sugar have been dancing like that all over. I haven't done that in a long time. That was fun," she said as she sat down at the table.

"Yes, it was," he said. "We'll have to do it more often."

❊

Columbus, Georgia

Five days after leaving Jefferson, Jasper and Sugar reached the Georgia line. Sugar awoke in the middle of the night and eased out of bed. She poured herself a glass of milk, opened the mini blinds above the booth-type table to look at the stars, and imagined her niece sitting at the table back in Jefferson, having a late-night snack before she went to bed. Tucker was there, but she could only see him in his stained jeans and shirt, like the picture Jolene had sent. He was a good-looking man with all that dark hair.

Her phone was lying on the table, so she picked it up and brought up the photograph again. Tucker looked happy. She flipped past that one to one of Jolene with a smudge of dirt on her face. Without thinking, Sugar tried to wipe it away with a fingertip.

"God, I miss home so much. I'm so homesick I could just cry," she muttered and then checked to be sure that she hadn't awakened Jasper.

What had she been thinking, leaving the place where she'd been born and lived her whole life? She had roots, not wings. She didn't necessarily want to go back to the inn, but she did want to go home.

Where are you going to live? a pesky voice in her head asked.

A few keystrokes on her phone brought up Dixie Realty. In only a few minutes she'd found several suitable places. She and Jasper didn't need a big house. Just a small one with two bedrooms would be fine. Jolene had her own place now, and Sugar's friends wouldn't be coming to spend the night.

Tears flooded Sugar's cheeks when she saw that the house next door to Flossie's was on the market. She'd been in that place when she was a little girl. It might be an older home, but it had been well maintained. She wanted to live there, next door to Flossie, but that was all a big pipe dream. Jasper had had his heart broken when Reuben sold his half of the inn. Sugar couldn't be the one to break it again. This gypsy lifestyle had been his dream for years, so she'd have to brace up and get over the homesickness—for his sake.

Chapter Nine

"Please excuse our mess. We're remodeling," Jolene said as she swung the door open before the ladies even knocked. She was glad to see these old gals. That they'd taken her under their wings and made her a part of their world meant more than they'd ever know.

"That sounds just like something Sugar would say. She called me last night, and Jasper is doing better now." Lucy carried in a box filled with something that gave off a delicious aroma. "I brought green bean casserole, rice, and salad."

Flossie came in behind her with a slow cooker. "I made my famous meatballs. I'm still mad at Reuben for what he did, but I'm glad he's not here."

Dotty brought up the rear. "I like to bake more than I like to cook. Like I've said before, I *can* cook, just like I *can* clean the bathrooms in the bar, but that don't mean I like either one. Anyway, my job is always dessert. Today we have chocolate cake."

Tucker took the box from Lucy. "Well, it all smells amazing. I'm starving. All Jolene would fix me for breakfast was a few scrambled eggs and some toast."

"I don't feel a bit sorry for you. You should have learned to cook," Lucy declared.

"I never learned to cook because I was learnin' how to put up drywall and repairin' floors *and* workin' all kinds of crazy hours as a detective." Tucker's drawl was more pronounced than ever. "I didn't have time to do everything, and besides, I ate a lot of fast food. Anyway, I'm real grateful for sweet ladies from Texas like y'all who bring Sunday dinner to me."

"Don't you try to sweet-talk me, boy." Lucy shook a forefinger under his nose. "And I wouldn't even give that recipe to Sugar, so don't ask. It's an old family recipe from down in southern Cajun country."

"What if he was a preacher? Would you deny the recipe to a man of the cloth?" Dotty asked.

"I wouldn't deny God anything. He's saved my soul," Lucy declared.

"I'll give you my recipe for the meatballs. Sugar found it in an old cookbook of her mama's, and we been making them for years." Flossie grinned.

Dotty cocked her head to one side. "I'm surprised that you're goin' to partake of them, Lucy. You know they've got half a can of beer in them, and if you're goin' to fuss at us about our sins, then you should practice what you preach. And by the way, was that a virgin daiquiri that you drank in the Gator last night?"

"Oh, hush!" she growled. "Just because Ezra's death caused me to reevaluate my standing with the good Lord does not mean I can't have a mixed drink or eat meatballs with a little beer in them."

"You didn't mourn long. You're already eyeballing another man," Dotty argued.

She stuck her nose in the air. "Ezra would want me to be happy."

"Lucy, you've been doing this for the past twenty years," Flossie said. "You get a boyfriend. He dies or breaks up with you. We have to go to every church in town so you can be right with the Lord. It's time for it to stop. We like our own church, where we've all gone since we were little kids."

"But what if it's not the right one for the Lord to hear my repentin' for bein' a loose woman with a man?" Lucy asked as she helped get the food on the table.

"God could hear you if you were prayin' in the ladies' room at the Gator. And when you repent, you ain't supposed to go out and do the same damn thing again," Dotty said.

Lucy shook her finger at her. "You haven't got any right to preach to me. We had to have an intervention to get you off alcohol after Bruce died."

"That's what gives me the right, *chère*." Dotty dragged out the endearment.

"Miz Lucy?" Tucker pulled out a chair for her.

"Thank you, and Jolene, I'm sayin' grace," Lucy said.

Tucker seated Flossie, Dotty, and Jolene before he took his place at the head of the table.

The moment he sat down, Lucy dropped her head to her chest and rested her forehead on her hands.

Dotty rolled her eyes toward Flossie, who just winked and smiled.

"Our most gracious heavenly father in heaven's glory," Lucy started, and she went on for a good two minutes before she finally blessed the food with an amen.

"If this food is cold, then it's your fault," Dotty said.

"But God is happy that we graced it," Lucy said.

Flossie pushed her chair back, went to the kitchen, and returned with a bottle of wine. "Almost forgot this. Jolene, darlin', would you pour for us?"

"Wait a minute," Dotty said. "This is our first Sunday dinner with Jolene at the Magnolia. Let's do it up right." She went to the china cabinet in the corner of the dining room and brought out four stemmed glasses.

"Be glad to." Jolene poured for all three ladies. When she reached Tucker, he put a hand over his glass.

"Not much for wine, but I've got beer in the fridge. Anyone else want one while I'm up?" he asked.

"Lucy can't have one. And she shouldn't have the wine. I'll drink it for her. She might not get her wings and halo if she has wine and beer both," Dotty said.

Lucy glared at her. "You can shut up about that now so we can have a nice, pleasant dinner. And Tucker, I would love a beer. Wine with my dinner and a beer with the chocolate cake."

Flossie whispered into Jolene's ear, "She can't hold her liquor worth a damn."

Tucker returned and set a glass and a bottle of beer beside Lucy's plate. "I take mine straight out of the bottle, but I got you a glass."

"Bottle is just fine," Lucy said.

He sat back down. "When we get done eating, we'll give you a peek at what we're doin' upstairs."

"Oh, really?" Dotty raised an eyebrow and winked at him.

Lucy downed her wine while the food was being passed. "If you're going to think lewd thoughts, then I'll need another glass of wine to get through this day gracefully. And I don't like it that y'all are tryin' to tell me how to live my life, what church I have to go to, and that I'm a repeat offender to God askin' for forgiveness."

Jolene wondered if her mother had ever asked for forgiveness or if she'd just barreled on ahead with her life, not giving a damn whose life she was ruining on the journey. Had she even realized or cared that she was breaking her daughter's heart? Jolene could see her mother dancing through the trailer, music blaring on either the radio or the CD player. She'd be flying high on street drugs before she even hit the lowest-class bars in the area to add alcohol to the mix. Almost without fail she'd bring a different man home with her, the two of them leaning on each other and giggling as they stumbled back to her mother's bedroom.

"Now, darlin'." Flossie's tone sounded like she was talking to a child. "You know that you don't do well on two glasses of wine. Remember the last time you splurged?"

"That wasn't the wine. It was the medicine I was takin' for my blood pressure. I can drink both of you under the table," Lucy declared. "Pour me another one, Jolene. I'll prove to these two doubters that I can hold my liquor."

Jolene picked up the bottle and handed it across the table. "Sorry, Miz Lucy, but it's empty."

Lucy glared at Dotty. "I saw two bottles in that oversize tote bag that you carry everywhere."

"Now, *chère*—I mean, darlin'—one glass plus a beer is your limit. Jolene will have to take your keys if you have any more. Just think of all those angels in heaven who will be cryin' if you fall off the wagon. You've only been ridin' it a couple of weeks," Dotty said.

Looking back, Jolene would've been glad if her mother had cared enough to put her problems aside and be a mother, or even a friend. Before her husband had died, Elaine had been so self-absorbed that she hadn't had much time for her daughter. The only thing she really enjoyed doing with her daughter was shopping for clothes, so Jolene did have a few good memories from those years. After her dad was gone, most of the time Elaine just screamed at her for not paying the bills or for not having her favorite food in the trailer.

"You open that bottle right now," Lucy demanded.

"Okay, but I thought you were going to church tonight to flirt with the preacher." She pushed back her chair, disappeared into the foyer, and returned with a big bottle of red wine. "I'm giving you this because you are my friend, but you know very well you can't drink."

"Enough already. I've got on my big-girl panties, and I can decide things on my own. Now pass those meatballs," Lucy said.

Dotty opened the bottle and set it on the table, close enough that Lucy could reach it. Then she returned to her seat and picked up the beans. "I've always loved green beans made this way, and no one makes rice as fluffy as Lucy. Not even my Louisiana grandmother, and she cooked it every day. I remember when she came to Texas the first time and we had potatoes twice a day. She told me the day she left that she could never live in a place where the people lived on potatoes."

"Thank you." Lucy's tone was still a little strained. "My granny was from over the line, too. She taught me to make it, and it goes so well with Flossie's meatballs."

"Yes, it does," Tucker agreed.

An intervention. A talkin'-to. Whatever it was called, Jolene felt guilty that she hadn't coerced her mother into the vehicle and driven her to the Magnolia. Aunt Sugar would have taken things in hand, and maybe, just maybe, Elaine would have gotten dried out from all the drugs and alcohol.

"I just got my first bite of green beans. Is that Creole seasoning that I taste?" Jolene asked.

"Might be a little, but that's not the whole secret." Lucy refilled her glass and took a long sip. "This is better than the last. What is it?"

"Blackberry," Dotty said. "I thought it would go well with dessert."

"Not as well as beer. I like it. Reminds me of that time when the four of us were teenagers and we found that bottle of strawberry Boone's Farm wine in the Big Cypress Bayou, back behind the Magnolia." Lucy giggled.

"We drank it all and then washed the bottle out with a little water and drank that, too," Flossie said.

"And you . . ." Dotty pointed at Lucy. "You were the only one of us who got drunk."

"I did not. It was all psychological. I didn't know how much it took to get drunk, and I just talked myself into thinkin' I'd had too much," Lucy argued.

"One more glass and she'll get funny," Flossie whispered to Jolene. "And then?"

"Hopefully she'll see that she's not an evil person for sleeping with her boyfriends, and that they don't die or break up with her because she's not good enough in bed. And we won't have to go to some church where we don't know the people next week," Flossie explained out of the side of her mouth.

"What are you whispering about?" Lucy asked.

"We're trying to figure out what else is in these green beans," Jolene said.

Lucy stuck her thin nose in the air. "I might tell the preacher tonight, but I'm not tellin' y'all. You've been hateful today."

"And here it is Sunday, when we're supposed to love everyone," Tucker piped up from the head of the table.

"That's right, sweet boy. I knew you had a good heart hidin' in that sexy chest of yours," Lucy said as she finished off the second glass of wine and poured another one. "Did you know that we had to have an intervention for Dotty?"

"I did." Tucker gave her his full attention.

"Let me tell you about it. She was drinkin' too much, so we had to take matters in our own hands." Lucy nodded with every word. "Know what we did?" She frowned as if she was trying to remember something.

"We had a long talk with her, but in those days, no one ever heard of an intervention," Flossie said.

"I was tellin' the story." Lucy pouted. "After we talked to her, I thought we needed a preacher to pray over her, but it was Thursday night and there wasn't a church service going on."

Dotty shivered. "It was a tent revival over the border in the Louisiana boonies. I half expected the preacher to bring out a dead chicken. I told Sugar if he let one of them rattlesnakes loose that he had caged up, I'd swim across the bayou, and that broke me from drinkin' more than one glass of wine at a time or havin' more than one beer a night. I laid my hand on Lucy's Bible and swore that I'd never get drunk again if they wouldn't make me relive that experience."

"And Sugar said that she'd be right behind you in swimmin' across the bayou," Flossie laughed. "I wanted to take Dotty to a strip club instead of a church. I figured what she needed was a young stud to go to bed with her. That revival thing was Lucy's idea."

Lucy leaned over and stage-whispered to Tucker, "I bet you could get a job in a strip club."

His smile grew into a chuckle. "I was a cop in Dallas and then a detective. I don't think the force would have approved of that kind of moonlightin' job. Besides, my uniform didn't have those breakaway snaps to let me get out of it real fast."

"Too bad," Flossie sighed. "I bet Dotty would have put all of her dollars in your cute little thong underbritches."

"Damn straight I would." Dotty threw a wink his way.

Tucker picked up the bowl of green beans. "Anyone want any more of these? If not, I'm goin' to finish them off."

"You go right ahead, honey. And don't let these two sinners make you blush," Lucy said. "Is it time for dessert yet? I'm lookin' forward to this bottle of beer."

"I'll get the cake," Dotty said. "Anyone want ice cream with it? I know Sugar always keeps half a supply in the freezer."

"Yes." Tucker raised his hand.

"Me, too," Lucy said.

"Wine, beer, cake, and ice cream?" Dotty shook her head. "You'll be sick for sure."

Lucy inhaled deeply and let it out in a whoosh. "Stop bossin' me."

Jolene had heard those three words before—lots of times. She'd beg Elaine to stay home on Friday and Saturday nights, to save the money for food or bills. And she'd get the same response—*stop bossin' me.* Only it would usually be followed up by Elaine yelling that if Jolene were a better daughter, she'd love her unconditionally and stop trying to change her.

"Miz Lucy, if you have a little hangover, Jolene has a magic remedy. You just call me and I'll tell you how to fix it," Tucker said.

Lucy tilted her chin up. "I won't need it."

And just what's the difference in what Tucker does and what I did? Jolene's mother's voice was so clear in her head that Jolene cut her eyes around the room to see if she was there.

For one thing, he doesn't have a teenage daughter who deserved a life of her own and who shouldn't have needed to worry about grown-up things long before her time, Jolene answered.

He got the hangover medicine this morning. What do you have to say about that? Elaine argued. Like she'd done so many times in real life, Jolene let her mother have the last word by forcing her voice out of her head.

Sometime in the middle of that mental conversation, Dotty had brought in the cake and ice cream. "We'll pass it around, and everyone can get however big of a piece they want."

Lucy twisted the cap off the beer and took a long gulp. "That'll clean my palate for the cake."

❦

Tucker shooed all four of the ladies into the living room with the rest of the wine after dinner was finished. "You brought the food. Jolene and I will do the cleanup. Go pretend like you are guests of the Magnolia Inn. No, don't pretend. You *are* our very first guests, even if you didn't stay the night here."

"I knew I liked that boy from the first time I met him." Lucy headed that way with a wineglass in one hand and a half-empty bottle of beer in the other.

There's no one who's all good or who's all bad. What comes out and makes them look either way are the choices they make. Jolene remembered Aunt Sugar telling her that when she complained about Reuben.

Did that apply to her drug-addicted mother? For years Jolene'd not been able to find a good thing about her mom, and then Elaine had died in that miserable, cheap hotel room. Maybe if Jolene would get over not having been there with her and not being able to stop the downward spiral, then she could hang on to a few of the good moments they'd shared.

Tucker followed Jolene to the kitchen with a stack of plates in his hands. "Now explain to me what just happened in there. That didn't look like an intervention to me, and why are they even having one?"

"It's complicated. From what I understand, Lucy feels guilty because she sleeps with men, and then they either die or break up with her. I think it might be her upbringing. Back in her day, sex before marriage was this big no-no." Jolene rinsed dishes and put them into the dishwasher.

Tucker frowned. "So this is to get her out of religion? Most of the time folks try to push a person into it, not pull them out of it."

"Evidently they know what they're doin'," Jolene said. "Their method worked with Dotty."

"Guess you can't argue with something that's already been proven." Tucker nodded in agreement. "Think Lucy can make it upstairs to see what we've accomplished?"

"If that 'sweet boy'"—Jolene put air quotes around the words— "will offer her his arm and go slow, I bet she'll make it just fine."

"Been a helluva long time since I was called a boy." Tucker chuckled.

"Oh, yeah! How long?"

"Well, honey, I was born in 1981. You do the math," he answered.

"Thirty-eight?"

"On my birthday in April. And you?"

"Never was called a boy," she told him. "I'll be thirty-two in April. What day is your birthday?"

He scraped the leftover rice into the trash can. "The thirtieth."

"Mine is the twenty-ninth," she said.

How did a mother turn her back on a responsible kid like Jolene? Tucker wondered. *How could a mother ever become addicted when she had a daughter?* If he and Melanie had had children, he'd have still hurt when she was killed, but he would have had something to live for.

You've got something to live for now, so why are you still hitting the bottle? That niggling voice in his head sounded like Melanie.

He blinked away the question he didn't want to answer and said, "Guess us partners ain't never gonna forget the other one's special day, are we?"

"Guess not." She smiled. "And now we'd better get in there before our children get into more trouble than a simple hangover remedy can get them out of."

"So we've adopted them?" Tucker asked.

"Aunt Sugar told me to watch after them, so I guess we have. But you don't have to be the father figure unless you want. Might be good, because you aren't the best role model, now are you?" She raised an eyebrow.

"Come on now. I only drink on weekends," he said.

"When the kids are home." Jolene walked past him out of the kitchen.

She's right again. Listen to her. Let me go, darlin'. You've got a life to live.

Tucker set his jaw and followed Jolene. They could hear the singing before they reached the living room. Lucy's voice, slurring the words, was the loudest.

"Eighty-eight sips of wine in the jug, eighty-eight sips of wine. You take one now and pass it around. Eighty-seven sips of wine in the jug." Dotty waved from the floor, where they were sitting in a circle. Lucy took a sip of wine and went on with the song, while the other two women only put the bottle to their lips and pretended to drink.

"They're here!" Lucy squealed. "We can go see what they've done upstairs."

Tucker extended his hand to Lucy. "Shall we lead the way, Miz Lucy?"

When she was standing, he tucked her arm into his and headed for the stairs. She was weaving a little, but he'd seen worse—he'd *been* worse the night before. If he'd been a praying man, he would have asked God not to let Lucy tumble backward, because the other three women were right behind them. One false move and all five of them would go down, ass over big hair. Dotty and Flossie would probably end up with broken hips.

He didn't realize he was holding his breath until they were all in the hallway and well away from the stairs. "Watch yourselves. Furniture is piled up everywhere."

Lucy giggled when they entered the first bedroom. "I thought you was the best carpenter in East Texas, boy. Look at that bathtub in the bedroom. Are you crazy? Everyone knows you don't put a bathtub in the bedroom."

Dotty slipped an arm around Lucy's waist. "Lucy, you put in the bathtub and then build the wall around it. It would be a devil of a job to try to get it through the door after the walls were built."

Tucker eased away from Lucy, leaving her in Dotty's care. "We'll build a wall right here where the tape is on the floor. And we're using the washstand out there in the hallway for the vanity. The tub and shower enclosure will be kind of modern. But we're going to try to keep the old-world flavor."

"That sounds wonderful, Tucker, but we really should be going. Don't you have an appointment to meet up with the church Prayer Angels?" Dotty asked Lucy.

"Yes, I do," Lucy huffed. "And for your information, I just sell antiques. I don't build houses." She turned her attention to Jolene. "But it looks good. Let's go back down to the living room and sing some more. I liked that better than lookin' at bathtubs in bedrooms."

"I'm sure you did." Flossie winked at Tucker. "You are doing an amazing job. Sugar would be so proud. You sending lots of pictures to her, Jolene?"

"Every day," Jolene answered. "I take before, after, and in-progress pictures. I've been sending them daily and talking to her at least every other day."

"I do sing well, and I will pray for you." Lucy poked Tucker in the chest. "I will ask God to take away your desire to drink."

Tucker didn't even argue. He could use all the help he could get, but if God had been standing watch, he thought, then his Melanie wouldn't be dead.

"You do that, Miz Lucy." He put her arm back in his and dreaded going down the stairs even more than he had climbing up them. But at least if she pitched forward, she would only take him with her.

They made it to the ground, where Dotty took control and chattered the whole time she helped Lucy into her coat. "Thank you for a wonderful visit. I can't wait for the construction part to be done and the pretty stuff to start. You can bring our dishes home next Sunday. Dinner will be at Flossie's house. One o'clock sharp. Don't be late. We've always taken turns hosting Sunday dinner." She paused for a breath.

"Yes, ma'am." Tucker jerked on his boots and followed them out to the car to open doors for them. "And you call me if you have a headache later on tonight, Miz Lucy."

"Honey, I never felt better in my life. I just wish we'd got to the end of the ninety-nine sips of wine song. I was havin' fun," she said.

Dotty winked at him. "Thanks for everything. Sugar would be proud of you and Jolene. And now that she's three sheets to the wind, we're hoping that Lucy'll get off this crazy merry-go-round she's been on." Dotty lowered her voice. "Sometimes it takes a good hangover to realize that you've been goin' down the wrong path."

Most of the time, a person has to want to take a step into the future, rather than living in the past. What do you want, Tucker? This time his grandfather's voice was in his head.

Chapter Ten

*J*olene could hardly believe that it was already Friday again, but the calendar on her phone didn't lie. She and Tucker had gotten more done the past five days than she'd thought possible. The bathroom walls were up, and the dining room now had a hole big enough for a door where he'd knocked out the wall to put in new water lines. That morning he was under the house working on getting the last bits of plumbing done. After that he said they'd be ready for drywall.

She rolled her neck a few times to get the soreness out. This construction business was harder on the body than standing on her feet eight hours behind a bar for sure. But she was beginning to get a picture of what he'd visualized all along. Maybe as Aunt Sugar and Uncle Jasper came back across the United States on their way to California, they'd stop by and see all the improvements. Jolene was almost giddy as she thought about showing off the new bathrooms and all the remodeling.

Tucker's hand stuck out of the crawl hole. "Hey, I need a crescent wrench."

She put a tool in his hand, but in five seconds it came back out. "A crescent wrench, not pliers."

"Sorry about that," she said. "Don't fire me. I'm still learning."

"No way." He chuckled. "At least you didn't give me a pry bar, like my last assistant did," he said.

"That's because I'm not an assistant. I'm a partner, and I work real cheap."

When he finished, he inched out from under the house on his back, face-first. She was sitting cross-legged on the cold ground, all the tools laid out before her like surgical instruments. "Man, you are organized," he said.

She raised a hand and grinned. "My name is Jolene Broussard, and I'm afflicted with a slight case of OCD."

He pulled himself on out and sat down beside her. "My name is Tucker Malone and I have a confession. I'm a weekend drunk, but my deceased wife keeps tellin' me to stop living in the past and get on with the future. I never have wanted to do it before, but now I kind of do."

"Maybe we should both listen to her." Jolene hopped up. "I didn't know that you did plumbing as well as construction."

"It's not my favorite part of remodeling. Electricity is even farther down on the list. But I got my license in both when I started flipping houses as a hobby."

"Why didn't you just do that rather than police work on top of it?" she asked.

"My grandpa was a cop. I adored him and wanted to be like him. But I always loved working with my hands, too." He rolled up onto his feet. "That should do it for the plumbing. Let's go up and turn on the water, and then I'll test for leaks before we cover up the crawl space."

She sighed. "Will this be the process every time we put in bathrooms?"

"Kind of, but not really. I can tie into the pipes in the dining room wall, but that hole won't be covered up until we get finished." He put his wrenches into his toolbox and carried it inside the house.

"I'm just glad you're the one crawling under the house. I'm claustrophobic," she admitted. "And I'm afraid of heights. Or maybe not so much afraid of high places as falling off them. Do you put roofs on houses, too?"

"Yep. I'm not afraid of being up high or in tight spots, as long as there's no spiders in either place. Here." He tossed an aerosol can toward her.

She caught it midair. "What is this?"

"Bug spray. I never go under a house without it." He grinned.

❇

Dotty met her at the back door of the Gator that night with a worried look on her face. "It's only five minutes until we open. I was gettin' a little worried."

"Time got away from me." Jolene put her coat and purse under the counter and grabbed an apron. "Tucker and I were putting up drywall. How did it go with Lucy? I've been meanin' to call all week, but we were so busy."

"I think we finally got her to see the light. She admitted, while she was drunk, that she felt like God was always punishing her for sleeping with men when she wasn't married to them, and that He was killin' them off or else making them break up with her. We got her to understand that wasn't the case. It'll take a little reinforcing along the way, but I believe she's going to do better. She can have boyfriends. She can sleep with them. That's not why they die. We'll just have to keep her reminded. She's pretty mouthy, but she's kept all this shit bottled up. Me and Flossie and Sugar knew *why* she was doin' it, but she had to finally admit it to herself. You know, it's kind of like smokin'. Until the one with the cigarette in his hands realizes he's got a problem, no amount of bitchin' from his family or friends will help him stop."

"You got that right." Jolene thought of her mother, who never one time had admitted she had a problem. "Anything I can do to help?"

"No, but we did have to get Sugar on the phone. We put it on speaker, and she really helped us out. I got to tell you, Jolene, Sugar was kind of the glue that held us all together. I'm damn glad we can call her and talk about all this," Dotty said. "Now tell me about Tucker. He must've had a hangover to have mentioned a hangover cure."

"I told him it was a onetime deal. I didn't want him to have a hangover when y'all were there, so I gave him the cure I always used on my mother," Jolene answered.

"Why is it a one-timer?" Dotty asked.

"I felt responsible for Mama. I don't for him. He's a grown man." Jolene waved at Mickey as he came out of the men's room and took his place at the door.

She picked up a bar rag and gave the counter one more cleaning and thought about her statement. Tucker *was* a grown man, but he was also a troubled soul. Neither was any of her business, but these past days she'd felt an attraction for him.

No! I will not get involved with someone who is still in love with his dead wife and who drinks. Lord knows I've already been through enough in that department—maybe not with the wife issue, but with the other.

"Time to open." Dotty signaled to Mickey to unlock the doors.

In minutes there was a group of young folks on the floor line dancing to "Cotton Eye Joe." The stools quickly filled, and people were lined up three deep waiting on drinks.

"Goin' to be another busy one," Dotty said as she pulled two pitchers of beer. "I should've hired a hot young bartender years ago."

"Oh, hush." Jolene hip bumped her.

"And, honey, don't judge Tucker too hard. I've been where he is. It ain't an easy place to be. He's got to work through the fog before he can see the light," Dotty said.

"I'm not judging." Jolene reached for a bottle of Patrón tequila. "But I'm not his keeper."

"You might be more than his keeper. You and the Magnolia might be his salvation," Dotty said.

"Don't know about that, but when we close up, I'll show you the pictures of what we got done this week on my phone," Jolene said.

"Aunt Sugar loves it, but I hear a little reservation in her voice about Tucker. Did she say anything to you?"

"It'll slow down in a little bit, and you can show me then. And Sugar is worried about him. She wants to help him get through his problems. You know how she is. Your aunt sees good in everyone, even Reuben. Anyway, she thinks Tucker was led to the Magnolia so he can realize he *has* a problem. But she and Jasper are mad at Reuben, and a little aggravated at Tucker for buying him out so fast. If Reuben hadn't had such an easy out, then maybe he would have partnered with you, and then you could have helped him."

"I don't think there's help for Reuben. But I do know that Tucker needs to move on."

Dotty shrugged. "You both need to do just that."

Jolene started to say something but stopped when she saw Lucy and a distinguished-looking elderly man coming straight toward the bar.

Lucy threw up a hand and made a beeline for an empty barstool. "Hi, sweetie. I want you to meet Everett. We're here to dance more than drink, but if you'd make us one of those daiquiris that you made me and Flossie the other night, we'd love it. And"—she leaned across the bar—"do not let me drink more than one. Kick me out if I even order a second one."

"Hello." Everett stuck a hand over Lucy's shoulder. "I'd rather have a rum and Coke."

"I'm Jolene," she said. "Two drinks comin' right up."

"I see an empty table. I'll grab it and wait for you there." Everett handed Jolene a bill. "Keep the change."

"Did I really sing 'Ninety-Nine Sips of Wine'?" Lucy asked.

Jolene nodded. "And you decided that Tucker was a good boy and not the devil."

"They goaded me into proving I could drink and I can't, but I forgive them because it was for a good reason. Flossie and Dotty got it started, but it was Sugar who really lined me out. I feel like a rock has been lifted from my soul." Lucy picked up the two drinks. "And that's not the preacher. He's the man who came into my shop last week and asked me out. I wouldn't make a good preacher's wife, you know."

Jolene smiled. "I'm glad you feel better, and you didn't even call me for the hangover cure."

Lucy leaned over the bar and whispered, "I was too ashamed to call, honey, but if I ever make that mistake again, I sure will."

Everett was tall, like Lucy—lanky, like Lucy. And he had a cute little gray mustache and mischievous blue eyes. *Lucy had better be careful,* Jolene thought, *or she might be doing more than dancing with that handsome old guy.*

She caught a glimpse of them every little bit, and they looked like they were having a great time. They were both very good at two-stepping and swing dancing, but they sat out the line dances. Neither of them came back to order another drink, so it looked like Lucy really had learned her lesson, for a little while at least. Now that she and Dotty had both been in the intervention spotlight, Jolene couldn't help but wonder when it would be Flossie's turn—or if Sugar had ever had it shined on her.

❧

Jolene stumbled into the kitchen the next morning looking, Tucker noticed, like the last rose of summer a big old hound dog had hiked his leg on. Tucker smiled at his grandpa's old adage.

"Mornin'," she grumbled.

He pointed at the coffeepot. "Just made a fresh pot. I drank what I made earlier while I was figuring out what we need to get ready for work on Monday."

She poured a cup and sat down at the table with a groan. "And what do we need?"

"We should go to the paint store in Marshall. You could pick out the paint for this first bedroom so that we'll have it on hand when we're ready for it. I'm thinking that instead of peeling off all that old wallpaper, plaster, and lathing, we just put up drywall over it. If you want to feminize it, you could put a border around the ceiling, but wallpaper is a real bitch to hang and to maintain."

"Sounds good to me," she said.

"We could get a burger or maybe hit a pizza buffet for lunch. My treat," he said.

"That sounds wonderful. Give me a few minutes to shower and get dressed," she told him.

He went out to sit on the porch swing, and Sassy followed him. The cat settled onto his lap and meowed.

"So I've been hearing Melanie's voice more lately, but the only thing she says is for me to move on. I didn't tell her good night last night like I always do. Does that mean I'm finally taking a step forward?"

The cat shut both eyes.

"Lot of help you are," Tucker said. "There are days now when I can't remember what she looked like without looking at her picture. It scares me, Sassy."

The cat opened one eye and then closed it again.

"If I don't remember her, then all those wonderful years we had together will be gone," he whispered.

Jolene pushed her way out onto the porch, and Sassy hopped down off his lap and made a beeline to the door. "Guess she doesn't want to get left outside," Jolene said as she started for her truck. "I can't wait to decide what color to do this first room. I think they should all be different, but we should keep the colors muted and light, and that the border should have magnolias on it. But I have been thinking of painting the front door purple and hanging a pretty magnolia wreath on it. Aunt Sugar talked about doing that for years, but they never got around to it."

"Sounds good to me. We can take my vehicle," he said.

She nodded. "Then we can keep the rooms separate by calling them by their color. Like, 'we've got guests in the blue room.' But today we only have to decide on one color, right? And we'll think about the front door before we make a definite decision."

"We could pick out two colors today." He rushed around the truck to open the door for her. "That way we'll have the paint here and ready."

"Let's find a pretty magnolia border and then match six colors to that. And no heavy drapes on the windows. We need to bring the pine trees inside, and . . ."

He started the engine. "You've given this a lot of thought, haven't you?"

"Yep, I have, and I'm really glad that you are able to finance it, Tucker."

It was a good thing that they ate their burgers before they went to the paint store, because there was no such thing as simply picking out a border. She pored over three massive wallpaper books, marking at least a dozen borders that had magnolias on them, but she couldn't decide. The flowers were too big on one, too small on another, and too stylized on another.

Tucker found an old metal folding chair in the corner, sat down, and leaned it against the wall on the back two legs. He pulled his hat down over his eyes and crossed his arms over his chest. He would have picked out a border in five minutes, but he was a man. Melanie and Jolene both took forever to make up their minds about anything.

He smiled when a memory of Melanie popped into his head. He had taken her out shopping, and she'd been in and out of a dressing room, trying on outfit after outfit to wear to the Dallas Police Department's Christmas Ball. He'd sat in a chair pretty much the same as he was right then, only it wasn't leaning against the wall.

He shouldn't compare Jolene to Melanie, he thought. One had been choosing a dress; the other was choosing wallpaper. They looked nothing alike and their temperaments were different. But the flutter in his heart when he'd been around Melanie was the same one that he got when Jolene was close by. He'd continue to fight it, but it was getting harder and harder not to acknowledge.

Finally, Jolene narrowed it down to six and asked his opinion. He took the book and carried it fourteen feet away from where she was sitting and held it up in the air. "This is the way the people will see it when they walk through the bedroom doors. Now what do you think?"

"Why in the hell didn't you do that an hour ago? I've been agonizing over this because it's the most important decision we'll make. We'll see it in every room of the house, and you didn't think to do that?" She narrowed her eyes at him and then shifted her gaze to the border. "Not that one. Hold up another one."

He remembered that Melanie had held up two dresses in the end. One was red and the other one was black. He'd told her to buy both and decide which one to wear the day of the ball. She'd done just that and worn the red one—the same dress he'd chosen to bury her in.

He held up the last border, and before Jolene said a single word, her smile told him she'd found the perfect one.

"That's it. That's the one. We'll need to order a bunch. Is that all right?" She bit at a thumbnail.

He thought about telling her exactly how much money he'd received when Melanie died, but he just couldn't. It didn't seem right.

"Of course. We'll order as much as we need." He didn't tell her that he would have sunk his last dollar into wallpaper to have the decision made. "Now let's go get a sample of it to take home."

Home!

Saying it didn't make it so, or did it? He thought about it on the way to the checkout counter. Had the Magnolia become home? And if it had, did that mean he'd taken another step out of the past? And was Jolene part of the future? If so, in what capacity?

"I'd like a sample of this border." Jolene pointed to the one in the book.

"If we have one, you can have it." The sales clerk opened a huge file drawer and flipped through until she found the right one. "Once these are gone, we won't be giving them away anymore. Folks will have to order samples from the internet. Kind of loses the human touch, if you ask me. This is our last one."

"Thank you. We'll need to order quite a lot because we're going to use it throughout a whole house. Could we call you Monday with the measurements?" Jolene asked.

"Just tell me how many feet of it you'll need. I'll do the figuring and send in the order. You might want to order a couple of extra rolls for matching and emergencies."

"Thank you. Now about paint. Two gallons of this color and two of this one." Tucker put the two samples on the counter.

The saleslady and Jolene started up a conversation about how well those two colors went with the border, and he bit back a long sigh. Women talked a helluva lot about nothing. *Just mix the paint and get on with it.*

Hey, now! Melanie's voice was back in his head. *Cut her some slack. Us women like to discuss things and think about them before we do them. This is a big deal for her.*

He cut his eyes around the room, but he stood as still as if he'd spotted a spider in the corner. Of all the times he might want her to talk to him—this wasn't one of them.

Well, it's a pretty damn big deal for me, too, but I don't have to discuss it to death, resurrect it, and talk some more, he argued. If Melanie would continue to drop into his head every now and then, surely he could get rid of these feelings that were developing for Jolene.

He listened intently, but Melanie had left the building. Did that mean she liked Jolene? Or was she giving him a hard time because of all the times he'd been impatient when she was trying to make a decision—like with the Christmas dress?

"We don't have time to do much this afternoon, so maybe we could go to the antique stores," Jolene was saying when he tuned back in to the conversation.

How long had he been zoned out, anyway? Evidently long enough for the saleslady to mix four gallons of paint, because they were right there on the counter. He pulled his credit card from his wallet and paid the bill, picked up the paint, and followed Jolene outside.

"So?" she asked. "What about the vanities? I love the way you used that washstand for one in the first bathroom. It's awesome."

He'd had compliments on his work many times, but the way that her eyes twinkled put a big smile on his face.

Chapter Eleven

otty met Jolene at the Gator door that night and put a key in her hand. "Now I won't have to watch for you anymore. How's the parking lot lookin'?"

"Like we're in for a rush." Jolene stashed her coat and purse under the counter.

"So what's goin' on at the inn this weekend? I tell you one thing for sure, that Tucker is one hardworkin' man. I can see that he's really tryin' to get past his troubles. And, for that matter, you seem happier these days, too," Dotty said.

Jolene was tying an apron around her waist when she realized what Dotty was doing. Maybe the whole bunch of them were even in on it. "Dotty Beauchamp, are you playing matchmaker?"

"Oh, no!" Dotty laid a hand on her chest. "Not me, *chère*. I'm just tellin' you not to slam the door in the face of opportunity if it's starin' you right in the eyes."

"That sounded just like Aunt Sugar." Jolene smiled.

"It should," Dotty sighed. "She used to say it all the time. You want to buy my bar? I might get me an RV and join her after all."

"No, thank you. Running the inn is going to keep me busy."

"Has he kissed you yet?" Dotty's eyes twinkled.

Jolene shook her head. "No, ma'am."

"You think y'all might ever get together if he sticks around?" Dotty said.

If he sticks around—her mother had said that so many times. *If this rich man sticks around, he's going to take me out of this damned trailer. If this wonderful guy sticks around, he's going to take me to Vegas for a whole week. This man is the CEO of a trucking company—if he sticks around, I'm going to quit my shitty job and go on the road with him.* And every time it all fell through, Jolene had to clean up the messes those men left behind. Just thinking about it made her mad all over again.

Dotty wiped up a spill from the bar. "Sugar wants an update on Tucker and you tonight. She says you change the subject when she asks about y'all, and I've got to give her something or I'm afraid she's goin' to turn that RV around and come home."

Jolene sighed. "Then don't tell her anything, and maybe she really will come on back to Jefferson. As far as me and Tucker, we're partners. That's all. I can't get involved with him, Dotty, not unless and until he unloads all that emotional baggage, and even then it's iffy."

"Life's too short to be carryin' around heavy burdens. You both need to get rid of the past. Treat it like it's a material possession. Like Sugar did. She gave you everything that wouldn't fit in an RV and drove off with Jasper like a couple of newlyweds," Dotty said. "I wish I'd really sold the bar, got me an RV and a feller to drive it, and gone with her. God, I miss that woman. She was the most levelheaded one of us."

"It's not too late. I bet you could catch up to them in a week, but I'd sure miss you," Jolene said.

Dotty patted her cheek. "I can't leave you now, *chère*. I promised Sugar that I'd look after you until you were settled. Got to get back to my end of the bar, now."

Jolene was glad that Dotty had shifted spots, but now Tucker was on her mind. She wondered if he would stick around after the remodeling was done. Or if he'd get bored with a B&B, move his trailer back to Marshall, and just collect the money from the place.

❀

Tucker waited until Jolene left for work that evening, and then he and Sassy made a couple of trips back and forth, bringing in the rest of his things from the trailer. He put everything away and laid out his date-night outfit—starched jeans, ironed pearl-snap shirt, polished boots— just like Melanie liked for him to wear on Saturday night. After a quick shower, he got dressed, told Sassy that she was in charge until either he or Jolene got home, and headed for the bar. Only this time he didn't turn north to go to the Tipsy Gator, but south instead. He'd been to a little dive in the backwoods down near the interstate, and that's where he planned to go.

"Don't matter if we go to a steak house or get tacos from a wagon and eat them in a park as long as we're together. I'm not letting go of her," he said out loud. "I will not forget that Saturday is date night." He turned on the radio to his favorite country music station and kept time to the music with his thumbs on the steering wheel.

He always thought about Melanie as he drove to the bar on Saturday night. It was his time to replay highlights of their years together. It might be every detail he could remember about their wedding or their first fight or just crazy incidents that had happened during their five-year marriage. But that night it was about their last night together.

They'd sat out by the lake on a quilt, talked about starting a family, but decided to wait one more year. After all, midthirties wasn't too old to be a mommy and daddy, and it still gave them time to have the children they'd always talked about. The stars had been bright that night, and the moon was full. If only he'd known that in twenty-four hours his world would fall apart, he would have done things differently.

When he reached the bar, finding a parking spot wasn't a problem, but getting inside the bar was a different matter. There was a note on the door that simply said the place was closed and for sale.

I want tacos, not beer or Jack and Coke, Melanie said so clearly that he could've sworn she was walking beside him.

"Not tonight, darlin'. I need a few drinks to sharpen my memories of you. I'm enjoying being around Jolene entirely too much," he said as he got back into the truck. "If I'd waited a few weeks, I could have owned a bar instead of a bed-and-breakfast," he grumbled as he headed to the Southern Comfort. The drinks were more expensive and the crowd a little high-class for his taste, but maybe Melanie wouldn't fuss about tacos if she saw he was taking her to a fancy place.

Everything happens for a reason.

"You're in my head again. Dammit, Melanie, the way you pop in and out makes me dizzy." He caught the interstate going west.

Let me go. You can only keep the memories if they don't destroy you. And it's okay if you have feelings for Jolene.

"*I* should have gone to the store that night," he said.

He listened intently, but she was gone. A song came on the radio that brought back a memory of the two of them dancing in their bare feet in the backyard one night when they'd taken their burgers to go and spent the night at home. He smiled and waited. Still no Melanie.

The parking lot at the Southern Comfort wasn't as crowded as the Tipsy Gator always was on Saturday night. He found a spot not far from the door and headed inside. There was a barstool open away from everyone else, which was a good sign.

It's a fancy place, a club, so don't fuss at me, Melanie.

"What can I get you?" the bartender asked.

The kid hardly looked old enough to be pouring drinks. He was dressed in skintight pants and a knit shirt. A lock of blue hair hung down over one eye. There was live music—a piano player, who had a fantastic voice if a person liked that kind of music.

Tucker didn't. He wanted classic country music coming from a jukebox and some boots stomping on the hardwood floor.

"Double shot of whiskey, neat," he said.

"Yes, sir. Want me to start a tab?"

Tucker took a bill from his wallet and laid it on the bar. "No, I'll pay as I go."

The bartender flipped his blue hair to the side. "You're almost a dollar short."

Tucker put two more dollars on the bar. "Keep the change."

He sipped at the drink for more than half an hour as he thought about what he planned to do the next morning while Jolene slept.

"Another?" the kid asked. "Or would you like me to make you something different?"

Melanie had stopped talking to him, so evidently she didn't like this place.

"No, thank you," Tucker said as he slid off the stool. "You have a good night."

The kid answered with a wave.

Tucker got into his truck and pointed it toward Jefferson. He intended to go straight to the Gator, but with his mind on Melanie, he suddenly found himself parked outside the inn.

"Dammit!" He slapped the steering wheel. "This is one sorry date night when we get home at eight o'clock."

Everything happens for a reason. Her voice singsonged in his head.

"Is that all you are ever going to say to me from now on?" he asked.

Nothing. Not a single word or aura answered his question.

"Okay then, ignore me. I proved last week that I don't need a bar." He stormed into the house, poured two fingers of whiskey, took a drink, and carried it to the living room. "Easier on the wallet, anyway." He kicked off his boots and sat down in the recliner. "And more comfortable."

He took another sip and set the glass on the end table. Without finishing his drink, he left it behind, wandered upstairs, and leaned against the doorjamb of the room he'd been working on. It was going to be a really nice room when they finished. Sassy wove around his legs, but when he ignored her, she went into the bathroom, jumped into the tub, and curled up. With a sigh, Tucker picked up his tool belt and began to cover the new bathroom with drywall. Sassy slept right through it all.

He didn't even hear Jolene coming in or walking up the stairs until he felt her presence behind him. "What time is it?" he asked.

"It's after three in the morning," she answered. "Why are you workin' now? I thought you didn't do anything past your four hours on Saturdays."

"Couldn't sleep," he said.

"I'm surprised. Last Saturday night you were still out when I got home." She yawned.

"No, I wasn't. I got home about two thirty that night. I was passed out in my bedroom when you got home." He removed his tool belt and laid the nail gun to the side. "That was the last piece. After it's bedded and taped, we can set the rest of the fixtures in here and put up the tub enclosure."

"Hungry?" she asked.

"Yep. I'll get washed up. We got any of them doughnuts left that we bought a couple of days ago?"

"They won't be fresh, but we can throw some butter on the top and give them twenty seconds in the microwave," she said as she started downstairs.

He went to the bathroom at the end of the hallway and washed his hands and forearms.

He noticed on his way down the stairs that the railing was loose near the newel post and made a mental note to get that fixed. Sassy caught up with him in the foyer, and he bent to pet her.

"It feels strange to be sober on date night," he whispered.

The cat meowed at him and led the way into the kitchen, where he poured out a dozen of her special treats. "That's payment for helping me get things done tonight," he said and then turned to Jolene. "You made hot chocolate?"

"Just the kind out of a package. I like doughnuts dipped in it," she said.

So had Melanie, he thought. And cookies and even peanut butter sandwiches. Sounded terrible, but it wasn't so bad.

"Guess who came to the bar tonight?" She didn't give him time to answer, but went right into the story of Lucy and Everett.

He was relieved that she didn't ask why he hadn't dived into the bottle that night, because he didn't have an answer, and he sure didn't feel like talking about it.

"Sounds to me like those old gals could hang out a shingle for therapy. Lucy has been cured, and according to Dotty, they took care of her problem a long time ago."

"Therapists keep you coming back so they can make a living," Jolene said. "It's easy to talk to a stranger who's bound by law to never breathe a word of what you told them. You can tell them anything, and they just nod and ask you how you felt about it. They never tell you how to fix it. You're supposed to figure that out on your own." She put two doughnuts on a saucer and put them in the microwave.

"Sounds like you're speakin' from experience."

"I went to one a couple of times." She took the doughnuts out and set the plate on the table.

"Did it do any good?"

"Yes and no. It taught me that I had to figure out things for myself. No pill or shot of liquor or talkin' to a stranger would help. Maybe some folks do better than I did, or maybe I didn't give it enough time, but . . ." She shrugged.

"I've been to therapists," he said and then wondered if he'd said that out loud.

"For detective stuff?" she asked. "Like on television shows when they fire their guns and have to go in before they can have their badge and weapon back?"

"That and . . ." He paused.

He wondered if she even heard him, since she didn't look up from her plate.

"When my wife was killed," he went on, "two years ago last fall. It didn't help me, either, but I can't blame it on the therapist. I was pretty self-destructive during that time. I drank too much, got fired because of it, and decided to move here, since this is where she grew up. I thought it would help, but it didn't. Started doing odd jobs for her best friend, who's in the real estate business. I've had all the work I can do."

"Are you still self-destructive?" She finished off her doughnut.

"Only on Saturday nights. That was date night for us." He'd never even told the therapist that, but it was easier talking to Jolene than that old guy the police department had sent him to. "But I've got this new partner who has a terrific cure for hangovers, and for the first time in a very long while, I won't need it tomorrow morning."

"Your new partner has a cure because she had to use it really often for her mother." Jolene covered a yawn with her hand. "I'm going to bed. I'm not goin' to pass go, collect two hundred dollars, or even take a shower until morning. Good night, Tucker."

Just like that, she was gone. He'd just told her about Melanie and she hadn't told him that he'd get over it or that time would help—none of those things folks usually told him when he mentioned her name. She'd listened—like he had when she'd told him about her mother. But talking to her about it made him feel better than he had in months.

A pang of guilt hit Tucker smack in the heart. He'd never want to inflict pain on Jolene like what he'd heard in her voice when she said that about her mother. She sure didn't need to take care of him every weekend like she had her mother. It was time for him to straighten up and move on, but the thought of leaving Melanie behind didn't seem right—not at all.

Chapter Twelve

"This is not what I was expecting at all," Jolene said as Tucker parked in front of Lucy's house that Sunday afternoon.

"I figured Lucy would live in a two-story painted lady," Tucker said.

"Me, too, but this is the address she gave me." Jolene checked her phone, then glanced up at the house number on the porch post and turned around in her seat to see if they were on the right street. It all checked out. "And there's Dotty's van and Flossie's car in the driveway, so I guess we are here."

"All those years you visited your aunt, you never went to any of their homes?" Tucker asked.

Jolene frowned as she tried to remember. "No, never. Aunt Sugar would have never, ever let me go to the bar, and the ladies always came out to the inn. It doesn't look like the home of an antique dealer, does it? Seems strange, but when I was here, we even had Sunday dinner at the Magnolia. I wonder when they started taking turns."

"Maybe the inside is different," Tucker said.

As she walked up the sidewalk to the porch, Jolene looked up and down the block. Lucy's little brick house built on what they used to call a ranch plan was the last one on the block with three other houses about the same size. Two were painted white and one was yellow brick. They each had a one-car attached garage and small, well-manicured front lawn. They looked like they'd all been built in the seventies, from the same floor plan—small porch, garage, and a picture window with drapes drawn back to let in the light. Modern houses in that day and age, and still pretty much so even now, but nothing like what Jolene had imagined an antique dealer would live in.

Tucker knocked on the doorframe and glanced down at Jolene. She could feel him staring at her and looked up into his eyes. There was a difference in him that day, as if he'd shed some of the stuff weighing down his soul. They both started to say something at the same time.

"You go first," he said.

"I was just thinking," she started, but before she could say another word, Lucy swung the door wide-open and motioned them inside.

She wore an apron printed with Hershey Kisses all over it. "Will work for kisses" was embroidered in sparkly gold thread across the bib. "Y'all come right in. We've just about got the dinner on the table. I was hungry for fried chicken today, so we skipped church and we've been cookin' since eleven o'clock." She raised her voice. "*The kids are here.* Y'all get them potatoes mashed and the biscuits out of the oven. I'm going to talk to them in the living room."

Jolene could hardly believe her eyes when she entered the small living room: a black leather sofa; shiny, modern black end tables; a soft, pure-white leather recliner with a bright-red pillow on it. She should make a comment, anything, but nothing came to mind.

Lucy pointed at the recliner. "Have a seat, Tucker. It'll be at least five minutes. You're shocked by my style, aren't you, Jolene? When you work around antiques all day, you don't want to come home and look at them all evening. You can sit right there on the end of the sofa, honey. It's real comfortable." She lowered her voice. "I've always been the modern gal among us four. Dotty was the wild one. Sugar was the sweet one that held us all together, and Flossie wore lots of hats, but mostly I think she was just someone to fuss at me."

"I'm sorry," Jolene said. "I didn't mean to be rude. And believe me, Lucy, I did not grow up around antiques in West Texas, either. This room looks like the living room we had when my dad was alive, except the leather furniture was brown."

"Shocked and rude are two different things. I bought this house back in the seventies and thought it would be a good starter home. Evidently, it's been a good permanent home, because I'm still here," Lucy said.

"It's very nice," Tucker said. "Reminds me of the house my grandparents had in McKinney, only theirs had some acreage around it."

"Dinner's on the table," Flossie called out.

"That's our cue," Lucy said. "Follow me."

Memories flooded through Jolene's mind. The house was built on practically the same floor plan as the one she'd grown up in. She remembered family pictures hanging in the hallway. There'd been one of her at her first dance recital in a little yellow outfit. Elaine had decided that Jolene needed to do something to come out of her shell and enrolled her in ballet. Jolene had been five years old that year and she'd hated the class, but it meant a time when Elaine had been proud of her.

She'd sat in her empty room and cried the day she and her mom had moved from the house to the trailer. The closet in the new place was small, but she took all her clothing. Her bed wouldn't fit in her new bedroom, so she wound up with the futon from the den. As she stared at Lucy's pictures, the pain of that day came back. She tried to push it and the memories aside, but a picture surfaced of her sweet sixteen party. Elaine had insisted on having it at the country club. Boys had been invited, and Jolene danced with a few of them throughout the night even though she hardly knew them. They were sons of Elaine's friends. The boy she'd been seeing wasn't invited because her mother didn't think he was good enough for her.

The emptiness of the whole evening came back to Jolene as she remembered. The only thing that was a positive memory was that her mother had been happy. But then, of course, she should have been. Jolene's dad was still alive and was willing and able to give her anything she wanted, and she was at the country club, where she was the queen of the party.

"Are you all right?" Lucy laid a hand on her shoulder. "You look like you've just seen a ghost."

"Your house brought back memories," she answered honestly.

And the feelings that went along with them, she thought.

"I hope they were good." Lucy led them on into the kitchen. "Now, Tucker, you can sit at the head of the table, but I will say grace. And you"—she pointed at Dotty—"don't say a word. I still believe in God even if I have skipped out on church today."

"Just don't pray so long that the chicken gets cold," Dotty said.

It was as if they had permanent seating arrangements wherever they went. Dotty and Lucy sat on one side of the table. Flossie and Jolene took up the other side, and Tucker got the king's chair.

Jolene's favorite meal was home-fried chicken with all the trimmings, yet she hadn't had it since Aunt Sugar made it for her more than three years ago. Her mind went back to the few visits she'd had in Jefferson after her mother died. Working six nights a week and playing catch-up on her errands the other day didn't leave much time to drive across the whole state of Texas for a fried chicken dinner. But she had been faithful about calling her aunt twice a week and had always looked forward to their talks.

"Amen," Lucy said.

Jolene hadn't heard a word of the prayer, but she said "Amen" right along with Tucker, Dotty, and Flossie. Her stomach growled as she looked over the table.

"It was three years ago at Christmas," she said.

Dotty put a chicken leg and a wing on her plate. "What about three years ago?"

"The last time I came home to the Magnolia. Aunt Sugar made me a meal like this. There's not a restaurant in the world that can touch this kind of dinner," Jolene answered.

The last Christmas she spent with her father, they'd gone to a restaurant because her mother didn't want to cook a big dinner for only three people. The last one she'd spent with her mother had been just another day. Elaine had spent the day drinking, and Jolene had worked a double shift at a twenty-four-hour truck stop. She'd taken supper home that night, but Elaine was already passed out on the sofa, so she'd eaten alone.

Even with friends surrounding her, and Tucker right beside her, a fresh wave of emptiness flooded over her—the same feeling she'd had those Christmas Days. She took a couple of big gulps of sweet tea to get the lump in her throat to go down.

"Speaking of good food." Tucker put two huge spoons of mashed potatoes on his plate beside a crispy chicken breast. "If I keep eatin' Sunday dinner with you ladies, I'm going to have to buy a bigger belt."

"When was the last time you had homemade fried chicken?" Jolene passed the sawmill gravy to him.

"There's been too many Saturday nights that fried too many brain cells for me to remember," he admitted. "But whenever it was, it couldn't have been this good. Is this fresh corn?"

Tucker hadn't gotten drunk since that first weekend after he'd moved to the Magnolia. Maybe he was putting down roots and moving forward, even if it was just baby steps. Having dinner with the old gals was enough to convince Jolene that he was at least trying.

"Straight from my freezer," Flossie answered. "I still have a little garden at my place. We'll have dinner there next week."

"Little garden," Dotty almost snorted. "She's got a quarter of an acre plowed up."

"How do you find time to garden and run a store both?" Tucker asked.

"She doesn't. She pays a guy to take care of it for her," Lucy tattled.

"I do not!" Flossie argued. "I provide the seeds. He does the work and we share the bounty. He has lots of friends that he gives fresh vegetables to, just like I do. That's not payin' him. I'm *helping* him. His wife took sick, and they had to sell the farm to keep up with her medical bills. He'd go stir-crazy livin' in town if he couldn't play in the dirt."

Jolene's thoughts went back to her father's flower beds. He'd spent hours out there every evening—watering, fertilizing, deadheading, and taking out every single hint of a weed. Had he really loved the work, or had it been an escape from her mother? They'd come from such different backgrounds. He'd been raised in Louisiana on a small farm, and she was a city girl from Amarillo. They'd met at a party given by mutual friends who worked at the bank with him. He'd been told when the company transferred him to Texas that it would only be for a couple of years. But when the opportunity came up to go back to Louisiana, he turned it down for Elaine. She liked living in the city. Jolene had never thought of it before, but maybe her father had been wishing he was back in his own world when he was out there in his flower beds.

Flossie nudged her on the arm. "You woolgatherin', darlin'? You've been holding that basket of biscuits for a full minute."

"I'm sorry. I was thinkin' of my dad. He never planted a garden, but he had the prettiest flowers in the whole county." Jolene hurriedly put a biscuit on her plate and passed the basket on to Tucker. "I like getting my hands dirty in flower beds. Maybe we'll put some in at the inn this spring."

"I like that idea, but right now I'm more interested in this corn," Tucker said.

"Person gets used to good fresh food and then that canned stuff don't taste good," Flossie said.

Tucker took a biscuit and passed them on. "I've lived on takeout for so long that two Sundays of this good cookin' makes me feel plumb spoiled."

Jolene stole a glance at him and remembered what Aunt Sugar said about no one being truly bad or good. Tucker was a good man, in spite of his weekend binges. He worked hard, had a sense of humor and a kind heart. But could he ever forget Melanie? The drinking seemed to be tied tightly to his deceased wife, and that would make it difficult, if not impossible, for him to get over it if he couldn't let go of the guilt surrounding her death.

She was still pondering those thoughts when Flossie bumped her on the knee and nodded toward Lucy.

"Having you around," Lucy was saying, "makes us feel like we did when we had our Friday-night girls' night."

Dotty yawned. "I agree, but I'm in bad need of a nap. Jolene and I were up until three this mornin'."

"I'll help y'all with cleanup, and then we can all go find us a nice soft bed for a Sunday afternoon nap," Jolene said.

"You don't need to help us," Flossie said. "Lucy's got a good dishwasher, and we'll have this done in no time. Don't forget next week is at Flossie's."

"Wouldn't miss it for anything, but please let us bring something," Tucker said.

"You can bring a half gallon of ice cream," Flossie said. "We'll have ice cream sundaes for dessert. But I'm going to put some of this cobbler on a plate for you to take home for supper. There's no way we can eat it all."

"I won't argue with you one bit. That was some fantastic cobbler." Tucker grinned.

Like that little compliment, Jolene thought. *It made the ladies feel special, and that was a good thing, so even a weekend drunk has good qualities.*

Jolene gave them all a goodbye hug, just like she had when she was a little girl. "Thanks for a great day. I can't wait to tell Aunt Sugar all about it."

"Well, that was strange," Tucker said when they were in the truck and headed down the highway toward the inn.

"What?" she asked. "Hasn't anyone ever sent leftovers home with you?"

"No, my grandmother always sent food home with me. But I felt just like I did when I went home with Melanie the first time to meet her parents," he answered. "Like I should be on my best behavior, and yet, it wasn't hard to do because they're so much fun to be around."

"What kind of food did your granny make?" she asked.

"They lived on a ranch, so it was usually steaks. But my grandma made the best cheesecake in the whole world. Didn't you notice all three of them making eye contact as if they were sharing an inside joke?" He turned down the lane to the inn and parked in front of the house.

It hit Jolene in a flash. Dotty had denied that she was playing matchmaker, but those old gals were up to something. "If it walks like a duck, quacks like a duck . . . ," she said.

Tucker's eyes went to every window in the truck. "Where's a duck?"

"I'm not talkin' about a real one." Jolene giggled. If he didn't know that Dotty, Flossie, and Lucy had united to play matchmaker, then she wasn't going to tell him.

"Oh, I see." Tucker grinned. "So you noticed what they were doing, too?"

"I did." She nodded.

"Well, honey, if it makes them happy and they make cobbler, then I don't mind, do you?"

She smiled. "Then it is true. The way to your heart is through your stomach."

"Today it is." Tucker changed the subject. "Guess we'd better go on inside and do some laundry while we take our naps, right?"

Jolene got out of the car and bent against a cold wind sweeping down from the north. "Does it seem strange to you when we combine our clothes?"

"Yep." He nodded. "But that's because my tighty-whities haven't been tossed in with a woman's underbritches in a long time."

She unlocked the door and led the way inside. "It's been a long time since I was in a relationship that got to the stage where we did laundry together. Guess it's a normal reaction, but it's nice to save water."

"Yes, it is."

Sassy came out of the kitchen, rubbed around Tucker's legs, and looked up at him with begging eyes.

Tucker set the cobbler on the cabinet and stooped down to pet her. "Sorry, darlin'. It's people food. It's not leftover steak, pizza, or even hamburger for you. We didn't think to bring home a fried chicken leg. How about a handful of cat treats?"

Jolene watched him shake out the special treats from a plastic container and let Sassy eat them from his hand. One more good thing— Aunt Sugar said you could judge a man's character by how animals and kids treated him. Dotty, Flossie, and Lucy weren't children, but they sure liked him, and the way Sassy was trying to eat and purr at the same time didn't leave any doubt about how much she loved him.

Jolene went straight to the utility room and put all the white things in the washing machine—his T-shirts, her white bikinis, and his tighty-whities. She adjusted the dials and poured in a capful of detergent. She had time for a thirty-minute power nap while that load ran, but she wasn't sleepy like she usually was on Sunday afternoons.

When she turned, Tucker was gone but had left a few more treats on the china plate that Sassy ate from. The cat followed her into the living room and jumped up on the sofa.

Jolene found Tucker stretched out in the recliner, his arms crossed over his chest. She eased down on the end of the sofa and stared her fill. His head rested at the top of the chair, but his feet hung off the bottom. He'd removed his boots, and he had probably fallen asleep as soon as he pulled the lever to put up the footrest. His hands were calloused from hard work, and he really did need a haircut, but then, he would look pretty sexy with a little ponytail.

"Don't go," he muttered.

"Go where?" she stammered.

He opened one eye. "I was dreaming."

"About?" she asked.

"Melanie." His eye slid shut.

She picked up a throw pillow and tucked it under her head as she curled up on the sofa with Sassy right beside her. The way he said her name was so sad that Jolene's heart ached for him. Would he ever get past the grieving process?

Chapter Thirteen

On Monday morning Jolene grabbed the broom and dustpan and started for the stairs, intending to clean up behind Tucker. Yet she hadn't even gotten out of the kitchen when her phone rang. When she saw that it was Sugar, she propped the broom at the end of the breakfast bar in the kitchen and sat down in a chair.

"Aunt Sugar! Where are you this morning? Is Uncle Jasper feeling better? I've been worried about him."

"He's accepting it but not liking it, though we didn't put any conditions on what we gave y'all. The place was Reuben's to do with what he wanted. We're just glad you didn't sell out, too. And we're still in Georgia, only now we're on the east side of the state. We found this little resort that we really like," she said.

"Speaking of selling, why didn't y'all sell this place? It would have sure helped increase your nest egg, and you had to at least wonder what would happen with Reuben," Jolene asked.

"Because," Sugar answered, "we didn't need more money, and Jasper was set on giving Reuben half the place. We had lots of late-night talks about it, but as you already know, I didn't win. Jasper hoped it would help straighten Reuben out. He thought your influence would be good. Reuben is on his third professor job. He had a wonderful position at Baylor and didn't make tenure. Then he got hired at a junior college in

Oklahoma and didn't make tenure. Now he's at another junior college and it's not looking good there, either."

"*Me* help *him*?" Jolene gasped. "I'm just a bartender. He's a professor. How was I going to help him?"

"Common sense and life lessons go a lot farther than book learnin'," Sugar said.

"Thank you for that much trust." A wave of guilt washed over Jolene for ever even having second thoughts about selling her half to Tucker. She wiped away a tear making its way down her cheek and changed the subject. "So tell me how you're managing cooking in that small space when you're used to this huge kitchen. And when did y'all start going to different places every week?"

"It's been an adjustment learnin' to cope with such a small space," Sugar said. "And we've been takin' turns with dinner for several years. Hey, speakin' of dinner, Dotty says that Tucker is a great guy. Tell me what you think."

Jolene giggled. "I'm pretty sure they're playing matchmaker, but"— she lowered her voice—"he's still not over Melanie."

"Some things take a little more time to get over than others," Sugar said. "Don't shut a door until you're absolutely sure about it. At least you're friends. It would be hard to work together if you didn't at least like one another."

Jolene could hear Tucker working, but she took the phone outside. Wrapping a quilt she'd taken from the sofa on the way out around her, she settled down on the swing. She had questions for Sugar that she didn't want Tucker to hear.

"We work together really well, but I can't go through what I did with Mama and with my last boyfriend, so I'm not going to start something that has no finish line," Jolene answered.

"Smart thinkin'," Sugar said.

She wasn't even sure how to begin her next thought.

"You still there?" Sugar asked after several long seconds.

"Yes, I'm here. I was trying to think about how to ask about Melanie. Maybe if I knew more about her, then I could understand Tucker better," Jolene said.

"You could be right," Sugar said. "She was a tall brunette, rather slim built, and when she and Tucker were home and came to church with her parents, they seemed like the perfect little couple. Her mother wanted grandkids, but she and Tucker didn't seem to be in a big hurry for them. She'd taught the little kids' Sunday school class, so it wasn't any surprise to us when she became a schoolteacher and got a job in Dallas. I'd worried about a small-town girl going to the big city, but Melanie did fine. Met Tucker and got married. Then she was killed in an auto accident, and you know the rest."

"Thank you," Jolene said.

"And now moving on," Sugar said. "Dotty raves about you working at the Gator. I wasn't real happy about that, but it's what you know, and I reckon you can take care of yourself."

"Had to have something to pay the bills and buy food after Reuben did what he did," Jolene said. "So you're having a good time?"

"Oh, sweetie, we've been having the best time. We spent a couple of days on that beach where we scattered your folks' ashes. We stood there in the edge of the water and remembered the day we scattered their ashes. It's such a peaceful place. I'm glad that you wanted to put them where they'd honeymooned. Then we fished and picnicked. I love this journey," Sugar gushed, "but I miss home. It's takin' a lot of adjusting, goin' from the Magnolia to an RV. Don't tell the girls I'm homesick—" Sugar's voice cracked. "If they knew, they'd beg me to come back, and I couldn't do that to Jasper. He's barely over the way Reuben . . . no need in talking about that anymore. It's crazy how a person can love a new life and miss the old one at the same time."

"I miss you, too, Aunt Sugar. Why don't y'all swing back through here as you zigzag across the states?" Jolene got up and went back inside.

"It's our secret, but if you change your mind, you can come back to Jefferson and live right here in the inn with us."

"Thank you. It's starting to snow." Sugar's voice wasn't still up to normal. "We're near Savannah, Georgia. Love you. Bye now."

"Love you right back. Bye." Jolene hit the "End" button and picked up the broom to carry it upstairs.

❧

Tucker was applying the final sanding to the areas in the bathroom that he'd already gone over with the electric sander. The process now was to hit it with fine-grit paper wrapped around a block of wood before he textured the walls. After that it would be ready to tape off and paint. He was listening to his favorite country music playlist through the earbuds of his MP3 player and wouldn't have even heard the phone if it hadn't been in his hip pocket. He jerked both wires from his ears and answered without even looking to see who was calling.

"Hello, Tucker, how are you this morning?"

"I'm fine, Carla." Of all the people in the world, his mother-in-law was the last person he wanted to talk to that morning. He didn't need the yearly reminder that it was close to Melanie's birthday.

"I hear that you bought interest in the Magnolia Inn and that you're remodeling it," she said.

"That's right," he said.

"I'm glad you're nearby. We're getting together again this year to celebrate Melanie's memory on her birthday. Just burgers cooked on the grill and homemade ice cream. We'll eat around seven, but come early if you can. You were a big part of her life, Tucker. We'd love to have you join us," Carla said.

"Thanks for the invitation. I'll see what I can do," he said. "Right now, I'd better get back to work. Thanks for calling."

He hit the "End" button before she could say anything else and then sat down on the floor beside the vanity. He didn't need to spend time with Melanie's family once a year to keep her memories alive. A lump the size of a basketball settled in his chest, making it hard to breathe. This would be Melanie's third birthday since she'd died. Her mother had called the past two years to invite him to join them in remembering her, but he'd never gone to one of their celebrations.

He laid his phone on the vanity and stared at the place where a mirror would hang later. The blank wall became a screen for memories. He could see his grandfather's face, standing proudly beside him as his best man at the wedding. His grandmother sat on the front row of the church, beaming and wiping tears at the same time. Cancer got his grandpa the next year, and six months later his grandmother simply didn't wake up. Tucker had always figured she died of a broken heart.

That was his entire family, gone in less than a year. His father had come over the border to work for his grandfather one summer. His mother, Debra, had gotten pregnant during that time, and his father had been deported. When Tucker was six weeks old, she'd disappeared in the night, leaving a note behind that she'd gone to be with Joseph, Tucker's father. She'd written several times, but before he was a year old, his grandparents got word that his mother and his father had both died in an accident when the bus they were riding collided with a semitruck.

If a person could really die of a broken heart, though, why was he still living? His chest tightened; his breath came in short gasps. He had to get away, even if it was just for a while. He passed Jolene on her way up and managed to get a few words out, saying that he needed something from the trailer.

A blast of cold air rushed out to greet him when he opened the door. Bright sunshine offered a little warmth outside the trailer, but the sunrays couldn't penetrate the metal shell to heat up the inside. One bottle of whiskey was left in the cabinet, so he poured a shot and carried it to the bed. He sat down on the edge and groaned.

"I don't drink on the job." He stood up, emptied the glass into the sink, and squared his shoulders.

Instead of going back to the house, he wandered down to the Big Cypress Bayou. The cold, dead grass crunched under him when he sat down and braced his back against a willow tree. Before long spring would push winter away and things would turn green again. But Tucker's heart was a different matter—he felt as if it had suffered a bitter, cold winter for almost three years now, and spring would never arrive again.

❧

Charleston, South Carolina

Jasper had walked up to the little store at the RV park that afternoon to get a loaf of bread and half gallon of milk, so Sugar used the time to call Dotty. The bar would open in half an hour and things would get hectic, but she and her friend could cover a lot of ground in that time.

"Hello, guess what. The kids came to Sunday dinner yesterday. Tell me that Jasper is better. We're still worried about him." Dotty sounded like she was out of breath.

Sugar had a vision of her having a heart attack and panic set in. What if one of her friends died and she was too far away to even get home for the funeral?

"Are you all right? You're panting?" Sugar asked. "Tell me everything. Is Jolene doin' all right? She says that she loves the work at the Magnolia and sends me pictures, but you're the closest one to her since y'all work together, so do I need to come home to take care of her?"

Dotty giggled. "I miss you like hell, but don't come back to Jefferson for Jolene. She's doin' a fine job of livin' with Tucker. And I think I can see some improvement. To my knowledge, he's only been drunk enough to have a hangover one time. Hell, who knows? Maybe Lucy's prayers are going higher than the ceiling."

Sugar laughed. "So what is Lucy praying for?"

"That he stays sober, especially after the grand opening in the spring, because she thinks it'll hurt business if he comes in drunk on the weekends," Dotty answered.

"Well, then praise the Lord for Lucy's prayers," Sugar said.

"Amen to that," Dotty said. "He don't know that he's fallin' for her, and we're tryin' our best to let them figure it out on their own. But he looks at her like Jasper used to look at you when we were all kids. And it's real hard for us not to play matchmaker."

"That's sweet," Sugar said. "But according to Jolene, he's not over Melanie. Sounds to me like Tucker and Jolene have been walkin' two separate paths. But then there was a fork in the road and they've met up to walk a single one. They've kind of got the same problems."

"You should've been a therapist, the way you can see inside people's souls," Dotty said. "Now tell me all about your travels."

"It's been great. We go as far as we want, stay in one place until we're bored, and then go on down the road again. It's like a long honeymoon," Sugar answered.

"I wish I'd got me a driver and an RV and gone with you," Dotty sighed. "Promise when you swing back this way, you'll stop here for a week or two. We miss you so much."

"Promise," Sugar said. "And here's Jasper with the milk so I can make fried chicken and gravy for dinner. Talk to you in a day or so."

Chapter Fourteen

Jolene's apartment out in West Texas had been so small that the only time Aunt Sugar came to visit, she said that she couldn't cuss a cat in it without getting a hair in her mouth. Now Jolene lived in a huge house, and yet after Tucker left that morning, it felt empty and cold.

"What's the matter with me?" She sat down on the top step of the staircase when she'd finished sweeping. "This kind of business is what I've dreamed about since I was a child."

Thinking that a breath of fresh air might straighten her out, she went downstairs, jerked her coat on, and headed to the bayou. As a child, she'd spent hours running up and down the edge of the water. Some days she made tiny boats from twigs and floated them. Others she'd dug a few worms or caught some grasshoppers and gone fishing. As a teenager, she'd found solace in sitting with her back to her favorite old willow tree and listening to the sounds of nature.

A cottontail startled her when it ran out from a thicket of dead branches not far from the water's edge, and she stopped to watch it zigzag back toward the house. She turned around and saw Tucker sitting against her tree, and it brought up something like jealousy in her heart. That was where she'd hidden from Reuben when she was a child. If she made herself very small, then he couldn't find her back in the drooping branches. It was where she'd poured out her heart in a journal the summer she was thirteen. And where she'd come to search for peace after her mother's addiction took a firm hold on her.

"That's my tree. It's not up for sale, not even half interest," she said.

"Then charge me for trespassing, and I'll pay my fine. What are you doing outside in this cold wind?" he asked.

"Same thing you are, probably. Needed some fresh air and a new perspective," she answered.

"Want to talk about it?" he asked. "You're not having second thoughts about the inn, are you? Because if you are, I'll be glad to buy you out."

She sat down beside him. "Not even for a million dollars."

He scooted over to give her room to lean against the tree. "My mother-in-law called. I guess that's what I should still call her. Melanie wasn't ever my ex. Maybe I should say my late wife's mother? She only calls once a year."

"In January? Not at Christmas?" Jolene picked up a rock and tossed it out in the water.

"Melanie's birthday was—is—again, I'm not sure how to even talk about this." His shoulders raised in half a shrug. "Anyway, January 19, this coming Saturday. Her family does this get-together to remember her."

"That's sweet," Jolene said.

"Her mother always invites me." His voice sounded hollow.

"Have you ever gone?" she asked.

He shook his head slowly. "I can't. Her father didn't want her to marry me. He thought she deserved better than a cop. Said I'd get killed on the job and leave her with a broken heart."

"That's real positive thinking." The wind whipped down from the north and blew Jolene's hair across her face. She dug around in her coat pocket for a rubber band and finger combed her hair up into a ponytail.

"I didn't come from such good stock, either. My grandparents were good people and they raised me. I don't know that my parents were ever married, so you know what that makes me." He went on to tell her more about his background.

She could hear more pain in his voice and reached across the distance to lay a hand on his shoulder. "You don't have to talk about it."

He picked up a twig and toyed with it. After a couple of minutes, he went on. "I kind of felt abandoned my whole life until Melanie. My grandparents were wonderful, don't get me wrong. Gramps was a cop and I adored him, but I already told you that. I thought I had a lot to prove, and so the reputation kind of followed me around," he said. "I usually don't talk about this to anyone but Sassy, and then only when I'm drunk."

He tossed a rock into the middle of the bayou, and they watched the water ripple out from it, first in little circles and then in bigger ones until the surface was smooth again.

"Did Melanie tell you what her dad said?" Jolene asked.

"No, *he* did." His tone had turned bitter. "I kind of understood where he was coming from. She was his only daughter. I assured him that I loved her and would take care of her, that he had nothing to worry about. I broke my promise."

"Hey, you can't carry that burden. That wreck wasn't your fault," Jolene told him. "You think she was a daddy's girl?"

He skimmed the water with another flat rock. "Oh, yeah. Big-time."

"She must've loved you a helluva lot." Jolene had been close to her dad, but she'd have told him to go to hell on a rusty poker if he'd talked to her like that about the man she was about to marry. She'd been a daddy's girl, too, but she'd never know the joy of walking down the aisle on her dad's arm.

"Why would you say that?" he asked.

"Come on, Tucker, think about it. She went against her daddy's wishes and married you. That takes courage, and from what I see on

153

television cop shows, living with a detective ain't all that easy, either, so it wasn't a bed of roses after she married you," Jolene answered.

"I could have been a better husband," he whispered.

"Yep, and if the situation were reversed and you were the one who died in that car wreck, she would be saying that she shouldn't have nagged you to take out the trash. Or fussed at you because you had a beer with the other cops after work, or forgot to pick up milk on your way home. Let it go and move on. She loved you enough to marry you, Tucker. She would hate for you to be punishing yourself all this time," she told him.

"You sound like the therapist I had to see at the station," he said. "I should be getting back to work."

"You should've listened to that therapist you talked to when you were in the service." She wondered if she was talking to him, to herself, or to both of them. The therapist she'd seen had told her that she had to realize she'd done all she could, but she hadn't believed him. Now she wished she'd worked harder at overcoming her own guilt. She'd buried it like a dog did a bone. And then she'd gone back every few months and dug it up again. Tucker was doing the same thing—only he never buried it to begin with. He carried it around with him, slept with it, and kept it close by his side.

"I probably should have, but talking about it with you sure helps." He leaned a little closer to her and their eyes locked.

For a minute, she thought he might kiss her, and she moistened her lips with the tip of her tongue. But then he turned away, focusing on the bayou again. She felt heat rise from her neck to her cheeks.

"Well, it helps me to talk about things, too. I've never been real comfortable tellin' anyone about my mother or Johnny Ray," she said.

"We're sure a couple of misfits, aren't we?" Tucker muttered.

"Yep, we are, and I for one am a hungry misfit. Want to share that cobbler we brought from Flossie's yesterday? We could heat it up and top it off with ice cream."

He stood up and offered her a hand. "Sounds great. And thanks for listenin'."

She took it and popped up to her feet. "That goes both ways. Sometimes we just need to get things off our chests." Chemistry sparked when he touched her, making her pulse race. "I talked to Aunt Sugar this morning. They're having a great time. You should sit in on her next call. She wants me to send pictures of us, not just the work we're doing. I thought maybe when we got into painting, we'd send one of us in our work clothes. Maybe we can even FaceTime and actually give her a tour of what's going on rather than just pictures."

Jolene talked too much and too fast for two reasons—either she was in trouble or she was running from her emotions. Right then, it was definitely the latter.

🌺

In mandatory therapy, Tucker would sit on the comfortable sofa and tell the guy what he needed to hear. He'd had to see him several times after Melanie's death. He'd been so full of rage and so self-destructive that he was put on desk duty. That's when he started drinking, and the last straw was when he had that little fender bender in his work car. He didn't pass the Breathalyzer test, and the doc said he wouldn't sign papers even for desk duty unless Tucker went to rehab.

But that morning, he felt better than he'd ever felt when he went to a therapist. Usually even the mention of Melanie's name made him want to drink. They walked back to the house together, past the trailer where he always had a bottle of whiskey, but the longing for a shot was gone.

They were close enough that their hands brushed several times. He couldn't deny that there were vibes, but until he was ready to close the door to the past, he couldn't do anything about the attraction. He'd wanted to kiss Jolene so badly back there under that tree, and even now, when he glanced over at her lips, he wanted to take her in his arms. But again, he had issues to take care of before that could happen.

When they reached the house, he held the door for her to enter before him. She removed her coat and headed straight for the kitchen. He did the same and got out the ice cream while she warmed the cobbler.

Food and work provided an escape after an emotional talk like they'd just had. Would it always be that way? Would they, someday in the future, really start a relationship? He was still wondering what that would be like with Jolene when she poked him on the arm.

"So?" she asked.

"So what?" He frowned.

"What were you thinkin' about? You didn't even hear me talkin', did you?"

"Nope. I was woolgathering. Tell me again," he said.

"I was asking you if you'll talk to Aunt Sugar with me. You can explain all the carpentry stuff a lot better than I can, and besides, it might do both of you good to get to know each other. This wasn't just her business. It was her lifetime home." She took two bowls from the cabinet and set them on the table.

He got out two spoons and the ice cream scoop. "Sure. Be glad to do that."

"Both Uncle Jasper and Aunt Sugar were so disappointed in Reuben that it'll be positive for them to see that the inn is in good hands," she said.

"You think they're kind of mad at me for buying him out? If I hadn't stepped up and got it the day after he put it on the market, he might have changed his mind," Tucker said.

She pulled the cobbler from the microwave. "I doubt that, but it is what it is."

He divided the cobbler into two portions and put them into bowls. She added the ice cream and carried hers to the table. He joined her and put the first bite of cobbler into his mouth. "This is better than it was yesterday."

Before she could argue with him, there was a rap on the door and Dotty yelled, "Yoo-hoo, I'm comin' in. If you ain't decent, you better hide behind a chair."

"I'm just glad I'm decent. I don't think there's a chair big enough to hide me," Tucker said.

"Little egotistical there?" Jolene raised an eyebrow.

"I wasn't talking about . . ." She hadn't seen a man blush in years.

"Talkin' about what?" Dotty draped her coat over a chair and sat down. "Got coffee made? If not, I'll have tea. I'm going to an estate sale that starts at eleven. They've got an old jukebox I want for the bar. It actually plays real records and might defend us from that damn karaoke."

Jolene cocked her head to one side. "Karaoke?"

"Thursday nights when you're not there. Bruce started it against my wishes, and I didn't know how to stop it once he was gone," Dotty said. "Listenin' to drunk people sing drives me crazy."

Jolene remembered her mother staggering through the door singing some song that she'd performed on karaoke night at a bar. Elaine had a voice like a screech owl when she tried to sing. Jolene had thought at the time that she was so glad she hadn't been there to see her mama make a fool out of herself on a stage.

"Y'all want to go with me?" Dotty asked.

"You go, Jolene. I should stay here and get some bedding and taping—" Tucker started.

Dotty reached across the table and patted him on the cheek. "You are your own boss now."

Tucker smiled. "You've got my attention. Tell me more about how an auction works."

Jolene poured a glass of tea and set it in front of Dotty.

"The first hour they'll sell off the junk while everyone looks round at the good stuff. Then from twelve to one, the crowd will all go to the food wagon to get a barbecue sandwich." Dotty took several long gulps of the tea. "It'll be a profitable couple of hours whether we buy or not, because old Buster runs that food wagon and he makes the best barbecue in the county. Y'all can follow me. I've got the company truck, and it only seats two people."

The auction was ten miles away, not far from Smithland, at a two-story house set back off the road in a copse of pine trees, not totally unlike the setting for the Magnolia Inn. A young guy directed the traffic to a pasture that was being used for parking, and Tucker pulled his truck in right beside Dotty's.

"First thing we do is go get us a biddin' number." Dotty started talking as soon as she got out of her vehicle. "Then we'll do a walk-through and see what they've got. Lucy said if I see something really nice to send her a picture and she'll tell me whether to bid on it for her."

They signed their names to the roster, and the lady sitting behind the table handed each of them a small booklet along with a piece of cardboard with a number written on it. "Everything is labeled in order that it will be sold, and the auctioneer will do the selling from the garage. So write down what you're interested in. Once you buy, you come back to me to pay and claim your purchase."

Dotty stuck her book and number in the hip pocket of her jeans and motioned for Tucker and Jolene to follow her. "I like this kind of sale. It's well organized. And if I see something I want to bid on, I'll write the item number down in my book."

"Oh, oh!" Jolene clamped a hand over her mouth. "I want this box of doilies and scarves." She whipped the book up out of her purse, located a pen, and made her first note. She could visualize them scattered on the dressers in each bedroom, and even matted and framed to hang on the walls. Crocheting was fast becoming a lost art, especially the kind with fine thread instead of yarn.

"You do realize that you'll have to wash them every single time a guest leaves, right?" Dotty frowned.

The box held dozens of doilies and at least ten embroidered scarves—one even had magnolia blossoms on each end with fancy work in between depictions of hummingbirds.

"I'm going to frame this one to go above a bed." Jolene held it close to her chest. She was determined to buy the box if it took all of her tips for the past two weeks.

"That's a lie." Dotty pointed at the scarf.

"No, I mean it. It will be lovely," Jolene argued.

"Not what you said, but the birds. Those little guys like red blossoms, not white ones."

Tucker chuckled. "I can just see our first guest tellin' us that they have to change their room because hummingbirds don't go around magnolia trees. How much would you give for that box, Dotty?"

"No more than five dollars, because I can't sell those things. People, even antiquers, don't like the effort it takes to keep them done up," she said.

Dotty found a secretary with a rounded glass door that she thought she might be interested in buying. Tucker's eyes went all dreamy over a gadget that Jolene thought was a piece of junk or maybe something like modern art.

He held it in his hands and looked at it from every angle. "This is a genuine hand planer. I'm hoping that there aren't any woodworkers here today so I can get it for a decent price. I could take a tiny bit of wood off the top or bottom at a time. I'm going to keep my eye on that for sure." He wrote the number in his book.

The box of doilies started at two dollars. Jolene didn't make a move until Dotty nudged her. "You got to raise your number, *chère*, or he'll put them with something else later, like a dresser."

Jolene's hand shot up, but she was holding her book instead of her number card.

"Wrong thing," Tucker said.

She raised her card with her other hand. "Sorry."

"I've got two bucks. Can I get three?" the auctioneer rattled off.

"Five," Jolene yelled out. The scarf with the magnolias was going to be hers.

The auctioneer grinned and went on. "Young lady in the back must like this kind of thing. Can I get six? Six? Anybody want them worse than she does? One more time. Six? Anyone? Okay, then, sold to the pretty blonde in the back for five dollars."

They broke for lunch before the box with the tools was up for grabs. They only had to stand in line at the barbecue wagon a few minutes.

"Man, you're so right," Jolene said after the first bite. "These are amazing sandwiches." She chattered on as she ate. "I can't believe I got that whole box of stuff for only five bucks. When you see what I've got in mind for that magnolia embroidery, it's going to blow your mind. I've seen plain doilies that've been matted and framed go for a hundred bucks. I wonder who did that work on the magnolias."

"Slow down." Dotty laughed. "You'd think this was your first auction."

"It *is* my first one." Suddenly she got serious. "I didn't see that jukebox that you wanted. Are they hiding it?"

"No, the sorry suckers decided to keep it," Dotty said. "That box of tools that Tucker wants is next, so we'll stay until they sell it. Then I'm ready to go home. My part-time help wants to leave before quittin' time. Anyone want another sandwich? I'm takin' a couple back with me for Flossie and Lucy's afternoon snack."

"I'm good," Tucker said.

"Maybe we will get on home after Tucker bids on his screwdrivers." Jolene smiled. "In our world a screwdriver is a whole different thing than in his, right, Dotty?"

"You got it, kid! And a planer isn't a funny-lookin' tool—it's talkin' about someone who doesn't dress to the nines, right? As in, 'she sure dresses plainer than her cousin,'" Dotty teased. "What's your top bid, Tucker?"

"I haven't decided." His hand brushed against Jolene's as he reached across the table to gather up everyone's trash and take it over to a big black can. She felt another rush of sparks, but the way she figured, it was like when she'd gotten a silly notion that she'd like to dye a blue streak in her hair a couple of years ago. She had, and she'd hated it. It took a while to grow out, but it taught her a lesson: never do anything on impulse again. So what if there were sparks—she was a woman and he was a very sexy man. If there weren't vibes, then she should be worried, right? Besides, she'd vowed that she'd never start a relationship with anyone who got drunk—even on weekends—and she intended to stand by that promise.

Dotty nudged her again, this time with a shoulder. "I'd give a pretty penny to know where your mind is, *chère*. I've got a feelin' it's not on a box of doilies."

"Nope, it's on how pretty that magnolia scarf is going to be with a dark-green mat and a pretty frame," she said.

"Come on, *chère*. Tell the truth," Dotty prodded.

"I'm attracted to Tucker. We were talkin' about things, heavy things, this morning, and I thought he might kiss me, but he didn't," Jolene admitted.

"Were you disappointed?"

"A little, but it's for the best." Jolene sighed.

Chapter Fifteen

*E*ight bucks!" Tucker couldn't expect Jolene to be as excited as he was to have just bought a two-hundred-dollar antique for only eight dollars, but he couldn't contain his excitement, either. He'd almost grabbed her and kissed her when he won the bid on the box of worthless tools that contained his planer.

She nodded toward the back seat at her box of doilies. "Big spenders today, aren't we?"

Tucker's grin widened with every word. "This same auctioneer is doing another one on Saturday, starting at noon, and Buster is going to be there with his food wagon again. Want to go?"

"Oh, honey, I've got the fever now." Jolene nodded. "Where is it?"

"Right in Linden. The sale bill is in the back seat. It lists a couple of washstands like we're lookin' for," he told her.

"We'll have to tell Aunt Sugar about our finds when she calls." Jolene reached for the green paper. "They've got a tiny picture of the washstands, and in the column that lists other things, they've got tools, crystal, and lots of miscellaneous. Wonder if they'll have doilies?"

"You've got enough in that box to outfit the whole house," he said.

"But for five bucks a box, I can hang them on the walls, use them in baskets where we'll put out cute little soaps and lotions in the bathrooms, and all kinds of other places. They'd even be beautiful sewn on the tops of pillows. They bring such an old flavor to a house," Jolene said.

He stole a sidelong glance at her as he parked the truck in the front yard of the inn. Several strands of hair had escaped her ponytail, and there was a tiny smudge of barbecue sauce on her jaw. But she still looked adorable in her ragged and faded work jeans and sweatshirt. What would it be like to really kiss her? To hold her in his arms and . . .

"No!" he muttered.

"No, what? You don't want me to use doilies in the house?" Jolene asked.

"No. I don't need any more tools. I didn't even need the planer. I wanted it because my shop teacher in high school had one like it, and I loved using it." It was lame, but at least it was the truth, and he didn't have to explain what he'd been thinking.

Good for you. Melanie's voice popped into his head. *Not for the lie covered with the truth, but for actually taking a step forward.*

"I'm not stepping anywhere, back or forward," he muttered to himself as he carried his box of tools inside the house.

Jolene had gone in ahead of him and was now sitting on the living room floor, dividing the doilies from the scarves. If they had a stain, they went in one pile. If not, then she stacked them on the coffee table.

The inn's phone rang, and he reached for it at the same time Jolene did. His hand closed around hers, but he quickly moved it away and told himself that the abrupt noise had startled him—that's what created the electricity between them.

"Magnolia Inn," Jolene said. She listened for a few minutes and then said, "I'm sorry, but we're closed for remodeling."

She put her hand over the receiver and whispered, "A lady wants to book a room, but we just can't, can we?"

He shook his head. "Don't see how."

More listening as she alternately shook her head and nodded. "Ma'am, the upstairs hallway has furniture stacked in it. The bathroom that the workers use is the only available one, and that bedroom hasn't been cleaned in weeks."

She laid the receiver on her chest. "It's an elderly lady who says that she and her husband spent their honeymoon here forty years ago. They want to come back and spend tomorrow night."

"Fine, tell her to come right on. I'll clear a path for them. Anyone who's been married that long deserves a little consideration," Tucker said. "But make them understand that we are in a major remodeling job."

She removed her hand. "Yes, ma'am, if you don't mind the mess, I think we can manage to have that room ready for you by four tomorrow afternoon. Great! We'll see you then."

❁

Jolene grabbed her head with both hands. "She wants the last room on the right side of the hallway. At least it's not torn up, but we'll have to move furniture around to get to it. I've got to get things dusted and clean cloths put on the dining room tables, and that room has to get a thorough cleaning. I'm going to put the doilies in the washer and use them, and I need to go to town tomorrow morning for some roses. I can get them at Walmart. Aunt Sugar has pretty vases somewhere, and maybe a few cookies . . ." She sucked in a lungful of air as if she was about to go on.

"Whoa, pardner." Tucker held up a hand. "You told her we were remodeling and she wanted to book a night anyway. Run the vacuum, chase away the dust bunnies, and make one of your fabulous breakfasts for them."

She folded her arms over her chest. "Their room should be nice, and the bathroom should be spotless. It's their fortieth anniversary, for cryin' out loud."

"Yes, ma'am, but roses and cookies?"

"That was something Aunt Sugar always did. A flower in a vase on the dresser and half a dozen cookies under a little dome. The guests loved that personal touch."

Tucker patted her on the shoulder. "How about one of those pretty silk magnolia things in a vase? I was going to make a beer run this evening anyway. I can go to Walmart and get one of those magnolia flowers and a dozen cookies. If I get there before the bakery folks leave, I might even get a cupcake with one of those 'Happy Anniversary' stick things on it."

"That would help so much. It'll give me plenty of time to plan breakfast and get things as straight as possible." Her mind was running in circles so badly that she didn't even realize he was touching her.

"Since the dining room is a total mess, we could put a small table in the corner of their room and offer them 'breakfast in bed.'" He pointed. "That little table right there with a lamp on it would be perfect."

"I love it. We can set it in the corner of their room and carry the food up to them on a fancy tray." She could visualize it with a breakfast tray set on it. "Now shoo! Go to work. I'll get busy making the living room presentable and then go on up to that bedroom. Good Lord, can you even imagine forty years of marriage and wanting to go back to an old bed-and-breakfast to celebrate? Me, I'd want a second honeymoon on a cruise ship or maybe in Hawaii. Wherever the first one *wasn't*!"

He disappeared up the stairs with his new box of tools, and she grabbed the basket of cleaning aids that her aunt always took to each room. Jolene had helped her aunt clean the rooms when she stayed there, but she didn't remember this one in particular. It was even shabbier than the one across and down the hall where she and Tucker had started renovations.

The only sound she could hear as she started dusting was the gritty noise of sandpaper on the wall as Tucker did his work. Then he started humming, and before long he was singing along with whatever song was coming through the earbuds of his MP3 player.

Jolene rolled her eyes toward the ceiling and noticed cobwebs in every corner. *My life is like this room. Needs some remodeling, and there's still old stuff in the corners that needs to be taken care of. Will I ever be able to trust my heart?*

Aunt Sugar had taught her to start at the top and work her way down, so she wrapped a rag round a broom and took care of the cobwebs first. That's what she needed to do with her life—start at the top and get all those pesky things out of the hidden corners. Judging Tucker by her mother wasn't right, for one thing. They'd both had horrible experiences that they tried to forget by drinking. It looked like Tucker was trying to overcome his problem, so that was a plus.

You're comparing apples and cow chips. Her mother's voice was loud in her ears. *Think about it.*

Jolene ran a wet cloth all around the baseboards to get rid of a layer of dust and muttered, "Why would I have to think about it? You both have or had the same problem, but at least if he dies in a sleazy hotel, he won't leave a young girl without parents. And he's trying to get his life in order."

She immediately felt guilty for her tone. *Why can't I sweep the bad feelings out of my heart and soul as easily as I did the cobwebs off the ceiling?*

Chapter Sixteen

Somehow Tucker managed to slide a piece of furniture into each of the other bedrooms and clear out the hallway, and they worked together to get the requested room ready. Jolene pretended she was the guests and slung open the door to get a first impression of the room. It certainly wasn't a five-star hotel, but she'd done what she could with what she had to work with, and there was a quaint beauty to the room. She only hoped that it didn't disappoint her anniversary couple.

Tucker's reflection in the mirror as he stood behind her said that he was as pleased with it as she was.

"It looks wonderful. Think about what the place looked like yesterday when we came home from the auction and how it is now. You've done an amazing job, Jolene."

His warm breath sent a rush of heat through her body, giving her the sudden desire to turn around and kiss him, but she wrapped her arms around her own body and said, "I've got this partner that helped me. You should meet him sometime. He's pretty great."

"Oh, really. Should I be jealous?" Tucker teased.

She whipped around, and for a split second, she again thought he might kiss her—their lips were that close—but he took a step back.

"Of course not," Jolene said.

"What if he had more money and was a better carpenter?" Tucker asked.

"Not even then. You don't have a reason to be jealous," Jolene answered.

Tucker scanned the room one more time. "Have we forgotten anything?"

"Not anything that I can think of. And your idea for that little table was great," she said.

"Thank you." He motioned with a nod for her to go downstairs before him. "Let's have a cup of hot chocolate while we wait for them. I hate that I'm losing time to work, but this is probably good advertising. We've got fifteen minutes until they'll check in."

"And if they're like Aunt Sugar and Uncle Jasper, they'll be here five minutes early," she said.

"Word-of-mouth promotion is the best in the world. These folks will go home and tell everyone how we worked to accommodate them."

"I hope so." She mentally ran through everything in the room and the bathroom to be sure she hadn't forgotten a single thing.

The older couple arrived at exactly four o'clock with one light-blue suitcase that had seen better days. The lady, tall and thin, had a magnolia corsage pinned to her white lace dress and shoes that dated back to the late seventies. Her salt-and-pepper hair was swept up in the back, and a circlet of faded silk roses held a shoulder-length veil.

"Hello, we're Jerry and Mary Anderson. We have reservations," the husband said.

"Your room is ready," Tucker said.

"Please forgive the mess," Jolene said.

"Honey, we don't care about all that. We just want to spend our anniversary in the same room as our one-night honeymoon, forty years ago," Mary said. "It reminds us of how much we love each other."

"I'll take that suitcase for you," Tucker said.

"No, thank you," the lady said.

"It's our little ritual. Same suitcase as forty years ago. Same clothes. Same room. And now I carry the bag upstairs and then . . ." He kissed his bride on the cheek.

"Jerry will set it beside the door and carry me across the threshold. We'll be in our room until tomorrow when it's checkout time." She tucked her hand in his.

"Since we're remodeling, we'll bring breakfast to your room at about eight in the morning," Jolene said.

"How sweet." Mary smiled. "We had blueberry muffins and the lightest pancakes. Sugar always remembered. Do you think that could be possible?"

"Of course." Jolene nodded.

"Okay, darlin'," Jerry said. "Shall we continue our honeymoon?"

"Yes, darlin'."

They went up the stairs hand in hand, with the suitcase bumping the wall every now and then. Jolene couldn't take her eyes from them, and when she heard the door shut, she sighed.

"What a beautiful tradition," she whispered.

"I need a drink. Want one?"

She shook her head. How could he drink now?

A memory of her mother when they saw a car with "Just Married" written on the back window in shoe polish flashed through Jolene's mind.

"It makes me sad to think of those happy days. I need a drink," Elaine had said.

When Jolene had returned home that night, Elaine was passed out on the sofa.

"All this work and they won't even use the living room or the dining room." She changed the subject and glanced toward the curtain and cornice that Tucker had hung in the dining room to cover up the huge hole where he'd torn out the wall to get to the plumbing.

"It don't matter. You sure you don't want a shot of whiskey or a beer?" he asked.

"No, I don't, and it matters to me, Tucker," she said.

"I had what they've got," he said. "Nothing's filling that hole."

"I assume we're talking about your heart and not the wall. What makes you think drinking will help?" She snapped, "You're a lucky man, you know. You had what I want so bad I can taste it, and instead of being grateful for what you had, you drown your good memories in a bottle."

"Don't preach at me," he growled.

"Don't make me." She flounced off to her room to find Sassy sleeping at the foot of her bed.

※

He wanted to slam the door to his room so much that it took all his willpower to shut it without a sound. Sassy wasn't anywhere in sight, so he didn't even have a cat to talk to. He went to the dresser and poured a shot of whiskey in a plastic cup. Sitting on the edge of the bed, he stared through the cup out the window toward the bayou. Nothing was in focus, just like his life. He set the glass on the nightstand without drinking from it, went back out into the foyer, got his coat, and tucked his keys into his pocket.

He drove to the Marshall cemetery and went straight to Melanie's grave. He sat down in front of the tombstone and ran his fingers over the engraved name. "I love you, Melanie Malone. Always will. You're my soul mate. You understood me."

"Hello," a deep voice said right behind him.

He didn't have to turn around to know that it was Luke Tillison, Melanie's father. Without being invited, the man sat down beside Tucker. Luke had been a big man the last time Tucker saw him—at Melanie's funeral. He'd lost at least forty pounds and aged twenty years.

Tucker started to get up. "I was just leaving."

"Don't go, Tucker. Life hasn't been good to either of us, has it? You're still grieving and I've got an inoperable brain tumor. They gave me a year and it's been nine months, but the upside is that when I'm gone, I'll see Melanie again."

Tucker eased back down to a sitting position. "I'm sorry."

"I'm not. I've missed her so much, Tucker. I've got two sons, and I should be focused on giving them support and love, but she was my baby girl. She stole my heart the day she was born, and she took it with her when she died."

Tucker took a blue bandanna from his hip pocket and handed it to the man. "Mine, too."

"Don't let this . . ." Luke wiped his eyes and handed it back to Tucker. He cleared his throat. "I've wanted to talk to you for a long time. She loved you, Tucker. And it was plain that you adored her. I'm sorry. But don't let her death define you. You are young. Move on and live a long and happy life. Don't wallow in misery like I've done. I've cheated my wife out of my last years and my sons out of a father. I hear you've bought interest in the Magnolia Inn. I'm glad to see that you're trying to move on."

"I should have gone into town that night. I should have spent more time with her. I shouldn't have worked late," Tucker said.

Luke laid his hand on Tucker's knee. "Could have. Should have. Would have. That's all in the past. Take a lesson from an old man who's made too many mistakes. Move on out of the pain and be happy. It's too late for me now, but you're still a young man. And accept my apologies for trying to talk Melanie out of marryin' you because you were a cop. You gave her years of happiness and joy, and I'm grateful to you for that."

"Accepted, but it's hard to move on after everything you had was so perfect," Tucker said.

"Sounds like a country song," Luke said. "It would sure be nice if you'd come to the dinner on Saturday. Bring your partner with you. We'd like to meet her. You know I've got two sons that still aren't married." He managed a weak grin.

"Can't make any promises—we've got plans. But if we get through early, we might pop in for a few minutes." Tucker laid a hand on the tombstone and then stood up. "How often do you come here?"

"Every day. Sometimes more than once. I've begged for her forgiveness for tryin' to talk her out of marryin' you, but I don't feel like it's happened yet," Luke said.

"In my opinion, she forgave you years ago." Tucker gave Luke's shoulder a gentle squeeze. "Take care of yourself."

Tucker drove a few blocks away from the cemetery and pulled into the parking lot of a trucking business. He laid his head on the steering wheel. The sobs racked his body and tears dripped onto the legs of his jeans. "Why couldn't *we* have forty years, darlin'?"

You can still have it if you'll let me go, Melanie fussed at him again. *I can't do it for you, but I sent you the strongest messenger I've got today. Listen to Daddy.*

He raised his head and dried his face, blending his tears with her father's on the bandanna. "I'll try, but it can't be with Jolene. We're partners. If it fell apart, we'd have a hell of a situation."

🌸

Armed with a recipe for blueberry muffins, Jolene left her room to check and be sure that she had everything in the inn to make them. Sure enough, there were just enough berries in the refrigerator, and all the other ingredients were in the pantry.

She picked up a bottle of water and carried it to the living room with Sassy right behind her. The cat jumped up on the sofa beside her and inched her way into Jolene's lap.

"You have a stubborn master." Jolene rubbed her long fur.

"Yes, she did," Tucker said from the doorway.

Jolene had never known a man who walked as quietly as he did. She didn't answer—just shot a look over toward him. "So do you still need a drink, or did you have three or four before you left?"

"Sassy was Melanie's cat to start with, and you're right. She could be as stubborn as the proverbial Missouri mule. Ever wonder why one from that state would be worse than, say, one from Texas?"

"No, and you didn't answer my question," she said.

"I didn't have the drink. I poured it, but . . ." He removed his coat and hung it over the back of a rocking chair before he sat down in a recliner and popped up the footrest. "I went to the cemetery to talk to Melanie. Her dad, Luke, was there. I need a friend, Jolene. Not a therapist. Not a partner. A friend."

"Me, too," she whispered. "So what happened with her father?"

"He told me to move on, that Melanie would want me to, but I'm afraid if I do that I'll lose the memories I have of her," he said.

His eyes were bloodshot, but she believed him when he said he hadn't had a drink. She'd swear to that. She knew the difference in eyes that had been crying and those that were caused by too much liquor.

"He has a brain tumor, and he hasn't got much longer—that was partly why he was there. He looked like hell. But he apologized and doesn't blame me for her death."

"That's good, isn't it? Not that he's dying but that you got things settled." She wished that she and her mother had come to an understanding before Elaine had passed on.

"It should feel good, but nothing's different." Tucker's tone said that he was miserable, but at least he hadn't gone straight for the bottle.

"Let it go, Tucker. Some of it you've got to do yourself, and that's a friend talking, not a therapist. No one can do it for you. Maybe the first step would be to go to the party they're having. It might bring you closure to remember everything, the good and the bad."

"But . . . ," he started to say and then stopped.

She could've finished his sentence for him if she'd wanted. He was about to say that there were no bad times, but she knew that was part of the letting go, too. To remember it all just like it was—black, white, or gray. There had been very few white—or good—memories in her world. Most of them had been either gray or black. Maybe it was the reverse in his, but she was learning to face it all. Like remembering the good times with her mother and her dad's flower beds. Remembering only the good times was just as unhealthy as remembering only the bad ones—there was no closure in either.

"I'll try," he finally said.

"You never know when a day is going to be your last one. We've both got the battle scars to prove that," she said. "Luke is dying. This could be the final time you get to spend with him and the family."

Tucker went to the cabinet and took out the peanut butter. "You're right, but it doesn't make it easy."

"Life is not easy." She opened the fridge and set the grape jelly on the cabinet.

They'd made sandwiches and sat down to the table when giggles floated down from above. Then they heard the old pipes groaning as someone turned on the water in the bathtub.

"Are they . . . ," he whispered.

"I believe they are reliving their honeymoon night by taking a bath together. Or maybe they're having tub sex." Jolene smiled. "I hope I'm still interested in taking a bath with my husband when I'm their age."

"I just hope I don't need those little blue pills to get in the tub with my wife when I'm that age," Tucker said.

Chapter Seventeen

Sometimes a springlike day will sneak its way into what is still officially winter. That was the case that Saturday morning as Jolene drove into town to shop for groceries. She rolled the window down to enjoy the fresh air. But instead of driving to the store, she found herself parked outside the Tipsy Gator.

"Guess this old truck has a mind of its own," she said. "I'm here, so I might as well go on in and talk to Dotty."

She opened the door with her new key and yelled, "Dotty, where are you?"

"Thank God you're here." Dotty appeared out of nowhere and pulled her inside by the arm.

"Is something wrong?" Jolene asked.

"No, *chère*, I'm just bored out of my mind. And when I get bored I want to drink," Dotty answered. "So come in here and keep an old woman company for a little while." She looped her arm in Jolene's and led her to a table. "Want a root beer?"

"Only if you're having one," Jolene said.

"I guess I can pretend it's a real drink." Dotty opened two bottles of root beer, handed one to Jolene, and then sat down.

"If you're so bored, why didn't you go to Flossie's or Lucy's to help them out?" Jolene asked.

"They didn't even open today because of this storm comin' in. It's supposed to get real icy, so we're callin' off the dinner tomorrow at Flossie's. She'll have it next week. I thought about closin' the Gator, but I figure that folks will find a way to a bar, even if they have to come on dog sleds. What're you out doin'? Layin' in supplies for the bad weather?"

"I was on my way to the grocery store and somehow found myself here instead, but if we've got ice on the way, I'd better stock up. You do still want me to come in, don't you?" Jolene sipped the root beer.

"Of course I do. If it ever gets too bad for you to go home, my couch makes out into a bed," Dotty said. "Now tell me about your first guests. I'm so glad you fixed things so they could stay. We heard all about their plans at church. They spent their first night there when they got married."

"We hardly saw them. They went straight to their room. I took breakfast up to them and Mary took it at the door. They came down at exactly eleven, which is checkout time, thanked us for making the arrangements, paid us, and left." Jolene leaned forward and lowered her voice. "They enjoyed a bath together."

"Every year." Dotty's green eyes twinkled. "Mary says she don't give a damn if Jerry has to eat Viagra like M&M'S, or if gravity has got her boobs, she will have sex in the bathtub like they did on their wedding night."

Jolene giggled. "Tucker was just sayin' last night that he hoped he didn't need them when he was past sixty."

"Oh?" Dotty cocked her head to one side. "Just what brought that conversation on?"

"What happens in the Magnolia Inn is like Las Vegas, remember? But we were talking about Mary and Jerry—sound travels along those pipes." Jolene blushed.

"If you didn't at least think about having bathtub sex with Tucker when all that was goin' on, then you're crazy," Dotty said. "I'm thinkin' about all the times Bruce and I did and I didn't even hear the noise."

The blush deepened. "Okay, so I dreamed about it last night and woke up kind of angry that it wasn't real."

"Then at least you've thought about having sex with him or you wouldn't dream about it." Dotty put a palm on her cheek. "Don't blush, darlin'. We're grown women with needs of our own."

"But . . ." Jolene started.

"Tell me all about the 'but,'" Dotty said.

"Until he gets over Melanie, what's the use in even thinking about such things?"

"It's tough to let go of someone you love, *chère*. You ever think that fate put him here . . ."

"Fate put who where?" Lucy arrived through the back door.

"What are you doing here?" Dotty asked. "And how did you get in?"

"You're gettin' dementia. You gave me a key when Bruce died so in case you passed away, the cops wouldn't break down the door. Remember?" Lucy asked.

"Of course I remember, but I didn't even hear the door open," Dotty told her.

"We came to get you to go to the store with us." Flossie hung her coat on the back of a chair. "You can't live on what's up there on that shelf." She pointed to the liquor behind the bar.

"Now what was that about fate?" Lucy removed her coat and tossed it on a nearby table.

"I was telling Dotty that Tucker is having a terrible time moving on," Jolene said.

"And before I was so rudely interrupted, I was about to say that fate might have brought him here so that Jolene could help him move on," Dotty said.

Flossie took a deep breath and let it out slowly. "Way I see it is this: he's got to get on with life and quit this weekend drinkin' for good. I'm with Dotty on this one. Fate brought him to the Magnolia Inn so that y'all could be friends and you could help him."

"Fate didn't have anything to do with it," Lucy said. "Honey, you know there ain't a single clock in heaven, don't you? That's because nobody gets in a hurry up there. God has been working out a plan for years that would eventually bring you and Tucker together so you both could go on a healing journey. Tucker will help you and you'll help him. Now start at the beginning and tell us all about everything."

Jolene told them about Tucker saying he needed a drink but going to the cemetery instead. "Lucy, you say I'm on some kind of spiritual journey that's been working on a higher plane for years." She turned to Flossie. "You think Tucker and I are destined to be friends." Her eyes went to Dotty. "What does fate say?"

"It says that you might help Tucker the most by just listening to him. But I believe he was sent to the inn to help you. His journey and yours are interlocked. He's forgiven his father-in-law and accepted his apology. Have you forgiven your father for dying so early? Or your mother for all the misery that she put you through?" Dotty asked.

Jolene shook her head. "I thought I had when I took their ashes to the beach, but when Tucker talks about his pain, mine surfaces right along with his."

Dotty patted her on the knee. "This forgiving business is not a sprint but a marathon, *chère*."

"But what happens at the end? If God or fate has predestined this whole thing, what is the endgame?" she asked.

"That, darlin'"—Flossie smiled—"is up to you. You get the final say-so. Whatever the universe did to put you where you are, including sitting here in the Tipsy Gator with three meddling old women, its job is finished. Now you make the choice."

"Run beside him for a while in this marathon," Dotty said. "If you don't like his speed, get ahead of him or fall back. The ball is in your hands now."

Jolene was glad that she'd wound up at the Gator, because she felt better. "Are you all speaking from experience?"

"We are," Dotty said. "For me, it's the life I had with Bruce. We were best friends all through our growing-up years. And, *chère*, it was not exactly the thing in those days. Girls' best friends were girls. Boys' were boys. I cried on his shoulder when my first boyfriend broke up with me. He did the same when his best friend died. We went down that path for many years, and then when we were in our twenties, we realized that somewhere back there we'd fallen in love."

"And for me, well, I'm still hunting for my Bruce. I saw what Dotty had and I won't settle for anything less," Lucy said.

Jolene shifted her gaze to Flossie. "What's your story?"

"Fell in love. Lost him to Vietnam. I had my girls here and your aunt to help me through it all. Sisters of the heart, darlin', are as important as romance. Not saying that whatever the end of your journey with Tucker becomes isn't important, but . . . how do I say this." Lucy stumbled over the words.

"You're stepping into Sugar's shoes with us and we need you," Dotty said softly.

"Good Lord!" Jolene gasped. "I'm not wise enough to do that."

Lucy fluffed up her kinky hair with her hands. "That's your opinion, not ours. And we need a fourth woman in this friendship wagon."

"But Aunt Sugar is still available by phone when y'all have a problem," Jolene said.

"Yes, she is, but she's on a decades-late honeymoon with Jasper. We'll talk to her about some stuff, but we don't want to bother her too much. So accept it, child—we're all in this together." Flossie giggled.

❁

Dark clouds hung in the sky as Jolene drove back to the Gator that evening. Cars and trucks were already parked and waiting for the doors to open when Jolene arrived. Dotty had been right about drinkers finding their way to a bar.

But then, Elaine had proven that years ago. And once Jolene started bartending, she'd seen it for herself. Once her mother had spent the night in her car when it slid off into a ditch. Thank God whiskey didn't freeze, because if it did, she had enough in her that she could have died from the inside out. But even that wasn't a speed bump for Elaine. The car had a few scrapes and a dented fender, but it wasn't messed up too bad. It ran well enough to get her back out on the ice the next night so she could go to the bar again.

Dotty threw an apron toward Jolene when she saw her coming inside. Jolene wrapped it around her waist, bringing the strings back to the front and knotting them in a perfect bow. She'd learned long ago to never tie it in the back when a customer reached over the bar and pulled the strings. Her tips had gone flying every which way, right along with her pen and notepad.

"So did you bring a go-bag so you can stay with me if it gets too slick to drive?" Dotty asked as she picked up an apron.

"No, I've driven in snow up to the runnin' boards and even outran a tornado a couple of times. I'll be fine," she said.

Dotty opened the door, and only five people came inside. Mickey was one of them, and instead of standing or sitting beside the door, he hiked a hip on a barstool. "I got a job with a beer delivery company out of Tyler, and I think every store in East Texas is stocked up and ready for this storm. I was wonderin' if you'd let me off tonight. My girlfriend is worried about me drivin' all the way home in bad weather. If you're not comfortable not havin' a bouncer, I can stay, but . . ." He let the sentence dangle.

Dotty reached across the bar and patted his cheek. "I got a sawed-off shotgun under the bar if things get too rowdy, but I'm not expectin' a big crowd. You go on home, and drive safe."

"Thanks, Miz Dotty. I've never had to toss anyone out yet, and since I've got the new job, you might want to reconsider keeping me on Friday and Saturday nights," Mickey said.

"We'll talk about that later," Dotty said.

Mickey disappeared, and Dotty turned to Jolene. "There was a time I thought maybe he might ask you out."

"Not my type." Jolene smiled.

Dotty wiped down the already clean bar. "What is your type?"

"Have no idea right now, just know what isn't," Jolene answered.

The door opened and a blast of arctic wind blew half a dozen cowboys into the place. Jolene took a minute to scan their faces, not finding Tucker among them. She was a little disappointed, and yet she hoped that he was home with Sassy, watching television or maybe measuring something for the next room they'd work on.

More than a dozen people filed in next—ready to drink and party, not a bit afraid of the weatherman's forecast. Dotty and Jolene became too busy drawing up pitchers and mugs of beer and even making a few fancy drinks to talk any more.

"Madam Fate, if you are real and you spent all these years setting this up, then I'd sure like to know what your endgame is," Jolene whispered.

❧

Montgomery, Alabama

Sugar was watching the countryside fly by at sixty-five miles an hour. When they left South Carolina, the plan was to take their time driving to Kansas and then head back west again in a zigzag pattern. They'd already called ahead and made reservations in an RV park in Alabama for tonight.

It wasn't until Sugar looked at the calendar that she realized that it was Saturday. If she were home, she'd be thinking about church in the morning—maybe ironing one of her Sunday dresses and making sure she had a decent pair of pantyhose. Girls these days had stopped wearing hose, but not Sugar. She had given up her girdle years ago, but she'd told Dotty that they'd damn sure better bury her in pantyhose or she'd come back to haunt all three of them.

If they were home, she and Jasper would get up on Sunday morning, have pancakes, and go to church. Bless his heart, he'd been so good all these years to have dinner after church with her friends. After Bruce died, he'd had to endure the women without the benefit of another man. And not one time had he ever complained, so she needed to buck up and stop feeling sorry for herself.

"How about pancakes tomorrow morning?" she asked.

"Of course. It's Sunday and we always have pancakes before church," he said. "And we agreed before we ever left home that wherever we were on Sunday morning, we'd find us a church with a parking lot to fit this vehicle, and we'd attend services."

"Yes, we did." She laid a hand on his arm. "And maybe this one will feel more like home than the last one did. It was just too big."

She got her phone from her purse and looked at the little house that was still on the market. There were others—one down the street from Lucy looked pretty good—but that white house with the big front porch was the one she liked best. She wished she had a picture of their little church to look at. Big, small, or in between, nothing could replace it.

Chapter Eighteen

Tucker polished his boots, ironed his shirt and jeans, dusted off his cowboy hat, and got into his truck with plans to go to Luke and Carla's place for Melanie's birthday celebration. Maybe it *would* be a level of closure to be there with others who loved her and share experiences with everyone that evening. He drove straight to their house, a redbrick place in a really nice area of town. He parked across the street and watched the family through the big plate-glass window. From the looks of it, they'd put aside the fact that Luke was dying and were laughing and having a good time.

A blast of icy wind hit Tucker in the face when he opened his door. He instinctively shut it again and drew his coat closer to his body. He should brave the wind and the family, but he couldn't make himself do either. Finally, he started up the engine and drove back to the inn. He took a full bottle of whiskey with him to the living room and turned on the television just to have some noise. He surfed through the stations until he found an *NCIS* marathon. He recognized it as the second season, the one where one of the team members got killed at the end, and thought it appropriate that evening. He drained the last drop of whiskey from the bottle and threw it back just as the shot rang out that killed the character Kate.

"Some of us don't have any luck," he slurred as he got up to go get another bottle, but he'd gone only a few steps when the room began to whip around him so fast that he couldn't get his bearings.

He sat down in the foyer with a thud. After a few minutes, he started to get back on his feet, but his legs wouldn't cooperate. Finally, he stretched out on the floor with intentions of shutting his eyes for only a few minutes. In an hour what he'd drunk would be out of his system, and he'd get up and go to bed before Jolene got home from the bar.

❦

Jolene slipped on the ice once as she made her way from the bar to her truck, but she was able to right herself before she fell flat on her fanny. She got inside her vehicle and started the engine and then got back out to scrape the ice from the windshield. Freezing rain stung her face as she worked, but neither a knight in shining armor nor a big strong cowboy on a white horse appeared out of the darkness to do the job for her.

Her teeth were chattering by the time she finished and hurried back inside the truck. She'd almost warmed up by the time she'd gotten out of town, but neither the windshield wipers nor the heater could keep up with the freezing rain. She pulled off the road into a closed service station. The awning over the gas pump gave her enough shelter that she could remove the buildup again, but she was already thinking ahead to other places where she could repeat the process.

"Dammit!" She realized that she hadn't switched the heat to the windshield. "No wonder it wouldn't warm up and melt the mess." She sat there several minutes until the heater melted the last of the ice.

What was usually a five-minute trip to the inn took fifteen just to get to the turn down the lane. The trees glistened with ice, and the ground crunched beneath the tires. Sleet still peppered the windshield and the top of the truck.

The foggy outline of the inn was in sight when suddenly a deer jumped right into the road in front of her and stood there, staring at her with big eyes. She braked and whipped the steering wheel to the right. The deer ran off and the truck slid right toward a big pine tree, coming to a gentle stop against it. Her heart raced and her pulse pounded in her ears. She laid her head on the steering wheel for several minutes until she could catch her breath, and then put the vehicle in reverse. The wheels whirred and spun out on the ice, but she couldn't get traction. She swung the door open and got out, only to see that the back wheels had dropped into a ditch about six inches deep. There was no way she'd be able to get the truck out that night, and maybe not until things thawed.

She dug her phone from her purse and called the inn. Surely that party for Melanie hadn't lasted until three in the morning. After ten rings she hung up and tried again. Still no answer. She called Tucker's cell phone, and it went straight to voice mail.

She grabbed her purse, shook her fist at the sky, and trudged the rest of the way to the inn. She was hungry, angry, and chilled to the bone with sleet hitting her in the face all the way to the door. Lord, even her eyelashes were frozen. A rush of welcome warm air greeted her when she unlocked the door and pushed it open. She took a step forward, reached up to feel for the string to pull on the light, and tripped over something on the foyer floor.

The fall knocked the wind out of her, but when she could catch her breath, she realized that she was lying on top of a person. Visions of a dead body flitted through her head as she pushed away from it. Then she got a whiff of whiskey, and a fresh rush of anger filled her heart and soul.

"Dammit, Tucker," she yelled as she stood up.

The last time she'd come home to a sight like this was the day before she'd kicked Johnny Ray out of her apartment. He'd taken her debit card and managed to wipe out her bank account, but even at that, it was worth getting rid of him. She'd decided right then that she might only be a bartender, but she deserved better.

"And I do," she said as she stepped over Tucker's curled-up body.

She made herself a sandwich and poured a glass of milk. She walked around him on her way to her bedroom. "Evidently, you like wallowing around in misery. Well, I might be your partner, but I'm not cutting you one inch of slack. You can sleep on the floor all night."

She flipped the light switch in her bedroom and heard a moan in the foyer, but Tucker Malone was on his own. If he didn't remember the hangover cure, then he could damn well suffer.

Sassy had followed her to her bedroom and curled up on the foot of the bed. "I don't blame you, girl. I wouldn't sleep with someone that reeked like he'd fallen into a barrel of whiskey, either."

The adrenaline rush from swerving to miss the deer settled down. The chill of the walk home also eased when she got into a pair of sweats and an oversize T-shirt and crawled beneath the covers. The hunger subsided when she finished the sandwich. She fell asleep before her head hit the pillow.

Sassy was sitting right beside her when she awoke at noon. "I bet you're hungry and needing to find your litter pan."

The cat meowed pitifully.

"Well, darlin' girl, I will feed you, but scooping the litter pan belongs to your master. Let's get you taken care of, and then I'm diving into a warm bath." Jolene crawled out of bed with Sassy right behind her.

Tucker was still on the foyer floor, in the same position as before. Jolene didn't feel a bit sorry for him. She fed the cat, took a long, hot bath, and washed her hair. When she finished, she went back downstairs and stepped over Tucker again. He groaned and grabbed his head. She ignored him and went straight for the kitchen, where she made coffee. While it perked she put three sausage patties in a skillet to cook and made a stack of pancakes.

She heard another groan around the time she sat down to eat, but she still had a big ball of anger in her heart. Seeing him like that caused her to remember the anger, pain, and disgust connected with her mother all over again. Sassy hopped up on the table, and Jolene fed her little bits of sausage as she ate.

Her cell phone rang, and she dug it out of her purse. "Good mornin', Dotty. Are you survivin' this ice storm?"

"I'm fine, but the regular phone lines are down. We're lucky we've got electricity. I'm just checkin' in to see that you got home all right. It sounds like shotgun shells goin' off all over town as the ice breaks down tree limbs. I tell you, it's going to be a real mess to clean it all up," Dotty said. "They've called off church services, and school has already been canceled for tomorrow. I guess we're all iced in for the duration. How're things there?"

Jolene told her about the deer, having to walk home, and falling over Tucker right inside the door. "I'm not so sure your fate thing was right. After living with a drunk, I'm sure not lookin' to hook up with this one."

Tucker staggered into the kitchen. His eyes were bloodshot and his hair was a fright. The only thing missing was the rancid smell of vomit on his breath.

"Hangover cure?" Both his hands went to his head.

She gave him a dirty look and crooked her finger for him to come closer. "Figure it out for yourself," she yelled right into his face, and then turned her attention back to Dotty. "Sorry about that."

"What's goin' on?" Dotty asked in her ear.

"Why are you so mean? You fixed me the cure last time," Tucker said.

She poked him in the chest with her free hand. "It's called tough love. If you want to wallow around in the past, get drunk and pass out on the floor, and make me fall when I come home, that's your business. But I'm not your nurse or your mama."

"But you're my partner," he protested as he poured a cup of coffee.

"That's right, and right now your partner is talking to Dotty. When I get done, I'm going to turn on some music and start laundry. Then I'm going to vacuum my room. Lots of noise fixin' to happen. You might want to start that cure."

Dotty's laughter echoed across the room before Jolene even got the phone back to her ear. "I guess you're not going to be an enabler again, are you?"

"Nope. If he can't stay sober enough to help his partner out so she doesn't walk the equivalent of two city blocks in sleet and freezing rain, then his partner isn't going to mollycoddle him because of a hangover."

"And we all thought he was getting better," Dotty sighed.

"Drunks are professionals at fooling people," Jolene said.

"Looks like you got your hands full. Call me later today and don't back down," Dotty said.

"Will do. I've been through enough of this to last a lifetime. You stay warm now." Jolene ended the call and poured herself a second cup of coffee. She carried it to the table and sat down to finish the last few bites of her breakfast.

"You are evil," Tucker groaned. "So I fell off the wagon. I had a good reason."

"No, you had an excuse. It's pretty plain that you like this misery that you put yourself through, so you're not getting a bit of sympathy from me," she told him. "You know my past, but if you want to talk about reasons why I feel this way, we can go over it again. And just so you know, my truck is out at the end of the lane. I had to walk in freezing rain and sleet all the way to the inn at three o'clock in the morning, only to fall over your drunk ass when I tried to turn on the light. I'm plumb fresh out of sympathy, so make your own eggs and toast."

"That was real? I thought I was dreaming," he muttered. "You wrecked your truck? Why?"

"Look outside." She carried her dirty dishes to the sink, rinsed them, and put them in the dishwasher.

He shielded his eyes and glanced out the window. "Good God! You drove home in that? Why didn't you call me?"

"I did. You were passed out. And now I've got things to do." She left the room with Sassy right behind her. "Your cat doesn't even like you this morning."

She heard him swearing and got a whiff of burned eggs. Then there was a scraping noise as he trashed those and started all over. She hadn't felt such a surge of anger in years, not since her mother had passed. If only she could hit something—anything that would make noise. There was nothing but a small plastic trash can in the corner. With one well-placed kick, it went flying across the room and bounced off the wall, sending wadded-up balls of paper scooting across the floor. Sassy flew off the bed and attacked them as if they were mice, batting them under the bed and from one end of the room to the other.

Even that didn't put a smile on Jolene's face. She hoped that he would move his ratty old trailer back to Marshall when they got finished remodeling. She'd gladly mail him his half of the profits if he just left.

She couldn't stay in her room all day. She had things to do, so she took a long, deep breath and headed toward the laundry room. That day, they wouldn't wash their clothes together. She'd separate them and do only her things. He could damn well do his own.

When she went back through the kitchen, he reached out to touch her arm.

"I'm sorry I wasn't here for you last night," he said.

"Prove it," she said.

"What does that mean? You knew that yesterday was a tough day for me. It was Melanie's birthday," he said.

"And it's her birthday the same day every year. Just like it was every year before she died. Are you going to get drunk every time? If so, I'll mark it on the calendar so we don't have guests that will stumble over you when they come downstairs for a cookie or a glass of milk," she said.

"I don't like you so much right now," he snapped as he stormed off toward the bathroom.

"Well, I don't like you at all," Jolene said.

She put her white clothes in the washer, and while the cycle ran, she dusted all the downstairs furniture, the pictures, and even the window ledge where a cardinal watched her through the glass. "You're not going to make me feel guilty. More than two years is enough for him to pull up his bootstraps and get on with life."

When she finished, she went back through the foyer and into the utility room to get the vacuum. She heard water running in the shower. He'd better enjoy it, because if they lost electricity, there would be no hot water. But maybe an icy shower was exactly what he needed.

When she came back through the kitchen, Tucker was sitting at the table with a cup of coffee in his hands. His eyes still looked like hell. His hair still sported a few water droplets, but it had been combed. And he was wearing clean sweats, even if they didn't match.

"You said to prove it. Just exactly how do I do that?" His tone was still grumpy.

"Don't do it again," she told him.

"Ever?"

"That's right. Think about it. We have guests on a Saturday night and they come in late from a family reunion or a movie and stumble over your drunk ass in the foyer. That's real good for business."

He sucked in air and let it out slowly. "You ever give your mama that speech?"

"More times than I want to remember, only it was about being sober enough to go to work and get through her eight-hour shift five days a week. And what sent my last boyfriend, Johnny Ray, packing was the same problem. God hates me. He keeps putting you drunks in my path," she said.

He took a sip of coffee. "So how long do you stay mad when you get to this boiling point?"

"Don't know. A week. A month. I've never been this angry before," she said.

"Never?" He raised a dark brow.

"Nope, because always before if I got mad, I could move out or kick whoever upset me out. I have to live with you, so it may take a while."

"Whew!" Tucker wiped his brow.

"You caused it. Now live with it." She left him sitting there as she went to her room to read a book for the rest of the afternoon.

Chapter Nineteen

Tupelo, Mississippi

*W*hile Jasper made breakfast that morning, Sugar used the time to give Jolene a call. It rang four times before Jolene answered.

"Did I call at a bad time?" Sugar asked.

"Hey, darlin' girl," Jasper called out. "I'm makin' chocolate-chip pancakes. Want me to send some over the phone?"

Jolene sighed. "I wish you could send pancakes over the phone, or even just be here today. It's never a bad time, Aunt Sugar. I'm glad you called this morning. I need to talk to you. I hope I handled a problem right. But maybe I just overreacted because of my past," she said.

Sugar poured another cup of coffee and said, "Tell me all about it, honey."

Jolene gave her a play-by-play and ended with, "So give me your straight-up, honest opinion."

"Ask yourself—are you mad at him because he reminds you of your mother in that same condition or maybe that last worthless boyfriend that promised you he'd change for your love? Or are you disappointed in him because you want more in a partner? What's the underlying reason?" Sugar hated that Jolene was dealing with the same problem that she'd faced in the past. But being asked for advice sure made her feel good that morning.

"Maybe all of the above," Jolene said. "I'm not even sure I want to help him after last night. I tried to help Mama. And I tried to help my boyfriend. Neither worked, so why would I even try a third time? But if I wanted to, how do I go about it when he won't help himself?"

"Listen to your heart. It'll guide you right," she answered.

"I've tried that before, and it—" Jolene started.

Sugar butted in before she could say anything else. "Whoa, honey. Did you ever really, really listen to your heart?"

"How do even I know when it's talking to me?"

"There's peace." Sugar wasn't sure if she was talking to Jolene or to herself—maybe it was to both of them. The agitation in her heart right then could match Jolene's for sure. She was tired of this roaming thing. She wanted her roots back.

🌿

Tucker was in the denial stage on Monday. On Tuesday, he went to the anger stage. He was mad at Jolene for treating him like she had her mother. She had no rights over his life, even if he shouldn't have gotten so drunk that he passed out on the floor. Maybe he should get some painter's tape and divide the inn into two sections. He'd tell her what he did on his half of the inn was his business and not a damn bit of hers.

On Wednesday he woke up thinking about Melanie. They'd had arguments, but they'd always settled things before bedtime, usually with some pretty fantastic makeup sex. The next couple of days, they might walk on a few eggshells around each other, but always by the end of the third day they'd be right back on familiar ground.

This was the third day since Jolene had said, "Prove it."

The sun had come out the day before, and the temperature jacked up thirty degrees, from freezing on Monday to sixty on Tuesday. That was Texas weather for sure—Tucker wished it was Jolene weather, too. She was still hovering down there around the freezing point.

The first bedroom was finished except for the border, and that was waiting to be picked up at the paint store in Marshall. Jolene had bought new sheets and bedspreads from a wholesale company online. That day they were in the process of hanging drywall in the second bedroom. The bathroom was in place and the closet framed out. This one was going faster than the first one, but then that's what usually happened—after the first, Tucker knew all the little quirks of the house.

Jolene did what needed to be done or what he needed her to do, most of the time before he even asked. But before it had been fun, and now it was a job. At midmorning, he finally had had enough. He felt bad enough about her having to walk in the bad weather, and then to find him passed out on the floor. But she wouldn't even look him in the eye after two whole days. Anger, hissy fits, even throwing things he could deal with—but the disappointment in her eyes was killing him.

"So how long are we going to keep this up?" he asked.

"I suppose until we get the remodeling done," she answered.

"That's not what I'm talking about," he shot back.

"We haven't even gotten past one weekend yet, so who knows?" She shrugged.

There was only one thing to do if he wanted things back on the footing they'd had before. That was to show her that he wasn't a drunk. He didn't *have* to have liquor or beer. It was simply a numbing agent for the pain. He'd prove to her that he could do without it just to show her that he wasn't like her mother or that rotten Johnny Ray.

She finished what she was doing and left without saying a word. He put in the last small piece of drywall and started down to the kitchen. When he was halfway down the stairs, he caught a whiff of pot roast and his stomach growled. It wasn't nearly noon, but he'd gotten spoiled with midmorning snacks. He found her sitting at the table poring over a set of big clothbound books filled with tidy handwriting.

"What are those things?" he asked.

"Aunt Sugar's ledgers. She kept track of the business transactions by hand. We really should start using a computer program. The books say this place is a gold mine, if we recoup the loss due to the place getting run-down. And that's drawing the equivalent of a teacher's salary for each of us."

Teacher. Melanie. Why did she have to use that for a gauge?

"Do we really need that much of a salary? If we took out less, we could get it paid back quicker and then share the profits at the end of each year." He put the last slice of something she called hummingbird cake on a paper plate.

"Go ahead and finish that off. I had ice cream for my break," she said without looking up.

He got a glass of sweet tea and carried it and the plate to the table. Finally, they were talking about something, and her expression had changed from disappointment to excitement. "So do we need an office? Anything we buy for it is a tax deduction."

She closed the ledger. "I hadn't even thought of it being a write-off—we'd have to really think about where we could shave a few feet off to set one up. Maybe the dining room?"

Tucker shook his head. "If we want to promote weddings here at the Magnolia Inn, that room needs to stay as big as possible."

She took a deep breath and let it out slowly, as if she figured he was about to disagree with her. "We need a website first. It's the way to do business in our day and age. Ledgers and newspaper ads are so outdated. We need a professional to set it up, but then I can manage it."

"What would it cost to have it done?"

"Depends on how fancy we want it," she answered.

He pulled his wallet out and laid a credit card on the table. "I'll be working on bedding and taping all afternoon. That's something that you can't help with, so could you get this started? Charge whatever you think you need to this."

"We can let folks know that we're taking reservations starting in March. You want to advertise that we'll be ready for weddings the first of May?" she asked.

"Do you have a bead on a photographer and a wedding caterer?" He was glad to have something to talk about with her, even if it was business. At least there was a little of that old sparkle in her blue eyes.

"I could probably ask Dotty and the girls about who's available for that kind of thing," she said.

"Are we okay?" he asked.

"As partners, yes."

"Friends?"

"The jury is still out."

"Got any idea how long that jury is going to deliberate?"

Her eyes met his. "How long are you going to keep riding this guilt trip?"

"What's that got to do with anything?" he said through clenched teeth.

"It's got to do with everything in our lives. Tell me, if Melanie was the amazing person everyone says she was, do you really think she'd want you to be doing this to yourself? To sit around feeling sorry for yourself?"

"I'll see you at noon." There were times when he thought he liked Jolene, maybe too much. Everything she said made sense, but he still didn't want to hear it. So he turned and left the room without a backward glance.

❀

Jolene had just pulled up the website guru she'd used to design the site for the Twisted Rope when someone rapped on the door. Before she could push back her chair and stand up, Flossie's voice floated across the foyer.

"Where are y'all? We were going stir-crazy."

"And we brought a cake. I made it for the bake sale that got canceled." Lucy carried it into the kitchen. "Chocolate with chocolate icing. I call it 'sin in a pan.'"

Dotty hung her coat on the back of a chair and whispered, "Sugar called us. Where's Tucker? Did y'all make up? Was there sex involved?"

Jolene's eyes rolled toward the ceiling, and she shook her head. "Not hardly. Didn't you feel the chill when you walked in?"

"Pay up." Lucy held out her hand.

Dotty fished a dollar bill from her bra and gave it to Lucy.

"Y'all are bettin' on me?" Jolene frowned.

"Honey, those two will bet on which mosquito flittin' around will land on bare skin first. Don't take offense. I'll get the plates and make a fresh pot of coffee. You can fill us in on what's happening while we eat. Is that pot roast I smell cookin'?"

"Yes, it is. And there's plenty. Y'all might as well stay to dinner. I've got a raisin' of Aunt Sugar's hot rolls in a bowl to go with it, and you've brought cake for dessert." Company would be nice to buffer the tension between her and Tucker.

Dotty held up a hand. "Yes, we'd love to stay. Flossie, put away those plates. We'll ruin our dinner if we have chocolate cake now. Let's just visit."

Flossie nodded, crossed the floor, and peeked around the doorjamb into the foyer. "I think the coast is clear."

"He works with earbuds. He probably didn't even hear you come in," Jolene said. "And I'm not sure this journey y'all talked about with us being more than partners . . ."

Lucy held up both hands. "Whoa now, sister. Tell us about that time right after your dad died."

What did that have to do with today? Jolene frowned but said, "I was sixteen and planning to go to college, but that dream went down the drain because there was no money. Mama was in a downward spiral.

Drinking. Pills. Most days she did make it to work, but Sundays were awful, and I was constantly afraid that she'd get fired. I didn't know how I could support us both on what I made," Jolene answered.

"Ever feel sorry for yourself?" Dotty asked.

"Sure I did, and I felt guilty because I couldn't keep her in things like Daddy did, and . . ." She clamped a hand over her mouth. "Whose side are you on?" she mumbled.

"Your side, of course. We're always on your side, but that don't mean that we can't help you see things better," Dotty said. "The heart doesn't know age, race, creed, or colors. It just knows happiness or pain. And when your partner is in pain, then you have the responsibility to help. Now, that said, I think a little tough love is good."

Lucy patted her hand and lowered her voice. "But that doesn't mean you should put up with him getting so drunk that he passes out on the floor."

"So since I didn't pamper him—" Jolene started.

"You did the right thing for sure," Flossie butted in.

"I swore when Mama died I'd never put up with that kind of thing again," Jolene said.

"So what are you going to do now?" Dotty asked.

One shoulder popped up in a shrug. "He's my partner. That can't change. He's a damn fine carpenter and a hard worker. I appreciate that. But . . ." She paused.

"And are you willing to make a few adjustments? Friendship is give and take," Lucy said.

Jolene cocked her head to one side and narrowed her eyes. "What do *I* need to change?"

"If he wants a beer or a shot, don't give him the old evil eye," Lucy said. "Practice tolerance and patience."

"But don't enable or put up with jack crap," Dotty said. "Did y'all hear that Alison Drummond finally left that cheatin', beatin' husband of hers? He's done blacked her eye for the last time."

While they dissected poor Alison's story, Jolene thought about the way she'd handled things since Sunday. She wouldn't change a danged thing about that, but then, Tucker hadn't had a beer after supper on Monday or Tuesday nights. Would she have given him the evil eye, as Lucy said, if he had?

She slowly shook her head. It wasn't the fact that he drank a little that bothered her. It was when he went past that into the drunken stage that left him passed out on the floor. And they really should have a serious talk about that, even just as financial partners.

Flossie patted her on the shoulder. "Honey, are you okay?"

"Of course," Jolene answered.

"I asked you if it wasn't time to make out those hot rolls for lunch." Dotty grinned. "And I bet you were thinking about this whole thing with Tucker, weren't you? Y'all will be all right. You just got to get over this hurdle."

Jolene slid her chair back and went to the cabinet. "You really think so?"

"Oh, yes," they all chimed in at once.

She uncovered the bread dough, shook a little flour in the bowl, and kneaded the dough a few times. "Why do you think that?"

"Because of the way he looks at you. He's just got to get past his problem, and you'll help him with that." Lucy got out a pan and greased it with butter.

Jolene pinched off a dozen rolls and placed them in the pan.

The sound of Tucker coming down the stairs shushed them all. The ladies found something to do while Jolene slid the rolls into the oven with the pot roast. She checked his expression when he walked into the room. He was smiling brightly—as if nothing at all had happened in the past few days.

"Well, hello. What a nice surprise. Is that chocolate cake? Now I'm really glad y'all are here. Can you stay and eat lunch with us?" He shifted his gaze toward Jolene. "I got to a stopping point. I'll wash up and set the table."

"We've got it," Jolene said. "But you could put that sheet up over the hole. Sassy pulled it down this morning, and a lot of cold air is coming through there."

"Sure thing." He smiled.

Chapter Twenty

*T*ucker awoke Sunday morning with a clear head and Sassy in her spot on the pillow beside him. The world felt right again for the first time in many months. He crawled out of bed, and the sunlight coming through the window didn't blind him. He'd worked on the third bedroom until after two the night before and had still been awake when Jolene came in at three. But he hadn't gone to the kitchen to meet her.

Now it was after ten, and he was hungry. He padded to the kitchen in his socks and put on a pot of coffee. His cooking expertise ended with hot dogs made in the microwave and cinnamon toast in the oven. There were no hot dogs in the refrigerator, but there was plenty of bread. He buttered a dozen slices, shook a thin layer of brown sugar on the tops, and then sprinkled that with cinnamon. He'd just shoved the baking sheet into the oven when Jolene appeared, looking cute as always in a pair of pajama pants that were too long and a T-shirt that would have been big on a three-hundred-pound wrestler.

"Smells good. So you cook cinnamon rolls?"

"Cinnamon toast. But in a pinch I can make really good bologna sandwiches," he answered.

"I love cinnamon toast." Jolene poured a cup of coffee and sipped on it for a few minutes.

"We need to talk." He pulled the toast from the oven and set it on the top of the stove. "I cooked. You set the table."

"Seems fair enough. Are you about to tell me that you are going to continue to be an investor and do the work on this place, but you can't live in the same house with me?" She got the table ready and poured coffee for them.

He moved the pan from counter to table. "Don't put words in my mouth."

"We need new paint, then?" she asked.

"Yes, but this is something else. I need to apologize about last weekend. There's no excuse or reason for that kind of behavior, and if the roles had been reversed, I would have sold my half, or even given it away, and walked away that night." He paused, biting off the corner of a piece of toast, giving himself time to put into words what he needed to say next.

"Apology accepted."

He swallowed and sipped his coffee. "Melanie pops into my head every so often, mostly to fuss at me, sometimes to remind me of the good times. Lately all she says is that it's time to let her go, but I don't know how, Jolene. Last night I saw her in a dream, and she kept getting dimmer and dimmer. All she would say was that if I couldn't let her go, then she'd have to take care of it on her own. I woke up in a cold sweat and grabbed her picture from the nightstand. For the first time, I had to turn on the light to see her face. Before, if I just touched the picture, I could get a clear vision of her. I don't know how to handle life without her."

❦

Jolene took a deep breath and let it out very slowly. "Three years after my dad died, I was a mess, too. I'd basically lost both my parents, and I didn't know how to handle life, either. My mom was barely staying sober enough to hold down a job. Of course, according to her, nothing was her fault. She blamed my dad for dying and leaving her with bills she couldn't pay, and most of all for leaving her a kid to raise by herself. I used to sit outside on the porch of that run-down trailer and beg Daddy to tell me what to do. The first night she brought a man home from the bar, I threw a cussin' fit. Two years later, when I was a senior in high school, I just hoped whoever she brought home would leave before breakfast so our food would last all week."

That empty, helpless feeling that Jolene had felt at Lucy's grabbed her heart again. It seemed that all the emotions she'd buried were surfacing since she'd returned to the inn.

"Did you get over it?" he asked.

"When I moved out into my own place, a trailer not much different than the one you've got parked in the backyard, it got a little better. But my mother was constantly calling me for money. I couldn't tell her no. I felt guilty for leaving her when she needed me, but at the same time, it was a relief to be away. Then she died in a two-bit hotel room from an overdose. If I'd been living with her, maybe I could have prevented it. If I'd made her get help, maybe she wouldn't be dead. If she hadn't had a daughter, maybe some rich guy would have come along and married her, and given her back the lifestyle she was used to having." Jolene realized she'd only packed the feelings away, putting them in a place where she could forget them. Talking about them brought back the hurt, and yet at the same time, she felt like she was letting go of some of it.

"Are you over it, even yet?" Tucker asked.

"I don't think you ever get over it, but you can get through it." Jolene could hear the hollowness in her voice and hoped that she was finally ready to get through it.

"What's the first step?"

"Get up in the morning and make the decision to take a step forward instead of two backward for that day. Let go of the guilt, and stop feeling sorry for yourself. Don't let the what-ifs drive you crazy, because they will if you let them. I'm speaking from experience. Some days it's still all I can do to stay positive."

He started on a third slice of cinnamon toast. "You didn't mention the step of not getting falling-down drunk."

"That's a by-product of the guilt and taking backward steps instead of forward ones," she told him.

"What was your by-product?"

"Trying to find someone to love me. Making bad choices in men. Settling into a rut instead of working to better myself," she admitted out loud, and even that relieved part of the heavy burden of guilt.

"Want to elaborate?" He picked up another piece of toast.

"Number one and two are pretty much the same answer. I needed to be loved for me, just the way I am, not the way someone wanted me to be. Mama wanted me to be a social butterfly, but I'm not. Johnny Ray wanted me to be a party girl, and I'm not. I worked in the same bar for the same grumpy old boss for ten years. In that time, I could have taken online courses and done something better with my life. But . . ." She paused.

He raked his hands through his hair. "But our choices, whatever and however bad they were, have brought us to this point in our lives. And who knows? Maybe we need each other to take all those steps you talked about. I damn sure know I need help."

She held out her hand. "Friends help friends."

He took it in his, but instead of shaking it, he brought it to his lips. "I'm glad that we're friends, Jolene. It's been a long time since I cared about anyone, since I felt like I needed anyone, or gave a damn what anyone thought about my lifestyle. But after this past week, I figured out that I like having a friend."

"Me, too." She blinked back the tears.

It turned out that Flossie lived right at the north edge of Jefferson on two acres of land. As Jolene and Tucker walked up the eight steps from the ground to the wide porch with its four huge columns, she could imagine Flossie, Sugar, Lucy, and Dotty as little girls sitting on a quilt and playing with dolls over there at one end.

She wondered what her life would have been like if her grandmother Victoria hadn't taken Elaine away from Jefferson. Would Elaine have married someone local and been a different person? Would she have had friends to play on the porch with her? Jolene had kept her childhood friends until her father died, but they'd drifted away when she and her mother had to move to a trailer park. After that, she didn't have time for friends, and besides, she could never invite people to her house anyway—not with Elaine's problems.

It startled her when Flossie threw open the door. "I thought I heard someone knocking, but it takes me a minute to get from the back of the house. Sorry I kept y'all waiting. Come right in and make yourselves at home."

Jolene and Tucker followed her and Flossie into the house and into a huge living room with a fireplace alight at one end.

"Y'all go on and have a seat. I've just got a couple of little things to do," Flossie said.

"Can I help?" Jolene asked.

"Nope. Got it under control," Flossie answered.

Jolene started to remove her coat, but Tucker was instantly behind her, helping her. He tossed both his and hers on a rocking chair and warmed his hands by the blaze in the fireplace.

Jolene waited for some emotion to overtake her, but nothing brought back memories of her mother or of Johnny Ray—thank God. The place made her think of Aunt Sugar, though. The fireplace drew her like a moth to a flame. She'd love to put one in the dining room of the inn.

Tucker turned to face her. "Nothing warms like an open fire. I've always wanted one of these."

"So did Aunt Sugar." Jolene smiled.

"Think we should put one in the dining room? That would be a nice addition if we had a winter wedding," he said.

"And when Aunt Sugar comes to visit, she and Uncle Jasper could enjoy it, too." Jolene's smile widened.

"We'll have to think about that while we're remodeling," Tucker said.

"Yoo-hoo!" Dotty carried in a long dish of what looked like a yummy cake of some kind. "Sorry we're a little late. Lucy is right behind me with the salad and bread."

"Can I help y'all carry anything?" Tucker asked.

"No, we got it," Lucy said as she came in behind Dotty. "Glad y'all made it. Follow us to the kitchen and we'll get dinner on the table."

"Oh, my!" Jolene exclaimed when she looked out the kitchen window. "That is one huge garden. Do you sell fresh produce at the store or something?"

Lucy rolled her eyes toward the high ceiling. "If it wasn't for Otis—that's the neighbor who lives next door to her—she couldn't have a half-acre garden. She's only one person. She could grow enough vegetables to feed herself in a flower box, but oh, no, she and Otis have to harvest enough to feed half of Jefferson."

Flossie yelled from the dining room, "Remember that when all y'all reap the harvest with me, so stop bitchin' and come to dinner. Lucy, you can say grace, but it better not take forever."

"Where's the restroom so I can wash up?" Tucker asked.

Lucy pointed. "Down the hall to the left."

The minute they heard the bathroom door close behind him, all three women circled around Jolene. Dotty was the first to whisper, "How's it goin' with Tucker?"

"We had a talk this morning. Things are lookin' up," Jolene said.

"Did he get drunk over the weekend?" Lucy asked.

Jolene shook her head. "Nope."

Flossie whispered, "He'll know we're talkin' about him if we're all right here. So what did you talk about?"

"Pretty much everything," Jolene answered.

"Did he kiss you?" Dotty asked.

Jolene blushed. "No, but I wanted him to. Is that wrong?"

"Of course not. He's a good-lookin' guy. If I was younger, I'd want him to kiss me," Dotty said.

"Well, I'm never doing the relationship before friendship again," Jolene said.

When they heard the door open and close, all the women suddenly took their places at the table. While Lucy said grace, Jolene opened one eye and glanced around the table. Tucker had his head bowed and eyes closed tightly. Lucy's hands were clasped together under her chin as she prayed. Flossie looked over the table as if she was making sure she hadn't forgotten anything. When Jolene looked toward Dotty, the old gal winked at her.

"Sounds crazy but I had this vision of y'all as little girls when I walked up on the porch," Jolene said when Lucy finished her short prayer.

"Oh, honey!" Lucy's smile at the memory lit up the whole room. "All of our mothers were affiliated with the women's church group, and they started a little book club here in town. So yes, we played together every week and always after church at one house or the other."

"That's because it gave our parents some personal time on Sunday afternoons. No kids. A bottle of wine. Some slow music. You get the picture," Dotty said.

"Good grief!" Flossie's hands went up to her cheeks. "I never realized that. How'd you know?"

"Because after Sunday dinner with all y'all was my and Bruce's personal time. I asked Mama about it, too, before she died. She blushed and said that was her business, but why did I think God set aside Sunday for men and women both to have a day of rest?" Dotty giggled.

Jolene couldn't remember a Sunday afternoon when her parents did anything like that. If her dad hadn't been working at the kitchen table, then he'd been sleeping in his recliner with the television turned to a ball game. Her mother was usually out of the house shopping with friends.

"Well, no wonder my folks were in a good mood on Sunday nights." Flossie started passing the food around the table.

Dotty giggled again. "Speakin' of Sunday, next week is at my house, so let's plan our menu. I thought Tucker could grill steaks for us, since I hate to cook. I'll make a dessert and pop some potatoes in the oven to bake. Flossie, you can do the salad and bread again. And Lucy, you can bring your corn casserole."

"What about us?" Tucker asked.

"The griller doesn't have to provide any food. Just whatever special sauces he uses," Dotty answered.

The conversation, as usual, turned to town gossip. Jolene knew that she should be listening because knowing the people mentioned would help when they opened the Magnolia Inn for business. As Aunt Sugar often said, "You can never have too much information. Gather it in and then sift it, and let the unimportant fall through the small holes."

But she kept going back to what Dotty had said about personal time on Sundays. If she ever got into another relationship, it was going to be like that—not stale after a few weeks, but always lively. One where she'd look forward to Sunday afternoons. Yes, ma'am, that's exactly what she wanted.

West Memphis, Arkansas

Sugar figured out that Sundays were the hardest of all for her. They found a place to go to church that morning, but as she sat there among strangers in a huge sanctuary, she pictured the little church at home. Dotty, Flossie, and Lucy would be on the third pew—if Lucy wasn't on some kind of religious kick where she was trying out all the faiths. Granny Alberta would be right up there on the front pew because she couldn't hear too well. And Mr. Thomas always sat on the back row because he wanted to be the first one out the doors when the last amen was said. He'd hurry to the Dairy Queen to save a seat for his old cronies for lunch.

And then afterward Sugar and her friends would go to one of the girls' houses for dinner. Jasper would doze on the sofa while a ball game of some kind played on the television. And she and her friends would have a gossip session in the kitchen.

When the services were over that morning, Jasper held her hand as they made their way out to the parking lot. "What's the matter, Sugar? You've been awful quiet today. Missin' Jolene? I do, too. I'm still disappointed in Reuben, but I'm proud of the way she's stepped up to take care of the Magnolia."

Sugar managed to keep it together until she got inside the RV. Then the tears began to roll down her cheeks. "I love you and I love being with you, but I'm homesick." She buried her face in his chest so she wouldn't have to see the disappointment on his face.

He hugged her even tighter. "Well, praise the Lord! I like our RV. I like traveling with you, but I hate not having roots, too. I've got a confession to make, darlin'. I've been lookin' at real estate in Jefferson and wishin' we'd just bought a house instead of this big RV."

Sugar brought his lips to hers for a long kiss. When it ended she asked, "Did you see that the one next to Flossie is for sale?"

"That's the very one I've been lookin' at." Jasper grinned. "But let's keep our RV for vacations. We won't use it for a way of life but just for short vacations."

"Do you think we should've kept the inn?"

He put a finger over her lips. "Not even for a second. It's time we retired, and neither of us needs to be climbing stairs. We should be home in three days, and there's RV parks in Marshall where we can live until we decide what we want to buy. I'll even be home in time to go bowling Friday night. I been talkin' to Herbert and they haven't replaced me on the league." His grin widened with every word.

"Why didn't you tell me sooner that you weren't happy?"

"Because this has been your dream for years. We've planned it for so long and I thought you were happy. But I'll gladly turn in my wings for the roots I had. We only thought we wanted to be free birds." Jasper chuckled.

"Maybe we can run away from Jefferson a couple of times a year in our new RV." Sugar took a step back and settled into her seat. "But not on holidays. I need to be home at those times. Jolene might need me. We're all the family she has."

"And she's all we've got left. Maybe Reuben will come around to thinkin' responsibly like she does in a few years, but I'm not holding my breath. I'll be glad to get back there and get some hugs from our girl," Jasper said.

Later, he was driving through Arkansas when the sky turned dark and great sheets of rain began to sweep across the highway. He gripped the steering wheel so tightly that his knuckles were white. "Darlin', find us the next RV park. We can't keep going in this."

Sugar hit a few icons on her phone. "There's one three miles ahead of us. Not this next exit but the one after that. When we get to the bottom of the ramp, turn right and it's a quarter mile down that road."

Half an hour later they were parked. Sugar made a fresh pot of coffee. She filled two mugs and carried them to the table. "Is it too soon to call Belinda about that house next to Flossie's? Should we wait until we get there and look at everything on the market?"

"I liked the looks of that place when I looked it up, so call her and say we're interested," Jasper said. "It's what we need—easy to maintain and yet big enough for our Sunday dinners. And for the grandchildren when Jolene decides to have a family."

Sugar laid a hand on his shoulder. "What about when Reuben has kids?"

"Deep down in my heart I don't think he'll ever be involved with us, not like Jolene will." Jasper's voice sounded so sad that Sugar moved closer and hugged him.

"You do know that Jolene's kids won't really be our grandchildren." Sugar sighed.

"Yep, they will. They're goin' to call me Gramps, and you're going to be Granny," Jasper said. "And we're goin' to spoil them. So we need to think about them when we buy a house. Do we want them to have some runnin' room between our place and Flossie's, or do we want them to live closer to town?"

"You've got your heart set on grandchildren, don't you?" Sugar said.

"Yes, I do," Jasper said.

Sugar slid out of the booth-type table and refilled their cups. "I can't believe that we're makin' this decision."

"Does it make you happy?" Jasper asked.

She nodded as she carried the full mugs back to the table. "Yes. How about you?"

"Yes, it does. Now make that phone call. And ask her to leave the utilities turned on so we can hook up to electricity and water. We can live in our home on wheels until we're ready to move into the new place," Jasper said.

Sugar hit the button to make the call and whispered, "But let's keep it a secret and surprise all of them."

Chapter Twenty-One

Jolene had barely gotten her coat off and hung on the back of a chair at the Gator when Lucy and Flossie came through the door. "I just thought I'd stop by a few minutes this morning. I had to come to town for milk and bread, and Tucker's gone to Marshall to order some more supplies, so I had a free hour. But I wasn't expecting to see all y'all here. Is it a bad time?"

"Definitely not. Lucy wanted to talk to us and you're always welcome," Dotty said.

Lucy slumped down in a chair and sighed. "Of course you're welcome. We should've called you. I've got bad news."

Jolene's heart jumped up into her throat. She'd felt like something was amiss for a couple of days now and she couldn't put her finger on why. Maybe it was just that things were going well and she was waiting for the other shoe to drop—like it always had.

"Me, too," Flossie moaned.

Dotty threw up both hands. "I don't have any news at all."

Lucy's hand went to her forehead in a dramatic gesture. "Everett and I broke up. I found out that sorry son of a bitch is married. He told me his wife was dead."

"How in the hell did that happen? We're supposed to keep up with the gossip better than this. And didn't he say she'd died of cancer two years ago?" Dotty fumed.

Lucy pursed her lips and nodded. "He's from south of the lake down where my folks took us to picnic in the summertime. Near Palestine. We can't confirm the gossip from a place that far away."

"Why was he even here in Jefferson?" Flossie asked.

Jolene wondered how many of the men her mother had brought home had a wife and kids at home. The thought had never crossed her mind before because all she'd wanted was for them to be gone or, better yet, to have never shown up in the first place.

"He came into the store looking for a special set of candlesticks for his sister's birthday. I feel like a fool," Lucy sighed. "A married man! My mama is probably rolling over in her grave."

"How did you find out?" Dotty asked.

"His wife came into the store this morning. If she has any idea that she's married to a philanderin' fool, she didn't let on a bit. She asked about the same set of candlesticks that Everett had looked at, and we got to talking. She bought a set of antique mixing bowls and gave me the credit card with Everett's name on it."

"Holy smoke," Flossie gasped. "What did you do?"

Lucy sighed again. "I asked her for identification since that evidently wasn't her card. She apologized, took it back, and handed me one with her name on it. She said that she'd taken her husband's away from him because he didn't have a lick of financial sense."

"What did you do then?" Dotty asked.

"I asked her how long they'd been married, and she said forty-five years. And believe me, she didn't look like she'd ever had cancer," Lucy fumed.

"You think she knows about you and her husband and was just letting you know gracefully?" Dotty asked.

"I have no idea, but I called him, and I'll have to pray for a whole year for all the bad words I used," Lucy said.

"What did he say?" Dotty asked.

"After I slung enough cusswords around to send me to hell, he just hung up on me."

"I've got three shovels in the gardening shed," Flossie said. "We can hide that body down by the bayou so good that it won't never be found."

Lucy shook her head slowly from side to side. "I apologized to God for my bad language and left it in His hands. But I did tell Him that I expected Everett to suffer the plagues of Egypt, and that if he ever stepped out on that woman again, that He had my permission to fling a bolt of lightning at him. Now what's your bad news, Flossie?"

"Otis's wife died, and he put the house on the market. What am I going to do about my garden?" Flossie groaned.

"You're worried about your garden when your neighbor died?" Jolene asked. "That's kind of mean." Vegetables could be bought at any roadside stand in Texas. The man had lost his wife. Guilt stabbed her. There she was feeling sorry for Otis when Tucker had been in the same situation.

Dotty got up and went around the table to hug Flossie. "I'm so sorry. We all knew that she died, but we didn't expect him to move, at least not so soon."

"Well, he's gone. Went to live near his son in Houston. There's a 'For Sale' sign on the front lawn."

"Put an ad in the newspaper for someone to help you out with it. I bet there's lots of retired men who'd love to have a project that didn't take all year," Jolene suggested.

"*I* don't get a hug? My bad news is worse than hers," Lucy fussed.

"Of course you do, *chère*." Dotty moved around the table to Lucy. "I'm sorry about Everett. I thought he might be the one you'd end up married to."

"I'm giving up on marriage. This is worse than when my last two boyfriends died. I may sell my store and go into a convent," Lucy whimpered.

"Now, darlin'," Flossie said sweetly. "We need you too badly around here for you to go to a convent. With Sugar gone, that would just leave me, Dotty, and Jolene."

"I'm not going to be a nun. I never did look good in black. But I'm expecting God to take care of Everett with a vengeance, not kid gloves," Lucy huffed. "I miss Sugar so much. Why did she have to go away?"

"She's following her dream, *chère*," Dotty answered. "And we couldn't stand in the way or all of us would have regretted it forever."

Jolene loved these ladies, but she wished Aunt Sugar was back in Jefferson, too.

🌸

Tucker and Jolene finished putting the final touches on the third bedroom later that afternoon. In the past it had made him happy when a client stepped into a room he'd done and loved it. But his happiness surged when Jolene clapped her hands like a little girl and then got busy putting the final touches on the three rooms. With the border up, the beds made, and pretty white doilies scattered around, all the rooms looked warm and inviting.

"Here we have the ivory room." She snapped several pictures with her phone from all angles.

While she moved to the next doorway, he followed her. "And now you have the green room."

She shot two or three pictures. "Later we'll give our website a personal touch with pictures of the owners. This is the *sage* room," she corrected him. "It sounds so much more inviting than 'green room.'"

Keeping up a running monologue, she moved to the next room. "And this is my favorite, the rose room. Hey, we might even get audio on the website. No, that's too cheesy. We'll just use the pictures. But honestly, Tucker, they're too pretty to rent out. Maybe we should just make the inn into a museum."

"We'd never make any money that way," he chuckled. "What are these other three going to be called?"

"The sunshine room, which will be pale yellow. I've decided on a pale blue like that highlight color in the leaves for one of the other ones, and then we have one left. What do you think?"

He stepped into the room so he could see the border better. "See that light tan in the top of the border? That would be nice for a groom's room if we ever get to do a wedding here."

"Perfect," she said. "Now what do we name the blue room?"

It would be worth giving up drinking to see her this happy all the time.

"The summer room, because it looks like a summer sky," he suggested.

"I love it. Now come up with something for the brown one, and we'll have it all done."

He chuckled again. "I hope when and if I ever have kids, it's this easy to name them." Had he really said that out loud? He and Melanie had wanted kids, but did he want them with another woman? Would he ever be ready for that?

"You want kids?" she asked.

"Oh, yeah, someday, if I'm not too old when that day comes. Do you want children?" He backed out of the room and rolled the kinks out of his neck.

"Yes, I do want kids. I always wanted a sibling," she answered. "And this is changing the subject, but I forgot to tell you, Lucy said that she'd picked up two little chest of drawer–type things that might work for vanities. We could go look at them today."

"What do you have to do to get ready?" he asked.

"Just got to pick up my purse." She hurried off down the stairs.

She'd be good for you. Melanie's voice popped into his head so quick that it shocked him. He waited for a full minute, but she didn't say anything else, so he went down to the foyer and got his jacket.

Jolene slipped her arms into an oversize cardigan. "It's fairly nice out today. No rain in sight. Maybe we'll have an early spring."

Tucker held the door for her. "My grandpa always said not to think spring was here until after Easter, and that's not until the end of April this year."

"The Easter snap." Jolene nodded. "That's what Uncle Jasper called it."

"Yep, my grandpa said the same thing."

The trip to Jefferson took only a few minutes, but Tucker kept thinking about what Melanie had said. *Would* Jolene be good for him? Here lately, he really had felt a lot less guilty every time he thought about how cute she was with paint smeared on her face or how gorgeous she was when she got all cleaned up for Sunday dinner.

"The work is coming along faster than I thought possible," Jolene said when they parked outside the antique shop. "And I love the way it looks. Do you think we'll have the rest of the upstairs done by the end of February?"

"Yes, ma'am, and then we'll have March to work on the downstairs renovations," he answered. "There's not as much actual work there, mainly just deciding how on earth to get a little office space and some basic cosmetic help."

Her finger shot past his nose. "Look at that, Tucker."

A whitetail doe and her fawn stood right inside a barbed-wire fence at the edge of the road. It was one of those Kodak moments, but neither of them had their phones ready, so they didn't catch the picture.

"Ah, man, that was postcard pretty," Jolene said.

"If we ever see any around the inn, we'll have to take pictures to go on your website. You are going to keep it updated by seasons, right?"

She leaned forward, no doubt looking for another deer. "You bet I am. And if we ever have a wedding there, I'll get permission from the bride to post pictures of that, too."

Lucy met them at the door with her arms spread out to hug Jolene. "I'm so glad to see you today. You kids are like a breath of spring after a long winter. What brings you to town?"

"I've been racking my brain trying to come up with someone to help with Flossie's garden."

Tucker held up a palm. "Don't look at me. I've got black thumbs instead of green ones. Melanie used to say that if I breathed on a plant, it died."

He'd mentioned her name, and no sadness swirled up around it. He glanced down at the wedding band on his left hand. Was he really starting to take steps forward?

"Me, either. Daddy taught me how to grow flowers, but I wouldn't know anything about squash or tomatoes," Jolene said.

"Maybe Sugar can think of someone who might be interested. Flossie loves that garden." Lucy sighed.

"Don't you worry. I bet there's someone who'll love to help Flossie," Jolene answered.

Her tone was so honest and caring that Tucker wanted to take her in his arms and hug her. There'd been attraction before, but then, who wouldn't be drawn to a woman like Jolene? She was strong and independent, and still sweet.

"That's right. I don't know why I fret about things like I do. But enough about us old ladies and our problems. I bet you're here to see the things I bought for the inn, right? Y'all just follow me to the storage room, and I'll show you what I've bought. Since I talked to you, I found another piece. If you want both, I'll give them to you for what I paid for them."

"We can't do that. You need to make a profit," Tucker said.

"No, I don't. I've got more money than Midas already and no one to leave it to when I'm dead," Lucy argued as she opened the door into a storage room. "There they are."

Two small burled-oak washstands, complete with the towel bars, were side by side. There was no doubt that the hardware was original, and they were in pristine condition. Jolene squealed and went to open all the little drawers and then the small door.

"They're both perfect. That's so sweet of you to give them to us at such a bargain. Thank you, thank you." She rushed over to hug Lucy.

Tucker couldn't help but smile as he pulled out his wallet. "At least let us give you a finder's fee."

"Nope. I paid a hundred apiece for them, and that's what I'm charging. You can back your truck up around to the back doors and load them up." Lucy smiled. "I'm glad that I did good."

"You did better than good." Jolene ran her fingers over the top of each piece. "You did fantabulous."

Lucy giggled. "Well, thank you."

❋

Tucker got into bed that evening and laced his fingers behind his head. Clouds kept shifting across the quarter moon, sending shadows and shapes across the ceiling. He turned his head to catch sight of Melanie's picture on the nightstand, but she was barely visible in the semidarkness. Then he turned the other way to find that Sassy wasn't in her usual place on the pillow but had curled up at the foot of the bed.

He shut his eyes, and sleep came immediately—as did the dreams. He and Melanie were back in the trailer that last night. He argued with her that she shouldn't go into town, but she laughed at him.

"It's okay, darlin'. It's my time and no one argues with God." She kissed him on the cheek, picked up her purse, and started out the trailer door.

"Lucy does," he said. "Lucy argues with God, and I believe He listens to her."

"Who's Lucy?" Melanie asked.

"This older lady who's a friend of Jolene's. Don't go, Melanie. I can't live without you," he begged.

"Yes, you can. Life goes on, and I want you to be happy, Tucker. You have to let me go. My soul won't be at peace until you do." She took him by the hand and led him outside. "Now walk me to the car, and tell me goodbye."

"I can't," he said.

"Be brave, like you are on the force." She kissed him. "I love you. Give Jolene a chance. I like her. She'll make you happy."

He tried to hold her back, but she slipped away. As she drove off into the fog, he reached out one more time, only to find her wedding ring in his hand.

He woke up in a cold sweat, his hand clutched so tight that it ached. When he opened it, there was nothing there. Shock filled him to see her picture was gone as well. He switched on the light and found the frame on the floor, the glass shattered into a hundred little pieces.

Sassy was sitting right beside it with a mouse in her mouth. That explained the picture. She'd probably jumped across the bed and the nightstand to get at it, but Tucker just knew that Melanie had probably caused it.

"I get it," he whispered as he cleaned up the glass, threw away the frame, and tucked her picture into the nightstand. "You can go. I'm going to be fine."

Chapter Twenty-Two

*J*olene stared at the calendar—January 29. There was something special about that day, but she couldn't put her finger on it. Mentally, she ran down the list of family birthdays and got nothing. She flipped the calendar pages and saw where Aunt Sugar had penned in birthdays for her friends and special days that she and Uncle Jasper shared—their first date, their first kiss, and their anniversary. Then there were other days, like when Sugar's mother, her father, Elaine, and even Jolene's father had passed away.

But there was nothing written on January 29, so why did she feel like she was missing something important?

Tucker looked over her shoulder. "Got something going today?"

Him standing that close to her created a heat that she didn't want to think about. A relationship of any kind would be nothing but a rebound thing for him.

What would it be for you? Aunt Sugar's voice was in her head.

Disaster, she thought with honesty.

Jolene put her finger on the date. "January 29. Does that mean something to you?"

"Can't think of anything, but you did tell me your birthday was on the twenty-ninth, so maybe you're thinking ahead." Tucker rubbed a hand over his chin. "Why?"

If she turned around, her lips would be within a few inches of his ruggedly handsome face. She folded her arms over her chest and took a side step. "Look at it and see if it jogs anything in your memory. I've got this nagging feeling that it should mean something, and it's driving me crazy."

With a little distance between them, the tension faded. "How about some chocolate-chip muffins this morning?" she asked.

"Sounds great." He flipped through the calendar. "I wonder why Sugar did this when she knew she was leaving."

She headed into the kitchen. "It was part of her ritual. In December she always got a new calendar at the grocery store and used the old one to write all the important dates on it."

"And she probably didn't want you to forget, right?"

Tucker got eggs and milk from the refrigerator and set them on the counter.

"I wonder why she didn't take it with her," Jolene mused. "Maybe she made two. She wouldn't leave home without something to remind her of important dates. I'm going to use hers and make one of my own next year. I want to remember all those days."

"Maybe I could add a few to it," he said.

Jolene wasn't sure how she'd feel about his late wife's birthday being on the calendar, too, but they were in this venture together. She'd gotten used to putting their laundry together, so this wouldn't be all that different, would it?

"Sure, you can," she said, hoping all the time that she'd never have to look at Melanie's name on the calendar.

"Hey, where is everyone?" Dotty's voice echoed through the house.

"Back here," Tucker yelled. "Come on in and join us for breakfast?"

"What're you doin' out this early?" Jolene asked when Dotty appeared in the kitchen doorway. "How did you manage to get through that rain without ruining your hair?"

"A good umbrella. A fine plastic rain bonnet. And the best hair spray on the market," Dotty answered. "What are we havin' this morning?"

"Muffins and cereal. But I'll make you an omelet if you want one," Jolene answered.

"Let's have oatmeal with raisins and brown sugar to go with the muffins." The other woman headed for the pantry. "I'll make it while you finish stirrin' those up, *chère*. Something ain't right. I don't know if it's good or bad, but I had to come see if you kids were okay."

"Must be something in the air. Jolene can't figure out why today looks strange on the calendar," Tucker said.

Dotty filled a small saucepan with water and set it on the stove. "Me, either. That's where I went first. Sugar always got four calendars at the grocery store and she filled them out for each of us with our birthdays, committee meetin's at the church, and so on. Then we put in our own doctor visits and personal things. There's not a thing on today for any of us. I checked with Lucy and Flossie before I left—they got this feelin', too—so I volunteered to come out here to check on y'all."

Jolene felt better knowing it wasn't just *her* feeling strange about the day. Maybe it had to do with Aunt Sugar. That was the only explanation.

"Why didn't you just call?" Tucker asked. "You could catch pneumonia in this weather."

"Oh, *chère*." She giggled. "Us Cajuns are a lot stronger than we look. It'd take a little more than rain to get me sick. Must just be this awful weather gettin' us all antsy."

"Or maybe it's spring fever hittin' us early," Jolene said.

"Could be. I'm tired of this damn weather for sure. I saw a single little daffodil at the old Ennis place as I was driving out here and got more excited about spring than I ever have before."

That would certainly explain the vibes when Tucker was close, Jolene thought. It was the same hormones that the birds and the bees get when spring is on the way. Her focus shifted toward him, standing there with bedroom hair, and she almost dropped the pan of muffins that she was carrying to the oven.

Bedroom hair? Spring fever was taking over for sure.

🌺

Conway, Arkansas

Sugar did up the breakfast dishes and checked her calendar like she did every morning. She picked up a pen and wrote HOME in the January 29 slot. With good weather and no hiccups, they could be hooked up at the house next to Flossie's by nightfall.

"Still happy?" Jasper wrapped his arms around her waist.

"Too much to describe. How about you?"

"Like you said, there are no words. Do you realize that our grandbabies won't be off out there in West Texas? I wish Dotty would have hired her when she was twenty-one."

"I was selfish back then and didn't want people to know that she worked in a bar," Sugar admitted.

"And she refused to come work for us in the inn," Jasper remembered.

"She said she could make her own way." Sugar nodded. "But, darlin', I'm not sorry we did this trip. It showed us where we belong, and we'd never have bought the RV just for vacations."

Jasper brushed her hair back and kissed her on the neck. "And someday Jolene and her husband might want to borrow it to take the kids to Disney World."

She laid her head on his chest. "If only we could have had half a dozen kids of our own."

"That would've been wonderful, but that wasn't in the cards for us. Reuben or Jolene's children can be our grandbabies. I just hope neither of them wait too long to get married. Are you ready to get started on the last leg toward home?"

She pointed to the wall where the calendar hung. "Yes, I am. See, I wrote it down already because it's such a special day."

She strapped herself into the passenger seat. "What time will we be there?"

"Six, maybe, but probably more like seven. We can run on generator power tonight if it's too dark for me to find things." He kept talking, but Sugar had her phone out and was picking out furniture for her new place.

At noon, Jasper pulled the RV off into a rest stop in Louisiana and parked it in the truck-only area. Sugar heated up a pan of tomato soup and made grilled cheese sandwiches. Jasper got out potato chips and opened cans of root beer for them.

She had taken the first bite of soup when her phone rang. She bit back a groan when she saw it was Jolene. She handed the phone to Jasper. "You talk first. I'm afraid I'll tell her and spoil our surprise."

"Is this the Magnolia Inn callin' me?" Jasper teased as he put it on speaker mode.

"No, this is your favorite niece." Jolene giggled. "Are y'all havin' a good time? Where have you decided to go next?"

"Where our hearts take us," Jasper answered.

"Aunt Sugar, is there anything special about today? You don't have it on the calendar, but I'm kind of antsy, and something tells me it's got to do with the day," Jolene said.

Sugar glanced over at the calendar and sidestepped the issue. "Maybe it's got to do with Tucker. Have you thought of that? Or maybe you're going to win that thing where that company shows up on your porch with a big check."

"No . . . wait a minute while I step outside," Jolene said.

In a few seconds, Sugar could hear the screech of the old chains on the porch swing. She pushed the "Mute" button and whispered to Jasper, "She suspects."

Jasper smiled.

Sugar hit the button again as Jolene said, "Okay, I can talk now. Is it just spring fever that makes me . . . how do I put this?"

"Put what? Don't beat around the bush. Spit it out," Jasper said.

"Here lately I'm really attracted to Tucker." Jolene sighed.

"Oh, dear," Sugar squeaked. "Does he feel the same?"

"I don't know, but he seems happy. Maybe that's just me wanting to see something. I was guilty of that with Mama a lot of times. And God knows I gave Johnny Ray all those chances to straighten up and he didn't. I'm afraid of getting disappointed or hurt again."

"Did Elaine ever stay sober for ten whole days?" Sugar asked.

"Not even one time," Jolene answered.

"Did the boyfriend?"

"He made it two days one time," Jolene said.

"Then there's your answer. Don't judge Tucker by your mama's or that other man's half bushel," Sugar told her.

"What does that mean? I've never heard that expression before," Jolene said.

"It means that your mama's half bushel of problems stay in her basket. Johnny Ray's stay in his. Don't pull out any of those and use it to judge anyone else. The way they handled their issues has nothing to do with Tucker, so don't judge him by your experiences with those two," Jasper chimed in.

Jolene laughed. "And never the bunch of them shall meet unless they share a bottle of cheap whiskey. Then I can throw them in a burlap bag together, right?"

"You got it, darlin'," Jasper said.

"Okay, I guess I just needed to hear y'all's voices. Travel safe today, and I love you both. Where are you now?" Jolene asked again.

"In a rest stop having lunch, and then we'll get back on the road," Jasper answered.

"Well, be safe."

"We will," Jasper said.

The call ended without any of them needing to say goodbye.

"Sounds like you handled that real good," Jasper said. "And, if I was hearin' right, we might get them grandbabies sooner rather than later."

"We just might at that." Sugar nodded.

❧

The windshield wipers had to do double time to keep up with the sheets of rain hitting Tucker's truck like a sandblaster. The fifteen-minute drive to the lumberyard took half an hour, and he had to sit in the parking lot ten more minutes until the rain slacked up enough that he could jog inside. When he carried the five-gallon bucket out to the truck, there was still a slow drizzle coming down, but at least most of the storm had passed.

He laid his hat on the passenger seat and started back to Jefferson. But when he drove past the road leading to the cemetery, he turned that way. That first year after Melanie died, he'd gone to her grave every single day. The second year he forced himself to only go once a week, but it had been two weeks this time, and he felt guilty about staying away so long. He wondered if Luke had already been there today and felt guilty that he hadn't gone to the party. With Luke's problems, he probably wouldn't be alive another year to celebrate with them.

Tucker parked and sat there for a while, just looking out across the brown lawn. Soon spring would arrive, bringing with it pretty green grass. Melanie had loved spring, but summer was her favorite season. That meant three months when she didn't have to teach and she could spend more time with her Tucker.

Finally, he got out and, taking cover from the drizzle under a tall pine tree not far from her grave, tried to get into the zone that he always felt when he visited her. Maybe it was the rain, or the fact that he'd wanted to kiss Jolene that morning, but something wasn't right. He took a step forward and dropped to his knees.

"You were serious in the dream, weren't you, Melanie? You're not going to talk to me anymore, are you?"

Nothing, not a clap of thunder or a bolt of lightning, came from the clouds. He shifted his gaze from the tombstone to the skies, and be damned if they hadn't parted enough to let a ray of sunshine filter through. When he looked back at the tombstone, it sparkled in the fresh sunrays.

"I had the urge to kiss Jolene this morning," he whispered.

More sunshine, but nothing, not even a faint whisper, from Melanie.

He touched the tombstone. "I guess that means you aren't jealous. You're okay with it?"

The clouds covered the sun, casting everything back into grayness— like shades of a black-and-white movie.

"Okay, I get the message. I'll do my best." He removed his wedding ring from his finger and his knife from his pocket. Digging a small hole at the base of the tombstone, he buried the gold band. "You gave me yours back in my dream last night. I'm giving you mine this way. I love you, Melanie. I'm not sure where this is going with Jolene, but I've got a good feeling about it. She's a good woman. You'd like her a lot if you . . ."

A loud clap of thunder rolled across the sky, and huge drops of rain began to fall. He rolled up to a standing position and started to run back to his truck when a horn blasted right in front of him, much closer than where his vehicle was parked. He shaded his eyes against the rain and could see an arm waving to him to come that way.

He dashed over there as Melanie's dad pointed for him to get into his truck. Tucker hopped inside and shivered.

"Cold rain is the worst," he said.

"Amen to that." Luke patted his shoulder. "How are you doing? We were sad not to see you at the birthday."

The story of the dream poured out. Then he went right on to tell Luke how he'd felt that morning when he was close to Jolene.

Luke nodded through the whole story. "Has she talked to you about Jolene?"

"She told me that Jolene was a good woman and I should give her a chance." Tucker rubbed the place where his wedding band had been. "But it seems so final. Like I can't go back, but I'm not sure I know how to go forward."

"It was final the day that we lost her. It just takes a while for us to get that settled in our hearts," Luke said.

"But how can I be sure that it is settled?"

"I think what you put in the ground says that. I saw that you were burying your ring."

Tucker glanced down at his finger and the pale line of skin marking the ring's absence. "Is it possible that there's more than one soul mate for some of us?"

Luke clamped a hand on Tucker's shoulder. "Listen to Melanie, son. You're too young to go through life alone and lonely. I'm sixty-five years old and Carla is the same age, but I told her to find someone when I'm gone. With her family history, she could live past ninety. She could have another thirty years with someone who adores her," Luke said.

"But . . ." Tucker started.

"You look at things different when you're lookin' the Maker in the eye, just like Melanie looks at things different from the side she's on now. If she said this Jolene is a good woman, then believe her."

"Yes, sir," Tucker said.

"Carla and I'd like to meet her," Luke said.

Tucker couldn't answer for the grapefruit-size lump in his throat.

"And it would have to be pretty soon. As you know, I've got a deadline to meet. Let's go for ice cream on Sunday afternoon. Meet you at the Dairy Queen here in Marshall at four?"

"We'll be there." Tucker opened the truck door and ran to his own vehicle. He was soaking wet when he got there and shivering from his ears to his toes. Whether it was from closure or the weather, he had no idea.

❦

Jolene hoped that by the middle of March the new website would be up and running. That would be a perfect time to start taking reservations and to join the ads for the tour of homes. She had made several phone calls to wedding photographers, florists, and bakeries. As soon as she'd compiled all her materials, she and Tucker would discuss how to price wedding packages. The way she saw it, they could range from simply renting the place for a few hours to a full-fledged turnkey wedding where all the bride had to bring was her dress. As she closed her laptop, the doorbell rang. She and Sassy both rushed to answer it.

"Why'd you ring . . . oh, you had your hands full." She swung the door open so Tucker could come inside.

Sassy rose up on her hind feet when Tucker carried in pizza and then hurried off toward the kitchen, where she jumped up on the countertop.

"She loves pizza. Meat lover's with extra cheese and marinara sauce," Tucker explained as he took the first piece out of the box and cut it into bite-size pieces for her.

"I can see that. She almost beat me to the door when the bell rang." Jolene got out paper plates and napkins.

"Like Pavlov's dog . . . or cat? Anyway, the doorbell means pizza to her." He chuckled.

"She never does that when it's the ladies."

"She can smell pizza a mile away." Tucker stacked three pieces on a plate.

That's when she noticed that his wedding ring was gone. That was a huge thing. She was glad that she had a mouthful of food, because her first idea was to ask why he'd taken it off. With the ring gone and the difference she could feel in him, she wondered if he'd found a final piece of closure that day. She tried not to stare at his hands, but it was impossible to keep her eyes away from the pale indentation on his ring finger.

She shouldn't ask about that, even though she was itching to know the details of why now, where it was, and what had made him take it off. The silence was getting uncomfortable, so she started talking about the first thing that came to mind—the website she'd been working on just before he came home.

"This is going to be a fantastic website. I sent pictures of the first three bedrooms for the webmaster to get into the site. We'll have tabs of each room with pictures and prices and the whole nine yards. We should talk about prices. I charged that little couple who stayed here Aunt Sugar's old rates, but we can't operate on those twenty-year-old fees and keep things running." She got a second slice and bit into it.

"Look online or call around to see what everyone else is charging. Then we'll make a decision," he said.

She felt a lot like she had that morning when she'd looked at the calendar. It reminded her of that eerie feeling out in West Texas when a tornado was blowing through the flat countryside, only this wasn't fear of getting blown away. Tucker had taken off his ring, and that was really big. She couldn't wait for the opportunity to tell Dotty. Maybe she'd even call Aunt Sugar that evening and talk to her about it.

She grabbed a third piece of pizza and started toward the table with her plate, stumbled over her own feet, and barely got control, but not before she got marinara sauce all over her hand.

Tucker was instantly on his feet to help her. "Hey, I like that sauce too much to waste it." He picked up her hand and licked it clean.

Jolene's breath came out in short gasps. Sparks danced around the room. Electricity flowed like a live current between his mouth and her palm. The chemistry was hot enough to curl her toes. She should do something, but she was frozen on the spot until he took the plate from her other hand and set it on the table. Keeping her hand in his, he led her to the sink and pumped a little liquid soap into her palm. Then he turned on the water and rubbed her hand with his.

Her eyes went to his mouth and then their gazes locked. Her breath came in short bursts like she'd jogged a mile. When he leaned forward and his eyes fluttered shut, leaving his dark lashes to float on his angular cheekbones, she tiptoed and met his kiss halfway.

It started sweet, but then it deepened into more, and by the time he pulled away, she was panting. All the voices in her head were screaming that she shouldn't have let it happen, and she knew they were right.

"That might not have been such a good idea," she whispered.

He brushed another kiss across her lips. "What if it was meant to be and we ignored it? What if this is what fate has in mind for us? What's that old sayin' about not fighting city hall?"

"That's a pretty big basket of what-ifs to think about. We need to cool off for a few minutes." She fanned herself with her hands.

"Maybe we should take a cold shower together." He brushed another scorching kiss across her lips.

"I don't think so," she laughed.

"Well, then you should definitely mark this on the calendar— today's the day we kissed for the first time."

Chapter Twenty-Three

Jolene dreamed about Tucker again that night. In this one, they were sitting on the porch swing together on a lovely spring evening. She realized that they'd both gotten old when she saw his gray hair, but it wasn't until he told her that he loved the fifty years they'd had together that she realized they must be close to ninety. She moved closer, shifted so that she was sitting in his lap, and put her arms around him.

She awoke with her arms wrapped around a pillow. When she realized it wasn't him, she slung it across the room. She threw on a pair of jeans and a shirt and headed toward the kitchen. A dirty plate on the floor testified that Sassy had eaten cold pizza for breakfast. Jolene poured a cup of coffee and opened the oven to find the last slice of pizza on a plate.

She'd planned on eating it, but Sassy jumped up on the cabinet and sent up something between a meow and a howl, so Jolene cut it up in small pieces. She could hear Tucker doing something upstairs, so she headed in that direction.

"Good mornin'." Tucker motioned her into the empty bedroom. "I couldn't sleep, so I carried all the lumber up the stairs to put up the bathroom walls. I tried to be quiet."

She sat down on the floor and stared at him.

"What? Do I have a milk mustache? I had cookies and milk." He wiped at his upper lip.

"No, I had a dream about you last night. You were pretty handsome at ninety years old," she said.

He stared back at her. "I can't imagine you at that age, but I'll bet you are still beautiful then, too. So what were we doin' in this dream? Were we sharing another hot kiss?" he teased.

"No, but we might have if I hadn't woke up when I did," she answered.

"Do you believe in dreams? Are we still going to be together at ninety?"

"I'd like that."

He moved closer to her, tucked his fist under her chin, and tilted it up. Then his mouth covered hers in another kiss that had them both panting when it ended. She moved so that she was sitting in his lap like she'd done in the dream, wrapped her arms around his neck, and brought his mouth to hers for another passionate kiss.

His hands slipped under her shirt to touch her bare skin. Rough hands on her back, his lips moving from hers to that soft sensual place below her ear—the whole world disappeared and they were the only two people left in that moment.

But it ended abruptly with her blushing scarlet when he stood quickly and pulled her up with him. "I heard the door open. Someone is here."

"Hey, anybody home?" A voice floated up the stairs.

"Sounds like Dotty is dropping in again," Tucker said. "We've got to start locking that door."

The voice carried up the stairs from the foyer. "Jolene, where are you?"

"That's not Dotty. That's . . ." Jolene ran to the top of the steps and went down in a rush. It really was her aunt and not just her imagination.

"There you are." Sugar opened her arms, and Jolene met her hug.

"Is it really you? How long can you stay? Are you just passing through?"

Please think my cheeks are scarlet from running down the stairs to greet you and that I'm asking so many questions because I'm happy to see you.

"We came home for good," Sugar said.

Uncle Jasper walked up behind her aunt. "We missed you. Now that you are here permanently, we want to be close."

Jolene wrapped them both up in a three-way hug. "We've got rooms finished. One of us can move upstairs and give your old bedroom back to you. And—"

"Thank you, honey," Jasper said, "but we don't want to live at the Magnolia. If we did, we wouldn't have given it away to begin with."

Sugar took her by the hand and led her toward the kitchen. "We're probably going to buy the house next to Flossie's. We parked at a campground down by Marshall last night, but if things look good, we'll park by Flossie's tonight. I wanted to get here so badly that I didn't even make breakfast. So I'm going to cook. Would you call the girls and tell them to come join you? That way I can surprise them all at the same time."

"I'm so glad you've come back. We've missed you so much, but really, y'all can live here and not have to buy a house," Jolene said.

"She's right," Tucker said from halfway down the stairs. "There's plenty of room right here."

Jasper extended a hand. "I'm Jasper and this is Sugar. You have to be Tucker."

"Yes, sir, and I'm right pleased to meet y'all." Tucker shook with him and nodded at Sugar. "I've heard so much about y'all that I feel like I already know you both."

"Same here," Sugar said. "You two don't need to worry—we don't want to live here. We're both getting too old for stairs and takin' care of guests. This is your place now. I'm excited about having a home I don't share with people!"

"We'll be glad to help y'all any way we can," Tucker said. "And you'll have to climb those stairs at least one more time to see what we've got done so far."

"After I see the girls," Sugar said. "I'm really anxious to surprise them."

Jolene wiped at her eyes. "I might cry, I'm so happy."

Sugar stopped long enough for another quick hug and whispered, "So I see that he's not wearing a wedding ring. When did he take it off?"

"Yesterday," Jolene said.

"Been sober how long?"

"More than a week."

"That's wonderful news. Now make that call," Sugar said.

❦

Dotty's sixth sense kicked in that morning when she first woke up. It had to do with that damned calendar, she was sure of it. Whatever it was had happened yesterday, and she was just about to find out about it now. She started to make her cup of strong black coffee, but the phone rang.

"This is it," she muttered. "Don't let it be bad news. Hello, Jolene, is everything okay?"

"Of course. Just wanted to invite you, Flossie, and Lucy to breakfast this morning. I've got some exciting news," Jolene said.

"Does it involve Tucker? Are y'all dating or whatever you young folks call it these days?" Dotty asked.

"Can't say right now. Want to tell you all three at the same time."

Dotty could hear the excitement in Jolene's voice. "Okay, then, I'll call Flossie and you get hold of Lucy. Tell them I'll drive and get them in twenty minutes."

"You got it. See you in half an hour."

The call ended, and Dotty called Flossie. She put the phone on speaker and laid it on the vanity as she touched up her hair, applied fresh hair spray, and put on the fastest makeup job she'd done in years.

"What do you think the news is? Is it about the Magnolia Inn or about her and Tucker?" Flossie asked.

"Don't know. She wouldn't say," Dotty said.

"I'm hanging up now. So see you in twenty. Just honk and I'll come right on out," Flossie said.

Dotty finished in the bathroom. She jerked on a velour pants set with lots of bling on the front of the shirt, shoved her feet into a pair of boots, and grabbed her coat and purse. She broke every speed limit posted to find Lucy waiting on the porch.

"So what do you think she's going to tell us?" Lucy was getting inside the vehicle before it came to a full stop.

"It's got something to do with yesterday. I was antsy all day," Dotty said. "No one died in town last night, did they?"

Lucy frowned. "Not that I've heard of. I talked to Sugar last night and everything was fine. And you went to the Magnolia yesterday."

"I bet you that Jolene and Tucker have been hiding something from us and they're engaged," Dotty said.

"No!" Lucy shook her head dramatically. "We'd have seen that coming. We're not so old that we're losin' it."

Flossie was waiting and hurried out to the SUV, crawled into the back seat, and said, "Y'all know anything more?"

Dotty shook her head. "Nope, but it's got to be big news. I could hear it in Jolene's voice."

"Well, drive faster," Flossie said. "If you get a speeding ticket, I'll pay it."

Dotty jacked it up another ten miles and slung a little loose gravel when she braked to turn down the lane to the inn. She parked close to the front porch, and they all tumbled out of the vehicle like little girls rather than grown women.

Dotty swung open the front door. "We're here. Something smells delicious."

Lucy hung up her coat. "What's the news?"

Flossie didn't take off her jacket but pushed past both the others and met Jolene in the dining room. "Tell me right now that this is good news. My blood pressure is risin' by the minute."

"Surprise!" Sugar made an entrance into the dining room.

"Oh. My. Gosh. Am I seeing things?" Lucy squealed.

"I knew something was going on." Dotty raced across the floor to hug Sugar.

Then suddenly they were all four hugging, hopping up and down as much as ladies their age could do on bum knees and hips.

"Are you here for a visit?" Flossie asked.

Each of them still had a hand on Sugar's shoulders, as if they were afraid she'd disappear if they weren't touching.

"So how long are you stayin'? Will you be here for the weekend so you can go to church with us? Where is your RV?" Dotty fired questions one after another.

"Let's get some food and sit down," Sugar said.

"Hey, ladies." Jasper came in from the kitchen with a coffeepot. "Y'all go on and get your plates ready, and I'll pour the coffee."

"Are you headed for the West Coast now? I heard it was snowing out east of here." Flossie led Sugar to the front of the line. "You go first. I don't know if I can even swallow food right now."

Lucy followed Sugar. "I want to know why you didn't tell us you were coming through here."

"Because we aren't coming through here. I got homesick, so we changed our plan. We stayed in Marshall last night," Sugar said. "We're thinking of buying the little house next to Flossie. Our RV is out back right now, but we're hoping to park it at the new house tonight and start to move in as soon as possible."

✿

Jolene stood to the side and watched them. Everything was right in their world now. Sugar had come home. Tucker slipped an arm around her waist, and her joy doubled.

"How does this make you feel?" he whispered, so close that his warm breath caressed her neck.

"Like everything is falling into place," she said with a slight shiver. "How about you?"

"They kind of remind me of my grandparents. Mine would be older, but they still make me think of them," he said. "Are you cold?"

"No, your touch just affects me that way." If they were going to have a relationship, then Jolene figured she should be totally honest with him.

"And yours does the same to me," he said. "Damn, it feels good for things to be right again."

"Yep, it sure does." She tiptoed and kissed him on the cheek, not caring if anyone saw but relieved that they didn't. This was Sugar's thunder, and she didn't want to steal a single bit of it.

"When did you figure this out?" Lucy asked Sugar.

"Sunday, but I wanted to surprise y'all," she answered. "You can't know how hard it was not to tell you every time we talked."

"We would have had a big party if you'd told us," Flossie said and then turned her attention toward Jolene. "Did you know?"

"Not until this morning," Jolene said.

They all took places at the table with Jolene sitting right next to Sugar. She could barely believe a whole hour had passed when Jasper said, "Okay, ladies, we've got to be at the house at ten. I'm sure y'all have to open up your stores, too."

"We can open late," Flossie said.

"Why do you have to be there at that time?" Jolene asked.

"Belinda is coming to show us the place, but we already know we're going to buy it. And Sugar spent two days on her phone with a furniture store in Marshall. They'll be delivering a bedroom outfit at ten thirty so we can sleep in it tonight," Jasper said.

"But I have a store full of furniture that you can choose from," Lucy said.

"And so do I," Flossie said. "Come get whatever you want, and I won't even charge you for it."

"I don't want antiques. I've never got to pick out what I want instead of taking what was left to me. Not that I'm complaining. The inn was very good to us." Sugar talked as much with her hands as her words. "I appreciate y'all's offer, but Jasper and I want soft, comfortable furniture."

"She says she wants stuff that's comfortable and doesn't require much dusting," Jasper chuckled. "So, Jolene, will you forgive us for leaving you with a mess? We really should be going. It takes a while to get that big RV backed up among all these tall pine trees."

"You're forgiven," Jolene said and then asked, "How did you ever get it pulled down the driveway and out back without me hearing?" Then she remembered how she and Tucker had been making out at the time they'd driven by the house.

Sugar giggled. "Remember when you were a little girl and said that the inn was your magic castle? Well, honey, it hasn't changed just because you grew up."

🌸

Tucker and Jolene stood on the porch and waved at Dotty's SUV until it was out of sight. Then they did the same when the RV came around from the back and disappeared. Jolene shivered as a gust of north wind blew across the porch, and Tucker slipped his arms around her waist from the back to hold her close to his chest.

Touching her like that felt, oh, so right.

She covered his hands with hers, and that wasn't awkward or strange, either. He felt as if he was truly ready to take a big step forward, and he wanted to do it with Jolene. But he still had some ground to cover to get her to trust him.

"I didn't realize how much I missed Aunt Sugar. How about you? How is this going to affect you?" she asked.

Sugar moving back made Jolene happy, and he liked that. She didn't want to move back into the inn, and he liked that.

"Honest or sugarcoated?" he finally asked.

"Honest. Always, always honest," she told him.

"I'm glad that they're buying a house of their own. They would have been welcome here, but I kind of like us having the place to ourselves," he said.

She shivered again. "Me, too."

He wanted to stand right there and hold her forever, but it was too cold. "We better get inside before you freeze. Let's share the cleanup and the work. I'll take care of loading the dishwasher if you'll put away the leftovers."

When he carried the butter and milk to the refrigerator, he stopped and stared at his finger, naked where his wedding band had been. The deep indentation would take years to completely go away, but it didn't bother him as much as he thought it would.

"You're looking at your ring finger, aren't you?" she asked.

He nodded. "I buried the ring at Melanie's grave. It was time."

"It's part of your past, Tucker. You have to get over it, but you also need to know that it was this experience that makes you the man you are today," she said.

"Thank you," he said around the lump in his throat. "The same goes for you."

She laid a hand over his heart. "We all just get a day at a time. It's up to us whether we fight the demons that plague us or if we give in to them."

4444

He pushed her hair back away from her face and stared down into her big blue eyes. "How did you get so smart?"

"Living a tough life," she answered as she tiptoed and brought his lips to hers for a kiss. "But when you kiss me, it don't seem so rough right now."

Jolene was a fresh start with someone who understood him. What she said about fighting demons made a lot of sense, but it was a whole lot easier to fight something if a person had a partner to watch his back. What they did with their lives beyond a few hot kisses was up to them now.

Chapter Twenty-Four

Tucker had just finished work and taken a shower that Friday evening when his phone rang. Jolene had gone to the grocery store that morning but had forgotten to get milk, so she'd run back out for it. But it was his mother-in-law, Carla.

"He's gone, Tucker," she said between sobs. "I found him an hour ago in his recliner with the newspaper in front of him."

"What can I do?" Tucker asked with a heavy heart. He should've gone to that birthday party. At least it would have been bittersweet. Today would be nothing but sadness.

"Can you just come and sit with me and the boys awhile?" Carla asked.

"I'll be there in half an hour."

"Thank you." Carla ended the call before he could say anything else.

He dressed in creased jeans, shined boots, and an ironed shirt. He threw the hood on his coat up and ran to his truck. Several cars took up the driveway at the Tillison house when he got there, so he parked on the other side of the road and sat for several minutes. Another car pulled in behind him. A man and woman got out and slowly walked across the street and up the sidewalk and knocked on the door. A few minutes later, Tucker got out of his pickup and followed them.

Carla met him at the door with swollen eyes. "Oh, Tucker, I'm so glad you're here. Luke told me about your meetings at the cemetery. I thought we had another couple of months, but his heart played out."

Tucker backed her up enough to close the door. "I'm so sorry."

"The funeral will be Sunday. Luke planned it all, and last week he had me add you as a pallbearer. I hope that's not too much to ask." She hugged him tightly and wet the shoulder of his coat with her tears.

"That soon?" He pulled a handkerchief from his pocket and handed it to her.

"His wishes. Just graveside at the cemetery. He'll be buried beside Melanie. No weeping, he said, but I can't help it." She dabbed at her eyes and gave the hankie back to him.

He shook his head. "Keep it. You might need it again. What can I do?"

"Just sit with me and the boys. It'll be like having Melanie with us."

"Of course," he said.

"Four o'clock Sunday afternoon. Strange—we were supposed to meet for ice cream then. He was adamant about the time, too. It had to be at the same time we had the service for Melanie," she said. "Maybe I shouldn't be mentioning her so much since . . ."

Tucker draped an arm around the tall woman who had Melanie's eyes and build. "It's okay. I'm finally making my peace with it."

She took him by the hand and led him into the living room. "Luke told me that talking to you helped him do the same. Now come on in here."

A lady appeared at his elbow. "Let me take your coat. Can I get you something to drink?"

"A cup of black coffee," Tucker said.

"It's good to see you again, Tucker." Melanie's brother Will stuck out a hand.

Tucker shook with him and then turned to Patrick, her other brother. "I'm so sorry, guys. I thought we had a little more time."

Patrick pointed to the chair beside him. "How's the renovations at the inn going?"

"They're going great. We should be open for business by spring." He remembered the anger he'd pent up inside himself when people meandered around talking about jobs, family, and the weather the day after Melanie was killed. That evening, he understood it better. In situations like this, folks tended to talk about everything under the sun just to get their minds off the sorrow and the pain.

"And how's the new partner working out? I remember her from church when we were all kids," Patrick said.

"Better than I could have ever hoped." Tucker took a sip of the coffee that the lady put in his hands.

Patrick took a deep breath and let it out slowly. "I'm happy for you."

"And Melanie would want you to move on," Will said.

"Life is tough," Tucker said.

Patrick clamped a hand on his shoulder. "We don't mean to get all up in your business, but we've learned that we don't get guarantees in life. Be happy. And don't be a stranger around here. We've missed you."

Tucker swallowed twice to get the lump in his throat to go down. "Moving on hasn't been easy."

"Not for any of us," Will said. "Melanie would've been real happy that all her favorite people were here."

Tucker managed a weak chuckle.

Carla sat down on a nearby sofa. "I'm glad that Luke met you at the cemetery and you two got things straightened out. You'll understand when you have a daughter."

He got a fleeting vision of a little blonde-haired girl with blue eyes. She wore bibbed overalls and handed him a hammer when he asked for it. Carla was right—no man would ever be good enough for her. Suddenly, he understood Luke better than he ever had before.

❧

The lights were on in the inn when Jolene arrived home at three in the morning. Sassy met her at the door, and the smell of cinnamon floated through the foyer. She hung up her coat and started to the kitchen but noticed that Tucker was sitting in the living room in the dark.

She flipped the switch. His hands went to cover his face, and when he removed them, she could see that his eyes were bloodshot and he looked like hell.

"Something is wrong. I can tell. Please tell me it's not about Aunt Sugar." She plopped down on the sofa beside him.

"Luke died this afternoon. Melanie's dad. Funeral is Sunday, and they've asked me to be a pallbearer. Would you go with me?" He looked absolutely miserable.

She moved closer to him and slipped her arms around his neck. "I'm sorry, Tucker, but I'm glad that you made peace with him before he died. That will mean a lot as time goes on. Of course I'll go with you. I'm just sorry that I didn't make things right with my mother before she died. The last words between us were said in anger. I told her for the gazillionth time that I wasn't ever coming back to see her if she didn't get her life in order. She told me to get out and go to hell."

"We're a sorry pair, aren't we?" he sighed.

"Maybe, but we make a damn fine whole person when you put us together." She kissed him on the cheek.

"Think so?" His big, strong arms went around her, and he rested his face in her hair.

"Oh, yeah," she said. "We make a great team."

"I had my doubts at first about us working together, but . . ."

"But what?"

"I was wrong." He stood up and held out his hand. Her eyes locked with his when she clasped his hand. He pulled her against his chest and looked down into her face. Slowly his eyes fluttered shut, and his mouth closed over hers. Then she was floating as he scooped her up like a bride and carried her toward his room. He started to the bed with her, but she put her hand on the wall and shook her head.

"Sassy is sleepin' on your bed. Let's take this to my room," she whispered.

He stopped just inside her bedroom door. "Are you sure about this, Jolene? Is our relationship ready for this step?"

She put a finger over his lips. "Can I trust you with my heart?"

"Yes, darlin', you can." He kicked the door shut with the heel of his boot.

Chapter Twenty-Five

Church services on Sunday morning. A funeral planned for the afternoon. That was a lot in one day, but Jolene would do both. The first because Aunt Sugar wanted them to go to church in Jefferson with her. The second because she wanted to support Tucker.

But churches and funerals reminded her of when her dad died. The service had been in a huge church. She'd sat flanked by Aunt Sugar and Uncle Jasper. Her mother had been on the same pew, but it was Aunt Sugar who comforted her through the whole ordeal.

When Elaine passed away, there hadn't been a service of any kind. Aunt Sugar had offered to pay for a memorial or a full-fledged funeral if Jolene wanted, but it had seemed more than a little hypocritical on Jolene's part to do something like that. Especially since she and her mother had been at cross-purposes for years. So when the funeral home called her to claim the ashes, she'd done so and mixed them with those of her father.

She loved the congregational singing that morning. Tucker had a fine voice, and the ladies would most likely be after him to join the choir if he came to services regularly. But when the preacher read some verses from Psalm 37 about not fretting, she quickly tuned him out. Living with her mother, she'd learned early on to focus on something other than what was being said, so that morning she turned her thoughts to everything that had happened in one short month.

Dotty poked her in the ribs and whispered, "Ever had sex on a church pew?"

Jolene blushed. "Shhh . . . God will aim lightning bolts at us for even thinkin' that word in church."

"What word?" Tucker asked from the other side.

Jolene mouthed, "Later."

She was thinking about sex with Tucker on a church pew, her pulse and heart both racing when she glanced over to find him staring right at her. He laced his fingers with hers and leaned over to whisper, "You look gorgeous this morning."

"Thank you," she mouthed.

She was thinking about the night before and what Dotty said about sex on a church pew when the preacher jerked her back to the present by asking Jasper to give the benediction. Not one to ever use fifty words when two would do, his prayer was short and to the point. Everyone said amen with him at the end and didn't waste any time making their way to the doors to shake the preacher's hand. Then they'd hurry on home or to a favorite restaurant for Sunday dinner.

Jolene remembered a side door and quickly ushered Tucker out that way so they could get to the Magnolia before everyone else. She settled into his truck and fastened her seat belt.

"That was slick," Tucker chuckled.

"Uncle Jasper showed me how to get out quicker when I was a little girl," she said.

He drove out of the parking lot and turned south. "So we have to do this every week now?"

"I'm afraid so. Aunt Sugar says it's good for the business and that it won't hurt us to be still once a week. Confession time—I didn't listen much to the preacher, but being there was kind of nice," she said. "I haven't been in church in twelve years, but we have this service this morning and then we have a funeral. Seems strange, don't it?"

"It sure does, but I'm glad you were sitting beside me this morning and you'll be beside me this afternoon."

✿

Tucker dragged out his black suit, a white shirt, and a tie and dusted off his best black boots. He'd sworn after Melanie's funeral that he'd never put that suit on again, but he'd show respect, and besides, maybe wearing the suit was moving forward still another step. He looked at his reflection in the mirror, and something different shone in his face. The tension was gone, but then Jolene had come into his life and heart.

He made sure his tie was just right one more time and then stepped out into the foyer to find Jolene pacing the floor. "Are you okay?"

"These are your in-laws and I haven't been to a funeral since my dad died—we didn't have one for my mother. And I'm nervous about what they'll think of me. I work in a bar and . . ."

"Well, *nervous* is a word I never thought I'd hear out of your mouth. I thought you were made tough as nails," he said.

"That's the exterior. The interior is a mixture of jelly and mush," she said.

He started at the toes of her black high-heeled shoes and traveled up the slim black skirt that hugged her body and on up to the cute little jacket she wore over a silky-looking white blouse. They matched—him with his black suit and white shirt and her in that pretty suit. Had she worn that same one to her father's funeral?

"You look as beautiful in that as you did in the blue sweater this morning, but I've got a confession to make." He slipped an arm around her shoulders. "I like you better in your skinny jeans and work shirts. You're downright sexy in those."

She looped her arm in his. "I like you better in work clothes, too. I think this kind of getup means sadness and our everyday things speak to us of happiness."

The wind had calmed down, and although it was chilly, the sun shone brightly. It was so unlike the storm, complete with thunder and lightning, the day that they'd held Melanie's funeral and that last day he'd gone to the cemetery to see her. Maybe this day was just a reflection of what was in Tucker's heart. On Melanie's day he'd been so full of anger that he felt as if he could throw lightning bolts from his fingertips. But today, even though there was sadness, he was at peace with Luke's passing.

When they reached the cemetery, Tucker helped Jolene out of the truck and took her hand in his. Just that much gave him comfort and courage. He slowed his stride to match hers, but when they reached the hearse, she let go and went on ahead to stand beside a tall pine tree. The funeral director opened the back of the hearse, and Tucker took his place with Melanie's brothers on one side. Three men he wasn't familiar with served as the other pallbearers.

As they carried the casket to the gravesite, Tucker could hear the rustling of last year's dead oak leaves in the trees above them. But once they'd positioned the casket on the stand and stood back in a line, he heard a button click and Garth Brooks's voice filled the air as he sang "The Dance." The words said that he could have missed the pain but he'd have had to miss the dance.

It wasn't what most people would choose to play for a funeral. It was actually a song to a lover who had left, but it wasn't difficult to realize that it could be written to Luke from Carla on that day. Tucker glanced over at Jolene to see her wiping her eyes. Evidently the song was hitting her the same way.

Tucker thought about everything he and Jolene had been through and realized he was ready to do more than just share a bed with her. He was ready to share his life with her.

Home was Magnolia Inn in a physical sense. But home was Jolene Broussard in an emotional sense. He'd fallen in love with the woman, and now all he had to do was give her enough time and room to fall for him.

🪷

Jolene felt every word of Garth's song, and as the words sank into her heart, she let go of the guilt and the pain of the past. She might have missed the pain, like he said, but she would have missed the dance. The good times with her father in his flower garden. The shopping trips with her mother when she was a little girl. She'd hang on to the good memories, however scarce they might be, and do her best to let go of the others.

There was a pause when the song ended, and then a woman in a bright-red dress stood up. She had a microphone in one hand and a hankie in the other.

"Saying goodbye to my precious husband is not easy, and y'all might think that song is crazy for a funeral. But it was our song. We had a rough year in our marriage the year that song came out. We lost both sets of our parents. The kids were young, and Luke had lost his job. We used up all our savings before he finally got another job. We were fighting a lot in those days about money and kids and everything else. One day he came into the house, put a cassette in the player, and held out his hand to me. He wasn't a romantic man, so I was a little shocked, but I thought maybe . . ." She paused and dabbed at her eyes before she went on. "I thought maybe that he was ready to try a little harder, so I put my hand in his. He pushed the button on the cassette player, and that song started playing. We danced and wept all the way through it. That was the turning point in our marriage. He still wasn't romantic, but sometimes he'd come in and put on that song again, and we'd dance. He didn't want a funeral. He didn't even really want this

259

much. He just asked to be buried by our daughter, Melanie, and for me not to grieve too long. I can do it all, and maybe when the grief gets to be too much, I'll just put on this song and remember that if I didn't have this horrible pain today, I would've had to miss the dance with a fantastic man. Thank you all for coming—the song as you leave was *his* choice for today. It's the one that we danced to the night before he went to be with our daughter in heaven."

Jolene didn't even try to keep up with the tears dripping on her jacket as Vince Gill sang "Look At Us." She watched Carla kiss a single red rose and lay it on the casket. Then Carla sat down, and her shoulders began to shake with sobs.

Tucker left his place with the pallbearers to hug her. "Call me anytime. I'm here for you and the boys."

"Thank you," Carla said.

He took a few steps toward Jolene. She met him halfway, and their tears blended together, washing away the past.

He handed her his handkerchief. "I need to say something right now, Jolene, because we might not have anything but this moment. I'm falling in love with you."

"I never believed that love conquered everything. But maybe, in our case, it could be right." She wiped her eyes and handed it back to him. "I feel the same about you. Do we go home now?"

"We should go to the house," he said. "Carla wants to meet you."

Chapter Twenty-Six

*C*onversation flowed in low tones as they reached the house. Tucker kept her by his side for a while, and then Carla looped an arm in hers and said, "You boys go on in the living room and talk. I want to show Jolene something."

Jolene sent a frantic look toward Tucker, begging him to make an excuse to take her home, but he just nodded and went into another room with Will and Patrick.

Carla led her into a study, shut the door, and slumped down in a chair. "I love my family, but I need a moment. Please sit down and let's catch our breath."

Jolene sat down next to her and crossed her legs at the ankles. She was reminded of how she'd sneaked away after her father's funeral. All those people milling around. Her mother in tears. She'd felt the walls closing in on her and gone outside. Uncle Jasper had finally missed her and had come out to sit beside her. He didn't say anything at all, but just held her hand for a long time.

Now it was her turn to be the one to comfort someone—a complete stranger, and yet grief is no respecter of persons. She reached across the distance and laid a hand on Carla's arm. "Your eulogy was wonderful. So heartfelt and personal. More funerals should be like that," Jolene said.

"Thank you so much. I want to say something to you, but I'm not even sure where to begin." Carla fidgeted with the handkerchief in her hands.

"It's only awkward if we make it that way, so let's don't," Jolene said. There wasn't going to be anything left of that hankie if Carla kept wringing it. "It's okay. Tucker told me all about Melanie and how he and her father had made peace with each other the week before he died."

Carla sucked in a lungful of air and let it out in a whoosh. "I felt like I'd lost two kids when Melanie died and Tucker didn't come around anymore. I didn't think he'd ever get over it, and I'm not so sure he would have without you in his life. I know it's a crazy thing to ask under the circumstances, but I'd like for us to be friends. We, my sons and I, want Tucker back in our lives, and this is going to sound insane," Carla whispered. "I had a dream last night. You'd think it would be about Luke, but it was about Melanie. I could see her sitting on her tombstone, wearing her wedding dress, of all things, and she told me that she had a new friend named Jolene that was going to help Tucker. Luke told me that you see things different when you're lookin' at death. I thought he was bat-crap crazy, but I've changed my mind since that dream. The last thing she said as she faded away, leaving just the tombstone, was that I'd like her new friend, too." She took several sips of her tea.

A cold shiver chased down Jolene's spine. Those two songs that were so unlike funeral music, hearing Tucker say that he was in love with her and saying it back to him, the way she'd felt when she awoke in the middle of the night to find him still in bed with her—it was all surreal, but not as much as Carla telling her about that dream. But then, looking back over the past month, not much *hadn't* been slightly weird.

Carla went on. "I won't smother you, I promise, but I do miss having a . . . well, maybe I should just say having a younger woman to go shopping with sometimes or out to lunch or maybe even just to talk to on the phone."

Jolene flashed her brightest smile, and it was sincere. "I'd like that."

"Let's just sit here a few more minutes. I need the time," Carla said with a weak smile.

"When you're ready," Jolene said. "Give me a call when things settle down."

A gentle knock on the door was followed by Tucker's face as he peeked inside the office. "I'm not rushin' you, but we probably should be getting home."

Jolene stood and then bent to hug Carla. "You don't have to call before you come see me. Just drop in anytime."

Tucker escorted her out of the house and into his truck, where he promptly removed his tie and tossed it over the seat. "Are you okay? What happened in there?"

She told him what had happened, and he leaned over the console and kissed her. It started out slow and sweet, but before long, his tongue was teasing her lips open. When he finally broke away, he was breathing hard. "You never cease to amaze me, woman."

"Because I told your mother-in-law we could be friends? That's as much to my benefit as to hers. I liked her honesty and the way she handled that funeral. We'll be good friends. I can feel it in my heart," Jolene said. "And you need a family, too, Tucker."

🌸

Jolene slung the door open the day after the funeral. "Aunt Sugar, are you sure you want to climb up into that attic today? It's going to be chilly."

"And dusty, but there shouldn't be any mice scampering around. Me and Jasper put out a fresh batch of poison before we left last month." Sugar started up to the second floor. "I wore my oldest work coat, so it won't matter if it gets dusty and dirty."

Jolene followed along behind her. "Why are we doing this today, Aunt Sugar?"

"Because I want to take some of the old picture albums to my new house, and there used to be a little library stand up there that I could use in the corner of the living room. I've about got all the big pieces of furniture in the house. I thought I wanted all new things, but I need a few old comfortable pieces. A house isn't a real home without some past, present, and future in it."

As they made their way, single file, up the narrow steps at the end of the hallway, Jolene asked, "And how are you going to put *future* in the house?"

When they reached the top, Jolene was amazed at all the stuff that had been stored. She'd known for years that the door led to the attic, but she'd always been afraid of mice and thought that there could be one hiding up there.

Sugar pulled a rocking chair over to a roll-top trunk. "I need some doilies, and I know there's a box of them in this trunk because I put them here years ago."

"You didn't answer me," Jolene pressed. "That's the past. The present is the new things. What about the future?"

"See that baby bed over there? I'll send Jasper out here tomorrow for it. Tucker can help get it down the stairs. I slept in that crib, your mother did, and so did you when she brought you to visit as a small baby. That is the future, because your children are going to sleep in it when I babysit them," she answered as she brought out a thick picture album. "I'm going to pick out several of these of you and have them framed to go in the nursery."

"Gettin' the cart before the horse, aren't you?" Jolene blushed. "Did Reuben ever sleep in that crib?"

"No, he didn't come stay with us until he was about seven. That's when his mama started letting him out of her sight for more than an hour for what you kids today call playdates," Sugar answered. "And I'm not gettin' the cart before the horse, either."

"Tucker and I've known each other less than two months," Jolene argued.

"I knew Jasper fifteen minutes when he proposed to me. He was the shyest boy I'd ever known. I was so surprised when he blurted out that he fell in love with me at first sight. I told him he was crazy, but he proposed again six weeks later and meant it. I'm just gettin' ready." Sugar pointed at the album. "I hope the first baby is a girl and she looks just like you. Jasper and I are so ready to be grandparents."

Jolene blushed again. "Aunt Sugar!"

"Oh, stop that blushing. I know y'all are sleeping together. I figure you're on the pill," Sugar said. "But me and the girls have been praying ever since I got home that they fail. We need a baby to spoil. We ain't had one in more than thirty years, and that's too long. Dotty is already knitting blankets. Lucy is keeping an eye out for one of those rocking cradles for her house, and Flossie is stockpiling diapers when she finds them on sale."

Jolene's hands went to her cheeks.

"And that's the picture of the future," Sugar said with a lilt in her voice. "I'm taking this album and going home."

"I'll walk you out," Jolene said.

"Not necessary. You stay up here and stare at that baby bed. Maybe it'll put ideas in your head." Sugar left Jolene speechless.

❦

Tucker waited until Sugar had left before he went up to the attic. "It's cold up here. Why didn't you come down with Sugar?"

"Because she shocked the hell out of me, and I'm trying to get my bearings," Jolene answered. "She's talking about babies, and the girls are already getting ready to babysit, and I don't even know where we are in this relationship, but it's sure not to the point where we discuss babies." She stopped to catch her breath.

He sat down beside her. "I'd ask you to marry me and have my children. But if it's too soon, I can ask later on. And babies sound pretty good to me."

"We've only known each other . . . ," she started.

He scooted over closer to her and took her hand in his. "I'm not in a hurry. Like I said, I can do this another time. This is not the most romantic place in the world, is it?"

Past.

Present.

Future.

The three words raced through her mind. They were sitting in the attic with the past all around them. They were living in the present and talking about the future.

"Why come back another time? We're right here, right now."

"Okay then." He moved around until he was on one knee. "Jolene Broussard, I don't even have a ring, and I can't say I loved you from the time we met. But I can say that I intend to love you until we are both old and gray and lots of babies have used that crib over there. So will you marry me?"

"Yes!" She wrapped her arms around his neck. "Want to go start one of those babies right now?"

"Now that sounds like a plan." He took her by the hand and led her down to the bedroom.

Epilogue

Eighteen months later

Jolene dressed in a pretty, lacy dress. She swept her hair up into a bundle of curls and tucked some baby's breath in the side. Aunt Sugar and Uncle Jasper were repeating their vows that day in the wedding/dining room of the Magnolia. Jolene had the urge to pinch herself just to see if this was all real or if she was dreaming. Her life had changed so much, and all of it was for the better.

Tucker knocked on the door of what they'd dubbed the rose room and poked his head inside. "Well, hello, gorgeous."

"Hello, sexy cowboy." She crossed the room, slipped her arms under his suit coat, and laid her head on his chest. After more than a year, that steady heartbeat still calmed her soul.

He'd been wrong when he said he wasn't romantic, but then, their definition of the word wasn't the same as other folks'. Bringing in the first daffodil of the spring meant more than a dozen red roses on Valentine's Day. Sneaking out of bed early in the morning to have the coffee ready or, better yet, giving her a whole hour with no interruptions for a long, hot bath after she'd had a rough night. What were those things, if not romantic?

"This is a milestone that goes on the calendar," she said.

He tipped her chin up with his thumbs and kissed her. "The day I bought half ownership in this place changed my life for the better."

"Oh, yeah." She pressed closer to him and tiptoed for another kiss.

"Hey, now." Sugar came from the bathroom.

Jolene stepped away from Tucker. "You and Uncle Jasper repeating your wedding vows is so special, and I'm glad you're doing it here rather than at the church."

"Seems like the perfect place, since we got married in the Magnolia. But, honey, I feel like Miss Piggy in a corset. I can't wait to get this show on the road and the whole thing over with, so I can come out of this. I never should have let you talk me into such a slim-fitting dress," Sugar fussed, but she turned this way and that to catch all the angles in the floor-length mirror. "You two should've gotten married here instead of going to the courthouse."

"You told me that you always wished you and Uncle Jasper had had a big wedding—well, here it is. Now bend down just a little so I can get this circlet of flowers on your hair, which looks amazing today," Jolene said. "Five minutes until the music starts. We've got to put on our shoes and then we're ready to go. Are you nervous?"

"Not as much as I was the first time I went down those steps on my father's arm." She smiled.

Tucker backed out of the room. "I'm going back across the hall. Jasper and I'll meet y'all at the front of the wedding room. Every chair is filled."

Jolene raised the hem of Sugar's pale-blue lace dress and helped her aunt with her shoes before she slipped her feet into her own. "I'll be glad to get out of all this and back into my jeans and T-shirt, but it is kind of fun to get all dressed up. And thank you for asking me to be your matron of honor."

"It's my way of apologizing for throwing that fit over y'all going to the courthouse. I always wanted to give you a big wedding," Sugar said.

Tucker and Jasper came out of the groom's room with Jasper in the lead. As if he could feel her watching him, Tucker turned around at the top of the stairs and blew her a kiss. She stuck her hand out the door, pretended to grab it, and held her hand to her heart.

Jolene scattered a few rose petals as she walked down the center aisle and stopped in front of an archway covered with ivy and red roses. She turned and winked at Dotty, who was sitting on the front row of chairs, along with Flossie and Lucy. Then Sugar appeared at the back of the room with her arm looped in Jasper's.

Everyone stood up, and it took only a couple of minutes for her to make her way to the front of the arch and hand off her rose bouquet to Jolene.

"You may be seated," the preacher said and began the ceremony.

❧

Tucker tried to listen to the preacher, but his eyes kept shifting from his beautiful wife to his baby daughter. The Magnolia had been the best thing that ever happened to him. Within these walls he'd come to grips with his grief, given up the bottle, and learned to love again. And now he and Jolene had a beautiful little black-haired daughter with big blue eyes.

"The ring," the preacher said.

Tucker reached into his pocket and handed it to him. Maggie continued to fuss. Dotty tried giving her a pacifier, but that didn't work. The preacher kept talking about the significance of the wedding ring, but Tucker's daddy instinct was on high alert. Finally, he could stand it no longer. He took a couple of steps and reached for his daughter. Dotty handed her over, and Maggie immediately settled down.

The ceremony ended, and the bride and groom quickly made their way to the office. Pictures would be done in a few minutes, but all the guests were invited to the reception in the Tipsy Gator.

Jolene looped her arm into his. "Aren't you glad we didn't do it this way?"

"Amen, darlin'."

With his wife on one arm and his baby nestled in the other, there was no place on earth that Tucker would rather be than at the Magnolia Inn.

Acknowledgments

Dear Reader,

Fate does have a way of showing up at the most unusual times.

On the way home from a big family Christmas vacation in Florida last year, Mr. B and I made a loop through Texas to find new sites for my upcoming books. When we reached the outskirts of San Antonio, it started to snow, and the weatherman said that there was bad weather to the west. That made us decide to go east instead, and we wound up going all the way to Jefferson, Texas, which isn't far from the Louisiana border.

We covered the whole little town, block by block, and I wasn't inspired. So we started back to Marshall, a few miles down the road, to our hotel. And that's when I saw the Magnolia Inn. A two-story house nestled in tall pine trees and set back off the road, it even had a big front porch. Instantly, I could visualize Jolene and Tucker meeting for the first time right there. The basis for the story came in bits and pieces over the next couple of days as we traveled from there back to our home in southern Oklahoma. If it hadn't been snowing west of San Antonio, if I'd found a spot I could live with right in Jefferson, if we'd driven east, west, or north out of town instead of back south? Yep, fate knew where to take us for sure.

Now you hold the story in your hands, thanks to Madam Fate sending us in the right direction. Speaking of the finished book, I want to thank Krista Stroever and Megan Mulder, my amazing editors, for helping me to bring out every emotion in all the characters. I'm so blessed to have them working with me. Thanks also to my publisher, Amazon/Montlake Romance, for continuing to believe in me. And to my awesome agent, Erin Niumata—we've been working together for almost twenty years. Without her I could never accomplish what I do. Also my thanks to Mr. B—the marriage that was only supposed to last six weeks has made it fifty-two years now. He's my best friend and soul mate, and he's always ready to drop whatever he's doing to read through a manuscript for me or to go on a road trip to make sure I have the details just right. And last, though not least, to all my fans for reading my books, for writing reviews, and for sending fan mail. I love you all!

As I write "The End," I'm leaving behind good friends that I've made with these characters. I hope that when you finish reading it these folks are your friends, also!

Sending all of you hugs until next time,
Carolyn Brown

About the Author

Carolyn Brown is a *New York Times*, *USA Today*, *Publishers Weekly*, and *Wall Street Journal* bestselling author and a RITA finalist with more than ninety published books, which include women's fiction and historical, contemporary, and cowboys-and-country-music romance. She and her husband live in the small town of Davis, Oklahoma, where everyone knows everyone else and knows what they're doing and when. And they read the local newspaper on Wednesday to see who got caught. They have three grown children and enough grandchildren to keep them young. Visit Carolyn at www.carolynbrownbooks.com.